Mutual
Feelings

Mutual Feelings

Billy Taylor

Book design by Maureen Cutajar
www.gopublished.com

ISBN-13: 978-1541036772
ISBN-10: 1541036778

For my mum

Without her none of this would have been possible. Just Friends wouldn't exist. And this book definitely wouldn't exist. She has supported me for every second throughout my journey, and I cannot thank her enough for it.

I love you mum x

31ST DECEMBER

I've always loved dinosaurs. Always. My love for them started when I was old enough to play with dinosaur toys, I guess. My mum bought me some when she could trust me to not try to eat them. I used to take them with me to nursery school every day in my dinosaur backpack. And I would have dinosaur-shaped meat on my sandwiches, which were stored in my dinosaur lunchbox.

My love for dinosaurs is how I became best friends with Ted. I was sitting in the sandbox one day at nursery school. I was only four, but I remember it so well. It's strange how you can remember some things from your childhood, and then others memories that my mum or sister will bring up are a complete blur. Most of them involve me running around naked somewhere, so maybe that's why I decided not to keep those memories.

Anyway, I was sitting in the sandbox one day. It was quite warm. I knew this because the sand was warm and I used my backpack as a seat to prevent it from burning my bum. I had my trusty dinosaur cap on though so it didn't hurt my eyes or burn my face. (It was one of those caps that came over your ears as well. I was such a cool kid.) And I was lining up my seventeen dinosaurs. Yes, seventeen. I counted them every day so I knew I hadn't lost one. They were pink and blue, my dinosaurs, but somehow clear, too. Sixteen were lined up against one. The smallest one, alone by itself. But this dinosaur was what I called a superhero dinosaur; he had powers to defeat all the other dinosaurs. And as he was about to kick every other dinosaur's ass, a shadow hovered over my seventeen dinosaurs and myself.

I glanced up and squinted. For a second I thought it was myself. I thought he had travelled from the future so myself and myself could play together with our dinosaurs. I'd never had anyone to play with because every other person at the nursery was a girl and they played with dolls. Apart from Josh, but he played with the dolls, too. I think he had a crush on the girls.

After a second I realised it wasn't myself, and I was very disappointed. This boy had blonde hair, and mine was brown. He was wearing khaki shorts and a T-shirt with a Chewbacca design on it.

"I'm Ted," he said, stepping into the sandbox.

"I'm Will," I said.

"Today is my first day. My mum said I have to be nice and have to make at least one friend."

"Do you like dinosaurs?" I asked.

"Yes," he replied.

"Do you want to sit and play?" I asked.

"Ok," he replied. He sat down and crossed his legs. I saw his shoes as he sat down and noticed that they had dinosaurs on them. And the soles flashed every time he took a step. I thought they were so cool at the time. A teacher came over a few moments later and placed a roof on the edges of the sandbox to protect us from the sun. The shade was very nice and it was like we had our own fort now.

"Why are all the dinosaurs lined up there, but one isn't?" he asked.

"Because this one is a superhero dinosaur, and he is about to fight all of the other dinosaurs. I call him Bob."

"What are Bob's powers?"

"He's strong and he can run really fast."

"Can he fly?"

"No, he doesn't have wings."

"Superman doesn't have wings."

"He isn't a dinosaur."

"Ok."

We sat and played for a couple of hours and had an awful lot of fun until it was time to go home.

"Are you coming tomorrow?" he asked.

"Yes."

"Ok. I will bring my dinosaurs tomorrow."

"Ok. Bye, Ted."

"Bye, Will."

He brought his dinosaurs the next day and soon we had an indestructible army of dinosaurs. We spent pretty much every single day after that playing with our dinosaurs until we moved into primary school and then we had to leave them in our backpacks because we had to pay attention in lessons.

Sixteen Years Later

It's approximately two or three minutes until midnight. Two or three minutes until the New Year. If I'm honest, New Year's Eve is just another day for me. I know the year is ending and a new one is beginning and that calls for celebration, but at the end of the day it is just another day.

I'm currently sat on the roof of the house where Ted's girlfriend lives. Before you worry about me falling off—the roof is flat. The surface is so large you could maybe play a tennis match on it. I'm not sure if I'm allowed up here, although there was a ladder on the balcony that led up to here, so I figured its purpose was to get people up here. The roof seemed like a nice spot to stand and wait for all the fireworks to start firing into the air. Also, everybody inside is gathered around Hayley, the girl Ted is seeing, who is crying about something. One minute she was fine. The next she started crying. Then she was fine. Then she started crying again. The only girl who wasn't bothering with her was Kate. But the only conversation she wanted to have was about Patrick Miller's TV show on Christmas Eve. She kept talking about this magician. I wasn't paying much attention. I just wanted to go home and watch the celebration on TV from my sofa.

The ladder began to rattle behind me, and then Ted Maguire, my best friend, rolled onto the roof in the least fluid way possible.

"That's not as easy as it looks," he said, walking over and standing beside me.

"How come you're not with Hayley? She'll need your lips to kiss in thirty seconds."

"She's still surrounded by her friends who are consoling her. She's upset about another friend who is being a bitch. I really don't know what's going on. I think I'm going to break up with her. Being with her is exhausting. I thought I would come and find you anyway. It seemed like a more interesting start to my year."

Everyone inside then started counting down from ten.

"I'm not kissing you. Let me make that very clear," I said, with five seconds to go.

"I wouldn't have wanted to kiss you anyway," Ted replied.

"Good."

Then everyone inside started to scream and cheer. One firework flew up and burst with a deafening bang. It spread across the night sky, illuminating it. It was shortly followed by a dozen more from different areas. Within seconds everywhere you turned you could see fireworks exploding.

"Happy New Year, bud," Ted said, holding up his drink.

"Happy New Year, man," I said, clinking mine with his. "Got a New Years resolution?" I added.

"To find a girl that I like. How about you?"

"Yeah, that's a good one, I think I'll join you with that one."

"I doubt it will happen," he said. "But we can dream." We laughed and then took a sip of our beers. The fireworks were still flying from every angle, providing a very nice image to begin our New Year with.

Ted and I have always done everything together. We went to the same school. We went to the same college. We live together. We work together. We work for a company called Ron's Ice Cream. Ted happens to be the great-grandson of Ron, creator of Ron's Ice Cream. And Ted's dad, Rob, is currently in charge. I don't think I have ever called him Rob. I've always called him Ted's dad. It's funny, I know. A twenty-year-old employee calling his boss "Ted's dad." It's been a habit since I was four so it's hard to suddenly stop calling him that after all that time.

Before you start to think we were gifted these jobs and aren't qualified for them, you should know that we studied business and all sorts of crap at school and then college for another two years. We could have skipped all of that and still been given a job, but we wanted to prove we could do them. The hard work at college also means Ted and I get to share our own office and we can sit around and relax if we have completed all our tasks. I think Ted's dad put us in our little office so we didn't distract everyone else every two seconds, too. Ted is expected to take over the company one day because his dad is going to want a break. So Ted will need to reliable and mature, not like the super unreliable immature Ted I know.

The apartment we live in we didn't work for. It was a present for Ted's twentieth birthday from his dad. We do work to pay the bills though. So, let me give you a tour of our apartment. It'll be brief, I promise. So you come through the door, and in front of you on your left is the living room, fitted with two sofas, a wooden table, and a television. My sofa has its back to you and is facing forwards. Ted's is to the right and is rotated at a ninety-degree angle, so his is facing the television in the back left corner.

An inch away from the back of Ted's sofa is the kitchen. It's not very big, but it has everything you need to make and store food.

My bedroom is past the living room, so if you come through the front door it's on the left. And Ted's bedroom is behind the kitchen, so if you come through the front door it's on the right. We both have our own bathrooms in our bedrooms. Obviously he chose me to be his roommate. But we hadn't seen the apartment before we moved in. We both stood in the middle of the living room and stared at each bedroom door. Since it was Ted's apartment he got to choose which bedroom he would have. But to make things interesting, we couldn't see inside them first. As we know, Ted chose the bedroom to the right, and he would later regret that decision as my bedroom is slightly bigger and also has a bath and shower cubicle in the bathroom, where as Ted only has a shower cubicle. I've hardly ever used the bath, but it's nice to have and it's more spacious.

You may think that Ted or we sound spoilt because of the apartment being bought by Ted's dad, but that simply isn't the case. Ted's dad has millions, and if he'd bought Ted a giant mansion or estate for his birthday, I don't think I would have been surprised. But instead he bought a regular apartment to start him off, so he remembers to stay humble and keep his feet on the ground. He believes it's something he needs if he is expected to take over the company in the future. Ted and I were extremely grateful for the apartment. We had originally planned to get a place together anyway. But now we can save up a little.

JANUARY 11TH

Sundiscussion Topic:
What is the best book of all time?

Before our Sundiscussion takes place, I should explain what a Sundiscussion is. It's a discussion that takes place between Ted and me every Sunday. Because Sunday + discussion = Sundiscussion. I'm sure you're thinking why not just call it a discussion, but we were fifteen at the time when we decided to create it, and we were very pleased with coming up with the name. And today's topic was: What is the best book of all time?

So we sat down on our sofas to discuss it.

"As I am a lover of J. R. R Tolkien, I'm sure you already know that I will be supporting *The Hobbit* and The Lord of the Rings novels," Ted began.

"I certainly do. And as you already know, I am a fan of Sir Arthur Conan Doyle and his Sherlock Holmes novels, so I will be supporting them," I replied.

"Yep," Ted said.

"You didn't really think this topic through, did you? I think it's taken less than thirty seconds to establish that neither of us will budge on our choices," I said.

"No, I didn't. I completely forgot to think of one, and

that was the first thing that popped into my head. I'll think of a better one for next week."

"We haven't done any 'who would win out of' ones for a while."

He nodded. "I'll think of a good one for next week."

"Please do. This was very disappointing."

JANUARY 12TH

"I ended things with Hayley last night," Ted said as we walked from the car park to our office.

"Why didn't you tell me when you returned to the apartment then?" I asked.

"Because I didn't end it with her then. I texted her before I went to bed. I've just had enough of her. She's no fun at all. She may be hot, but she's so miserable and boring."

"That could come back to haunt you. You could have at least told her in person."

"She would have gone on for hours and hours about unnecessary crap. So I took the easy way out."

"I see. So what are you going to do now?"

"I don't know. We were only seeing each other for a month or so. I don't think I want to be in a relationship to be honest. The girls I seem to take interest in are such high maintenance."

I shrugged as we walked through the automatic doors to the reception area. "I'm sure you'll meet someone you like soon, man."

Ted and I said hello to Ellie, who works behind the reception desk, and then we walked up the first flight of stairs to the office. After you've walked up the first flight of stairs, you come to a small landing and have to turn left to walk up the next flight. Then once you have walked up the stairs you reach two doors and they lead into our main office.

The main office is where most of our departments are based. Everyone has their own desk; they're all connected, but they have those opaque glass separator things so no one can see what you're doing. The first desk you come in contact with is Jeremy's. Jeremy is our office manager. He's one of the youngest in our office, at the age of twenty-two. But he's very good obviously. He makes sure everyone is working hard and if they need any help, then he makes sure that they get it. And he makes sure that the social media sites and websites are updated appropriately every day, which Ted and I are in charge of. He sends us what needs uploading onto them, and at what time, and then we make sure that happens. It's as simple as that really. Jeremy could probably do both of our jobs by himself, but it would take up much more of his time. Then Ted and I would have nothing to do, which isn't what his dad would want.

We have lots of different workers doing lots of different work in the office. But the main ones I know are admin and emailing. Admin make sure all deliveries and orders for everything are sorted. So they organise all the ice cream ingredients for each day and for each factory.

We have three factories. We have this one, here in England. Then we have another one in America and China. The admin team calls the guys who are working in those factories and makes sure they know what deliveries are coming so they can prepare to make certain flavours on certain days. And then they also handle the simple things, like making sure we have enough paper in the office. Then we have accountants, who take care of money obviously. And then we have mailers. They handle all the emails that are sent to Ron's Ice Cream. For example, if somebody emails in explaining that they found a toe in their ice cream, then this issue would need to be addressed and taken care of. (Just so you know, no one has ever found a toe in their ice cream. Nobody should ever find a toe in their ice cream unless they put it in there themselves.) But we don't reply to emails such as:

Plz tell me what ur recipe is for the cookie 1?

They don't get replied to. Because they're silly.

"Good morning, Jeremy," I said. "How was your weekend?"

I ask Jeremy this every Monday morning. Now there are only two possible answers from Jeremy to the question I just asked. If he says, "It was ok, thank you. How was yours?" then it's a normal conversation. But if he says, "So listen here, right," that means buckle up because he has some gossip to share.

"So listen here, right," he began, swinging around on his chair to face me. My ears pricked up and I leant my behind on his desk. "I went on a date with this guy from my gym who I've been meaning to ask out for a while now."

"Ok," I said.

"So I asked him out and we went for some dinner on Saturday. I took him to this Indian place that is always so quiet and lovely. Anyway, we had some wine, had a laugh, and had some good food. We fed each other and stuff, you know. It was going well. *Really well*. And afterwards he asked me if I wanted to go to his house."

"No," I said.

"I know, right? So I'm thinking 'ok, ok, now this is getting exciting.' We got a taxi to his house and opened up another bottle of wine. We sat down on the sofa and had a chat about puppies. Because I had just bought one with my flat mate."

"Of course," I said.

"Then he placed my hand on my knee. You know, all casual, but at the same time very implicative."

"Did you kiss him?" I asked.

"This is where shit just turned upside down. We had been kissing no longer than a minute and we hear the front door open. And we stop and frown at each other thinking someone is coming in to murder us. And then his ex-boyfriend comes into the living room with a bottle of wine."

"No!" I shouted.

"Yes! It was so awkward! I turned to him obviously to see what the hell he was going to say. And then he asked me to leave so he could speak to him! So I left and went home, feeling like a fool. Then Sunday he messages me saying they have gotten back together."

My eyes bulged. "What a dick!"

"I know. So now I have to find a new gym."

"I can't believe it. I'd kick his ass if I were you," I said.

"I've been thinking the same."

"You'll meet someone, Jeremy. Your Prince Charming is out there somewhere."

"Thanks, Grandma. Is Ted still seeing that Hayley chick?"

"He actually broke up with her last night."

"Marvellous. Do you think I should ask him out?"

"I think it may be a bit too soon to ask Ted out. He's also not gay, so that isn't exactly convenient either."

"You're probably right. And you're out of my league, Will. I can't date someone better-looking than me."

"That's very true," I replied. We wished each other a good day, and then I walked along the office corridor, past a third of the desks, and then I came to a door on my right. This door leads to mine and Ted's small office, which I already told you about. Our office is nothing special. You open the door and then my desk is facing you as you enter, and then Ted's desk is to the right as you enter. We have our own desks and computers, and that is it really. And we have a tray on the edge of our desks for paperwork, but we haven't used those for a long time.

JANUARY 15TH

"We're going to the cinema later," Ted said as we sat at our desks just after lunchtime.

"Do you mean 'Will, can we go to the cinema later, please?'" I replied.

"No, I mean we're going to the cinema later. We live together so don't say that you have other plans."

"What are we going to see?"

"*Role Models.*"

"Who is in it?"

"Paul Rudd."

"I love Paul Rudd."

"Everyone loves Paul Rudd. It's a natural thing like breathing."

I propped my feet up on my desk. "If you say so. Are we going straight from work or are we going home to get changed first?"

"We'll go home and change first. I spend enough of my day sitting in a suit."

"Ok. You can buy the popcorn, though."

"Fine," he muttered.

"So all that clicking and concentrating you've been doing at your computer is to look at what time the film is on at the cinema?"

"Yep. I'm super busy."

So, after work we returned to our apartment and got changed. And then we drove over to the cinema. Ted bought us some popcorn and then we went to sit in the cinema screen. The cinema we go to is quite big, but it's always quiet when we go in. But I guess most of the people who are there are already watching a film. Ted kept flicking popcorn at me before the film started. We kept pushing each other and throwing popcorn at each other. And then Ted took it a step too far and threw his shoes at me. The screening was over half full so there were plenty of people to see us acting like children. *Role Models* is a very strange film. It's hard to describe the plot without telling you the entire film. But I can tell you that it is funny, and random, and weird. Paul Rudd was as funny as ever. I wish he were our friend. We'd have endless laughs.

We waited until everyone else had left the screen. When I say waited, I mean I waited because Ted was reading the longest text message ever from Hayley. I thought she must have sent him a script to a play or something. He showed me the full message, and it seemed like I was still waiting for the message to end after a minute of scrolling.

"What are you going to reply?" I asked.

"Ok," he said with a grin. "She may possibly erupt from frustration."

"That's mean, Ted."

"I haven't done anything! I told her I didn't want anything serious, and then when I said I didn't want to see her anymore she acted like I've ended a five-year relationship out of nowhere."

"Ok, whatever you say. I'm not going to interfere."

I checked my phone as we exited the screen to see that I had zero messages and zero missed calls. Which was relieving as well as disappointing. It's always nice to see someone cares about me, but most of the time it is work-related anyway.

I put my phone into my pocket as we came to a set of stairs to the first floor. We walked down those and then we walked around to the staircase to the ground floor. It was like a winding staircase, I guess you could say. I glanced up before walking down the final sets of stairs, and standing at the bottom of the stairs behind a lectern, in a black cinema polo, was the most beautiful girl. Even from the top of the stairs the first thing I noticed was her bright blue eyes. And she had wavy, thick, fluffy, light caramel hair. She looked quite small, too...well, the stand made her look that way.

"Oh my wow," I said, and then I frowned at myself for whatever that was meant to mean.

"What?" Ted replied, but he became background noise. I was already walking down the stairs toward her. I walked over to her once I reached the bottom. I stood there silently and waited behind two people who were giving her their tickets to check. After they walked away I stepped forward. Attached to her black polo was a nametag that read Emily. Her skin and lips looked so soft, and she had a small amount of rosiness in her cheeks. Her hair was chest length, maybe a tiny bit longer. And I'd say she was five foot three or four.

But it was her eyes. They were just so blue and beautiful, and her eyelashes complemented them so well. This girl was perfect. Everything about her was perfect.

"Hi," I said. "I'm Will." I thought to myself that no one can be this perfect. And I was expecting her to have all of her teeth missing and have a really high-pitched squeaky voice.

She smiled a tight-lipped smile. "Hello, Will, do you have your ticket?" I can confirm that her voice wasn't high-pitched or squeaky. I'm not going to describe her voice as a soothing melody or anything like that because that would be an exaggeration. And I hate when people overdo it when they're describing things. She just had a lovely voice, and her teeth were fine, too; none of them were missing. I really wanted to ask her out, but we'd only met three seconds ago, and she most likely had a really handsome and muscular boyfriend.

"Erm, no, I just saw *Role Models* two minutes ago."

Ted then stood beside me. "Why are you being— *Oh ok...*" he began to say before he saw Emily and realised my actions made complete sense. The cinema was almost empty, apart from everyone leaving the screening we had come from, so I didn't need to worry about holding anybody up.

"Did you enjoy the film?" Emily asked.

"Yes we did, thanks."

"Good," she replied.

I wanted to keep the conversation going so I could show how funny and hilarious and amusing I am. "How are you?" I asked.

She briefly looked away. I'm sure she was wondering why I was talking to her if I didn't have a ticket. "I'm very well, thank you."

"Good," I said. "You have really beautiful eyes."

At this moment I wanted to run away and cry like an embarrassed little boy. But Emily didn't seem to mind my compliment. She grinned and blushed. "Thank you."

"You're welcome." I couldn't think of anything else to say so I said, "I'm going to go now. It was nice to meet you, Emily."

"Ok," she said. "It was nice meeting you as well, Will."

Without a moment's hesitation I turned away and walked to the exit. And then I began to think over the encounter I had just had, and how weirdly I had acted.

Ted strolled alongside me. "What did I just witness?" he asked.

"I'm calling it," I said.

"Calling what?" Ted asked.

"My 'I'm going to marry that girl.'" Ted laughed and patted my back. "I'm serious," I said.

"You only get to say that once, remember? There is ten pounds at stake here."

"I know. So you better pay up because you just met the future Mrs. Evans."

I should explain that when Ted and I were younger we came up with a bet that if we could call the girl that we were going to marry—like they did in the old days when a guy would gaze across the room in a smoky bar and see a beautiful girl, and he'd watched her for a moment, and their eyes would meet, and she'd smile briefly before looking away, and then he'd turn to his pals and say, "Hey, fellas, you see that girl over there, I'm going to marry her."—then the other had to pay him ten pounds. It's just a bit of fun between us really.

Ted laughed again. "Fair enough. So how are you going to make that happen?"

"We're coming here again tomorrow."

"Oh, no, Will, don't make me do this." He moaned.

"It's not like you have anything better to do. We'll come and see another film."

"I tell you what, I'll make you a bet."

"Ok, what bet is that?" I asked with a cautious look.

"I bet when we return tomorrow, she doesn't remember your name."

"How much?"

"Five pounds."

I offered my hand for him to shake. "Deal."

"What do we do if she isn't here?"

I shrugged. "We go home."

"Ok, cool. I hope she has a boyfriend because that will be so funny."

JANUARY 16TH

So, after work we returned home, got changed, and then drove over to the cinema. Ted was being as supportive as ever, and teased me every two seconds. Emily wasn't behind the same stand like she was yesterday. And I thought that was it. I'd never see her again. I'd given up after twelve seconds.

And then I spotted her. Everything was fine again. She was standing behind the counter that sold popcorn and hot dogs and other items. Ted and I walked over and lined up behind a couple that were buying some popcorn.

"Do you want some popcorn?" I asked him.

"Are you offering?" he asked.

"I just did."

"Ok, I'll have some salted popcorn."

"You're so awkward, you know I like sweet popcorn."

"I'm doing you a favour, Will, this means you will have a longer excuse to stand and talk to Emily."

"You're a genius."

"I know."

The couple in front of us grabbed their popcorn off the counter and then Ted and I stepped forward. Before I could say hello, Emily said, "Hi, Will."

"Ah, fuck," Ted said, instantly realising he'd lost his five-pound bet.

"Ignore him," I said. "How are you, Emily?"

She smiled a tight-lipped smile and then said, "Ok, thanks. How about you?"

"I'm good, thank you."

"Good. So what can I get for you both?"

"We'd like some popcorn, please."

"Ok. What flavour and what size?"

"Two large popcorns. One sweet, one salted."

"Ok," she said, lifting up the lid to the popcorn and beginning to shovel popcorn into the boxes.

"Any plans this weekend?" I asked.

"Not really sure. Probably watch a lot of TV."

"Are you not working?"

"Nope."

"That's good."

She placed the popcorn onto the counter and said, "Six pounds, please."

I stood aside and allowed Ted to step forward. "Ted lost a bet so now he has to buy me popcorn," I said.

Ted sighed and retrieved his wallet from his pocket and paid for the popcorn.

"What film are you two going to see today?" Emily asked.

"We only stopped by for popcorn," I said. "We were passing and thought we'd stop by to get some."

"Ok. Well, enjoy."

"Thank you. Good-bye, Emily. Have a lovely weekend."

"You too, Will."

As we walked away, Ted threw a piece of popcorn at my face. "That was so embarrassing to watch," he said.

"What?" I said.

"She said she didn't have any plans and she wasn't working. You had the perfect opportunity to ask her out."

"Well, we can—"

"No," Ted interrupted.

"What?"

"You're going to say we can come back Monday. I'm not coming here for a third time."

"Aw, why? One more time and it'll be the last time, I promise."

Ted moaned at me and then said, "Fine. But if you make us come all the way over here again so you can have another thirty-second conversation with her, then I will tackle you into the sweet stand."

JANUARY 18TH

Sundiscussion Topic:
Who would win a fight between Will and his hot sister Rosie?

"Really, Ted?" I asked with a questionable look.
"You don't think she's hot?" he replied.
"No, of course I don't think my sister is hot."
"Suit yourself. So who would win?"
"She would. She'd kick my ass."
"I agree."
"You forgot to come up with another topic, didn't you? You just made this one up."
"Indeed I did."

JANUARY 19TH

After work we went home, got changed, and drove to the cinema, again.

"Are we going to see a film?" Ted asked.

I don't know. Should we? Would we look strange going in for popcorn again? It depends where Emily is standing. Is there any other good films on we could see?"

"Yes. Going in for popcorn is a bit weird. And I've no idea, it was your idea to come again, I thought you would have thought it through."

We entered the cinema, and once again, Emily was no-where to be seen. And we stood there casually and discreetly for a couple of minutes before Ted spotted her on the top floor, taking people's tickets.

"We can't just walk up there. We need to buy a ticket so we can go up there and actually have a reason to be there," Ted said.

"Fine. Let's go and buy a ticket," I said, walking over to the counter.

"How can I help you?" the lady behind the counter asked.

"What films are showing on the top floor now or in the very close future?" I asked.

She frowned for a moment before glancing down at her

screen. "The only one that meets your request is *Bride Wars* in seven minutes."

I could sense Ted wanting to tackle me as he was now about to be forced to see a chick flick. "We'll have two tickets to that, please."

She processed the tickets and then we immediately made our way up to Emily.

"I wish I never agreed to this," Ted said. "I should have left you to come alone. Now look what you've done."

I laughed as we got to the top of the stairs, and then we strolled over to Emily's stand. It seems that every time I see her she becomes more and more beautiful.

"Oh, hello, fancy seeing you here," I joked awkwardly.

"I know," she replied. "It's almost like you're following me, Will."

"Ted and I have become big fans of the cinema recently," I said, expecting Ted to nod his head in agreement, but he just looked miserable and uninterested.

"What are you going to see today?" she asked.

"*Bride Wars*," I answered cautiously.

Emily bit her lip in an attempt to prevent herself from smiling. She had definitely figured out why we were here. She took our tickets and then ripped them before returning them to my possession. "Enjoy the film," she said.

"We shall. Will you be here when it is finished?" I asked.

"Yes," she answered.

"Good," I said. "We can tell you what we thought about the film."

"Ok," she said with a smirk. I turned to Ted, who had somehow managed to make himself look even grumpier. And then we walked forward and found the screen and then our seats. The cinema was again half full. We walked straight to the back and sat in the corner.

"If you don't ask her out when we leave, I will never

speak to you again," Ted whispered as he grumpily stuck his feet up on the chair in front of him.

"Don't worry." I said, patting his knee. "I will."

The film was a lot better than we expected and we found it quite funny. Well, I did. Ted was still being grumpy for being made to watch the film. Once again we waited for everyone to leave so I could speak to Emily on our way out. And just as we were about to talk to her she was called over by another employee. She told us she would be back in two seconds and then walked away.

I turned to Ted. "What should I say to her?" I asked.

"Would you like to go out sometime?" he replied.

"I can't say that."

"Yes, you can. Show some courage."

"Do I need to say anything else? Like, do I say how much I like her first?"

"Will, it's like you have forgotten everything. How have you asked girls out in the past?"

"I text them."

"Just ask her out and let's go home."

"So would it be ok if I told her that I think she is beautiful and I would like to buy her dinner sometime?"

"I don't know," Ted replied. He leant to his side and looked past me. "Would it?"

I sighed and realised he had set me up. I turned and faced Emily. "Oh, hey, Emily. How's it hanging?" I asked. *How's it hanging? Why not just ask her how she is?*

"Well, I sat down on them earlier and it really hurt," she replied.

I frowned, not understanding what she meant. "What hurt, sorry?"

Her innocent blue eyes blinked a couple of times before she said, "My balls."

I found it really funny, but I just smiled and froze, because it caught me completely off guard. Clearly I wasn't expecting that response. After a moment or two I laughed and said, "Well, I hope they're feeling better now."

She smiled a tight-lipped smile. "They are, thank you." I could feel my heart beat rising, and I could feel myself backing out of asking her.

"Will would like to ask you out, Emily," Ted then said. "It was painful watching you struggle," he said into my ear. I could see his smug smile out of the corner of my eye. I didn't know what to do or say, so I just stood there and waited to see what she would say.

Her eyes flicked between us a few times and then she brushed back a small piece of her hair that had fallen forward. "How about you give me your number and maybe I'll text or call you."

"Excellent. Will, give her a business card," Ted said, patting my chest. I turned my head and his smug face met my unamused face as I reached into my jacket and retrieved a business card, I always keep a couple on me. Ted snatched it from me and handed it to Emily. "We can stop coming to the cinema to see ridiculous films now. You take care, Emily," Ted said, forcing me to turn toward the exit.

"My name isn't Emily," she quickly replied.

I removed Ted's arms from my shoulders and turned back to her. "Sorry, I assumed that was your name since it was on your name tag," I said.

"My name is Zac," she said, as she examined my business card.

"But that's a guy's name," Ted said.

"Why don't you go and wait in the car?" I said, removing the keys from my pocket and tossing them to him.

"Fine," he replied, walking away. I shook my head and then took a step closer to Zac's stand.

"That's why I don't have a name tag with it on. Because everyone asks why I have a guy's name."

I nodded. "Well, I'm sure I can hear all about it if I hear from you."

"Yes you will, Will." She smirked at the "will, Will" part and covered her mouth to try to prevent me from seeing. I lifted an eyebrow at how funny she found herself. "Sorry," she mumbled.

I laughed. "That's ok. I'm gonna go now. I hope to hear from you soon, Zac." I wanted to stay and talk to her, but I didn't want her to get into trouble for chatting to me, even though nobody was around.

"Good-bye, Will."

"Good-bye, Zac."

JANUARY 21ˢᵀ

According to "the rules of waiting for someone to call you," I had to wait three days before I could presume that Zac wasn't interested in going on a date with me. And since Monday, I have done nothing but stare at my phone, wishing she would call. And then as I returned to my office from the toilet just before Ted and I were about to leave, my phone started to ring on my desk. Ted and I shared a glance, and then I dove onto my phone to answer it.

"Hello."

"Hi, Will, it's Zac. Is now a good time?"

"Oh, hey! Yes, it is. How are you?"

"I'm ok. How are you?"

"I'm good thanks. I'm glad you called."

"You're lucky that we met really because the past couple of weeks I've taken on extra shifts as someone is away."

"Oh really? I'm very fortunate then."

"I guess. Anyway, I thought I'd see if you still wanted to go out?"

"Yes, of course."

"I was wondering if you wanted to see a film with me tomorrow? It's the last showing of this film I've been meaning to see. I thought you could maybe watch it with me?"

"Yeah, of course, I don't have any plans. What time does the film start? We can get some food afterwards as well if you like?"

"Maybe. The film starts at 6:00 p.m. So I'll see you ten minutes before then?"

"Ok, 6:00 p.m. See you then, Zac."

"Ok. Bye."

"Bye."

JANUARY 22ND

I spent the rest of my evening grinning. I was looking forward to seeing her, and spending the evening with her. It'd be good to find out more about her as well since I know nothing about her apart from her name and where she works

I didn't have time to go home and get changed so I wore my nice black suit today. It was date appropriate anyway. I was just slightly overdressed for a trip to the cinema. Ted walked home while I took the car. Home is only a fifteen-minute walk from work so don't feel too sorry for him. By the time you've sat in traffic it probably takes the same amount of time to drive there, too. I called a flower shop earlier and ordered a bouquet. A beautiful girl always deserves beautiful flowers. Unless she's allergic. Then get her something else.

I stopped by the flower shop and picked up Zac's flowers. They had a small bag of water attached to the bottom so they didn't need putting into water right away. Normally I'd feel quite stupid walking into a cinema wearing a suit with flowers in my hand. But I was about to go on a date with a seriously beautiful girl, so other people's views were the last thing on my mind.

The cinema was maybe over half full, mostly people waiting in line for popcorn. A group of girls were leaving the cinema and they seemed to check me out, which was a reassuring sign that I looked appropriate for my date. I stood in the centre of the cinema and swept my eyes across everyone, but I couldn't see Zac. So I walked over to the café and joined the line of three or four people to grab her and myself a hot chocolate to kill some time.

After staring at the board for a couple of minutes wondering whether to have cinnamon with it or not, I felt a hand on my arm. I looked down and saw Zac looking up at me with a tight-lipped smile, and she'd tied her hair back. I'd never seen her with her hair tied back before. Somehow it made her eyes stand out even more. I had to remind myself not to stare into them. She was wearing a grey jacket with the zip undone so you could see her black work polo. She was also wearing black ripped jeans and original Timberland boots.

She flapped her hand up quickly and waved and then stuck it back into her pocket. "Hi," she said.

"Hi," I replied.

"I like your suit. You look smart," she said.

"Thanks. I didn't have time to go home and get changed," I answered. "I was going to get us a hot chocolate, is that ok?"

"I'm ok, thank you," she replied.

I nodded. "Ok." We stood in silence for a moment before she looked at the flowers, which I had forgotten about. "Oh, I bought you flowers."

"You bought me flowers," she said, taking them from me. "I've never had flowers bought for me before; this is so weird."

"Really? None of your ex-boyfriends bought them for you?" I asked.

"No, my ex never did."

I was very surprised, but did my best not to react and just did a few casual nods. I turned back to the queue and noticed that the woman who was stood at the counter ordering when I arrived was still ordering now. "I'm not really interested in a hot chocolate so shall we go find our seats?" I asked.

"Sure. I picked up the tickets before I came to find you," she replied.

"Ok, great. Would you like me to put the flowers in my car?"

She shook her head. "No, it's ok. I'll keep them."

"Ok. I shall let you lead the way," I said.

Zac had reserved our tickets for the aisle seats on the third row from the back. The film hadn't started yet, but the adverts were running. She took the aisle seat and obviously I took the seat next to her.

"So what is this film about?" I asked.

"I'm not really sure. I know these two girls are in a police station and then everyone suddenly starts shooting everyone. Something like that," she replied. Before I could reply she started talking again, "There's a burger place two minutes down the road from here. When the film finishes, we could walk to it and have a drink at the bar there."

I smiled. "Ok."

She nodded at me and then looked down at her hands she was fiddling with, still nodding. "I'm just gonna go to the bathroom before the film starts. I hate having to leave the cinema halfway through a film."

I smiled again. "Ok." So she got up, made sure her flowers were not going to fall over, walked down the stairs, and exited the cinema screen.

I sat back and could sense what Ted would say if he was seated next to me. *Jesus, Will, stop saying ok. Actually talk and say something, anything. Find out if she likes Star Wars or what her favourite colour is.* The screen then went black and a statement appeared saying if you record this film illegally you'll be fined or could face further prosecution. Zac still hadn't returned and I thought that she might have abandoned me and ran off. And then the film title *Twisted* appeared in bold capitals. Zac then reappeared and made her way back up the stairs and returned to her seat beside me.

"Everything ok?" I asked. She quickly looked at me and shushed me very loudly. Her beautiful blue eyes trapped me in an intense glare. I tensed up and froze like my mum had just told me off in public. "I'm sorry," I whispered.

She then sniggered at me. "Oh my God, you looked so scared."

I opened my mouth in disbelief. "That was so mean!" I whispered.

"I thought it was very funny. You looked like a dog that had been told off for peeing in the house again."

My mouth seemed to open further in disbelief. "And now you're comparing me to a dog!" Thankfully there was no one sat that close to us because my whispering really wasn't very whispery.

"I had to pop out and speak to security because I got a text from my friend who's on her shift, she said there was a suspicious gentleman wandering around in a suit, carrying some flowers, and she asked if I had seen him."

I hadn't clicked onto what she was saying and then I glanced down at my suit, and then at the flowers in front of her. Now I started to glare. As I looked up to her she began sniggering again.

"That's twice I have got you now!" she whispered. "The film really is about to start now though," she said, turning her attention to the screen and tucking her legs up onto the seat and wrapping her arms around them. I kept my eyes on her and watched her for a moment. She really was beautiful. And she's funny, too. Zac maintained her position, but her eyes peeked over at me and she smirked slightly. So I turned my attention to the screen too as the film began.

Twisted was such a surprise. It was nonstop action after the first ten minutes. It's about a girl who witnesses a murder, so she sprints to the nearest police station straight away and tells them what happened. And her new friend, whom she had started at university with, comes to comfort her. And then the group of people who arranged the murder comes to the police station, because one of the cops on the inside is a traitor and informs them. And they barge in and shoot the whole place up. Then the two girls suddenly turn into assassins and shoot them all back. The girl who witnessed the murder used to shoot with her dad so she was pretty good with a gun. To put a long story short, they manage to kill everyone and escape.

I recognised Eleanor Walden, the super-hot brunette actress; she played the new university friend. She has done loads of films. Ted and I have seen most of them. But the other actress, August Bishop, I've never seen before. She was also extremely hot. I can't believe Ted didn't want to come and see this film. This would be his definition of the perfect film.

I put Zac's flowers in the car while she went to grab her bag from her locker. By the time I walked back toward the entrance, Zac was already making her way out.

"Ready to go, Will Evans?" she asked.

"I am, Zac... umm..."

"Williams," she added. Before I could make the comparison of my first name and her second name she joked in a silly voice, "Yes, that's like your name."

I smiled. "Williams, Zac Williams. Got it."

"My full name is Zachary, but only my parents call me that when they're shouting at me."

"Zachary. So is there a reason you're called that or…?" I asked as we began to walk down the road to this burger place she'd mentioned.

"My parents wanted a boy. And they were one hundred percent convinced they were having a boy. I'm sure you can imagine their excitement when I entered the world without a penis."

"So, they called you Zac anyway?"

"Well, my dad is called Zac and my grandfather is called Zac. So I'm actually Zachary Williams the third."

"That is pretty cool, though. Not many people can introduce themselves as the third, or any other number for that matter."

"So are you a Will or William?" she asked.

"Just Will."

"Ok." She stuck her hands in her pocket and started shivering.

"Do you want my jacket?" I asked.

"No, it's ok, thanks."

"Are you sure?"

She nodded. "So what did you think of the film?"

"I liked it," I replied.

"I liked it, too," she began. "That was the blonde girl's first role, she'll be huge soon. I think I may have a small crush on her."

"Oh really? I think I'd still rather date Eleanor Walden."

"Yeah, she's hot, too, but August seems more like my type," she said with a sarcastic squint.

"Yeah, I agree. You two would make a lovely couple."

She sniggered. "I'm glad you agree."

I paused for a moment before saying, "But if I had to choose between the three of you, I would choose you." I almost winced after saying it, and thought that it was way too cliché, and she was going to think that I was weird. I could sense Ted beside me laughing.

Zac looked at me and then her tight-lipped smile grew into a grin as she blushed. She looked unbelievably cute. I really wanted to kiss her.

"I like your smile," I said.

She covered her mouth with her hand and mumbled, "Thanks."

As I looked ahead I could see the glowing lights from the burger restaurant. But halfway between us and the burger restaurant, was a small everyday shop. I saw this as an opportunity to quickly pop inside and call Ted to update him with how it was going with Zac. I suppose I could have called him from the bathroom of the burger place, but that might be a little weird. There could be another guy peeing, and then there's me stood beside him on the phone talking about my date. "I'm just going to head into this shop for a second. Is that ok?"

Zac was fiddling with her flowers so she didn't seem too bothered. Then her eyes flicked up and nodded. "I'll wait here."

I opened the shop door and walked to the back and called Ted whilst searching for something to buy.

"How's it going, you handsome devil?"

"I think it's going really well. She finds me funny, I think, and she's funny, too. She's kind of like a tortoise. One minute she'll poke her head out of her shell and be funny and excited, then the next she's all shy and quiet."

"Does she like Star Wars?"

"Thanks for listening. I haven't asked her if she likes Star Wars yet."

"It's an important question, Will."

"I don't have much time. I'm quickly came into this shop to update you with how it was going."

"Just make her laugh. Making a girl laugh is probably the most important thing. But don't try too hard, just make it natural."

"Surprisingly helpful advice. Thanks, man, I'll see you later."

"I'm going to bed now, so you can tell me about it in the morning."

"Ok, bye."

"Bye." I stared at the magazine rack and grabbed a magazine about movies. It seemed like a sensible thing for me to enter the shop for. As I pulled out my wallet and looked up at the shopkeeper, I noticed a stack of blue beanies behind him, hanging on the wall. And they were almost the exact same blue as Zac's eyes. I instantly knew I had to buy it for her. She was cold, too, so I had two reasons to buy it for her. And when we get married she can tell everyone that I bought it for her on our first date. So I bought the magazine and the beanie.

When I made my way out of the shop and returned to Zac, she was on the phone, too. "I'll speak to you later," she said. "I have to go. Bye."

"Everything ok?" I asked.

"Yep," she answered.

"I bought you a beanie," I said.

"You bought me a beanie?"

"You were shivering and you wouldn't take my jacket so I thought it might warm you up a little. It's also a similar colour blue to your eyes." She smugly raised her eyebrow and examined it. "Will you please put it on? I don't want you to catch a cold."

"Ok, ok. Whatever feeds your panda," she said, taking the beanie from me.

"Feeds my what?" I asked.

"Panda. I should explain that it's my saying. You know

how people say *whatever floats your boat?* Well, I decided to make up my own."

"Right...so whatever feeds your panda? Is that correct?"

"Yes, that is correct, Will."

"Can other people say it?"

"Absolutely not, make up your own saying! You can't steal mine!"

"Ok. I was only enquiring."

She removed the bobble from her hair, allowing her tied-up hair to fall, then placed the beanie onto her head and wiggled into place. "Have I put it on right or do I look like an elf?" she asked.

I took a step forward and adjusted it marginally. "Now you don't look like an elf."

Zac didn't want to talk about her family, which I completely understood, so we spoke about our friends since Ted had been with me every other time Zac and I met. So we sat at the bar and ordered a chocolate milk shake each.

"I live with my best friend, Natalie. She was using her spare room in her apartment as, like, storage and stuff and had some of her clothes in there. But she cleared it out and I moved in. I spent most nights at hers anyway, either on the sofa or shared the bed with her. The spare room isn't huge, but it's fine for sleeping in and stuff; the rest of the time I sit in the living room. My parents kicked me out nearly two months ago, so that's why I don't want to talk about my family."

"So are you at university or college as well as working at the cinema? And I understand. You don't really know me either so don't reveal too much to me."

She sniggered. "No, I'm taking a year off to figure out what I want to do. I don't even know what I would study."

"I understand. It's a lot of money to go to university, too."

"Exactly."

"So how old are you? If you don't mind me asking."

"Why, are you slowly trying to find out more about me so you can find my address?"

"No, I'm just trying to find your bank details. I've had your address for hours now."

She sniggered and then took a sip from her milk shake. "I turned twenty last month. What about you?"

"I'm twenty, too. I turn twenty-one in a few months."

"You have quite a baby face. So I thought you might be a few years older than me, and you can't grow facial hair, or you might be younger and just haven't started yet. But it turns out you're neither."

So we sat there and talked. I told her about working with Ted at Ron's Ice Cream. And I told her if she ever wanted a tour, I would happily show her around the factory where the ice cream is made. And it seemed before we'd started to get to know each other, it was already 11:00 p.m.

I offered to drive her home as she normally gets the bus, but I wasn't going to allow her to sit outside in the cold and wait for it. She told me she didn't have work tomorrow so she didn't mind.

I was really was lucky that I met her. She normally works Monday to Thursday from 10:00 a.m. to 4:00 to 4:30 p.m. Somebody was away on holiday so she had taken on some extra shifts. And she rarely does that.

We stayed for another twenty minutes before we strolled to my car. "You're cool, Will Evans," she said as we slumped into our seats.

"Thanks, you're cool, too, Zachary Williams the third." She smirked at me calling her that, and she looked out of the window.

I watched her for a second. And then she looked back at me. And our eyes met. And then she leant over and kissed me. Then she went all shy afterward and returned to her seating position, twiddling her thumbs.

"So, where are we going? Like what is your address?"

"We could...we could...go back to your place if you like?" she said, her eyes quickly meeting mine before they looked back down.

"You want to come back to my place?"

"Yes, if that is ok."

"Ok... My place it is," I said, starting the ignition.

JANUARY 23RD

Zac was still asleep when I woke up. At least I think she was. I couldn't see her face as it was covered by her hair. I had to hold my breath to prevent myself from laughing. It was a cute look.

It was only 7:30 a.m., so I had two hours before I needed to be at work. I thought about staying in bed and lying with Zac until she woke up, you know, like they do in the films and then they smile at one another and say good morning and stuff. But since all I had to stare at until then was a wall of hair, which at any second could have made me laugh, a lot, I decided to have a shower. I thought I would wait for Zac to wake up to have breakfast, then we could eat together.

When I returned from having my shower, she was no longer in the bed. And for a brief moment I thought she'd left, and I didn't know whether to panic or feel upset. But then I saw her phone on charge next to the bed, so she must still be in the apartment.

I quickly dried myself and put on my suit. I figured she was maybe trying to make herself some breakfast. But she was sat cross-legged on my sofa when I came out of my bedroom, watching TV, sipping a glass of water.

"Hey, good morning."

"Morning," she said, turning with her tight-lipped smile. "I'm watching SpongeBob." She'd tied her hair up, but there was a tiny bit that she'd missed at the back that stood alone, all curly.

"I can see that." I said, sitting next to her. "Are you ok?"

"I am. Are you?"

"I am."

"Good."

"Would you like some breakfast?"

"No, thank you."

"Ok. Would you like a hot drink? Tea, coffee?"

"Tea sounds nice."

"How would you like it?"

"Just with milk, please."

"Ok," I said. "Ok," I said again, and got up to make tea. I put on the kettle and grabbed some mugs from the shelf. And then Ted emerged from his bedroom.

I didn't know what to tell him about Zac, I didn't know if he'd already seen her this morning or not. And I didn't want to say anything that would make her feel uncomfortable or make her frustrated with me. He took two steps and then stopped, with a look of sheer delight exploding onto his face. His eyes bulged as he turned to me. And then he just grinned and nodded, not once or twice, he nodded like a bobblehead for a good ten to fifteen seconds. Zac was sat with her back slightly to him so she hadn't noticed his emergence. Then he said, "Good morning, Will. And good morning, unexpected guest on the sofa. Zac, is that you?"

Ted walked over to his sofa and sat on it. I said good morning before returning back to the kettle to pretend like I was busy making tea.

"Hey, Ted," Zac replied.

"I didn't realise we would be having your company this morning; it is such a pleasant surprise. Did you and Will enjoy your evening?"

I thought maybe I should intervene so I said, "Yes, we did. The film was great. I think you would have really liked it. Then we went and had a milk shake at a burger place not far from the cinema. And then we came back here for another drink. And then I slept on the sofa and Zac slept in my bed."

Ted placed his arm on the back of the sofa and swung himself around. "Oh, Will. 'Twas a noble effort, William, but I came into this room at 3:00 a.m. for a bottle of water and you were nowhere to be seen. This means both of you can only have been in one place." A small smirk appeared on Zac's face as her eyes met mine. I decided to shut up and stick to making the tea. "Anyway," Ted continued. "'Twas nice chatting, but I must flee. I'm going to walk to work now and on the way I shall pick myself up some breakfast. Then I have an enormous amount of nothing to do at the office, but since I'm awfully generous I'm going to let you have the car so you can drive her home."

"That is very kind of you, sir. I wish you all the best on your incredible quest," I said as I walked over and sat next to Zac, placing our mugs on the table.

Ted stood without another word being said. But he walked around to the back of my sofa and stuck his head between us. "Before I go... Was Zac the best sexual intercourse out of *all* the other ladies you've had the privilege of having sexual intercourse with?"

I didn't stall, I didn't blink, I didn't breathe. I replied right away and said, "Yes."

He then turned to Zac. "Same question for you, lady Zac."

But I pushed his head away. "Ok, leave now, please." He laughed and swiftly left Zac and I alone in our apartment.

"I'm sorry, he's very immature and doesn't have much consideration," I said to her.

"That's ok," she replied. I watched her as she went to pick up her mug. She was about to take a sip before she noticed me and then said, "What?"

"Nothing." I said. "You're incredibly beautiful, and I had a great time last night."

We drank our tea and then I drove Zac home. She was quiet in the car as I drove her home. Her apartment is about twenty minutes away from mine, so I'd make it to work with plenty of time to spare. But she sat there, all shy. I was expecting her to poke her head out of her shell at least once or twice. But no, she sat there peacefully, with her new blue beanie on.

"Thank you for driving me home. I had a nice time. And thanks for my beanie," she said as we pulled up outside her apartment. She wasn't making eye contact with me. And she was about to say good-bye and open the car door.

And before the opportunity slipped away I said, "I'd really like to see you again."

She turned and looked at me and didn't say a word.

"Would you like to see me again?" I asked, sensing that maybe she didn't, which was quite upsetting.

"I—" she began. "I'm not good at relationships or titles. They scare me now. I don't want anything serious. I don't want another relationship or feelings."

I listened to what she was saying and acknowledged it. After a second of taking it in I replied, "Well, we don't have to give it a title, and it doesn't have to be anything serious."

"I don't understand what you're trying to say?" she replied.

I pondered as I tried to figure out what I wanted to say next without sounding rude. "We could just do the final part of last night sometimes?" I soon noticed that my pondering had indeed had no improvement and I almost felt like stepping out of my own car and walking away.

"Will Evans, are you implying that we become fuck buddies?" Zac had now appeared from her shell and I felt like saying, "Ah, there's the tortoise!" But then I realised she was nothing like a tortoise appearing from its shell. Zac was more like a dormant volcano. One minute it's a nice calm mountain, and the next minute it's erupting. I feel like that's a fairer comparison.

"That's a little bit explicit," I said with a small squeak in my voice. "But I suppose that is one way of putting it."

Zac's smug smile grew. "I see. Maybe I'll text you, Will."

"Ok. I look forward to you maybe texting me, Zachary Williams the third."

"I'm going to regret telling you that if I maybe text you," she said, holding up her hand in front of me.

"Why are you holding your hand up?" I asked cautiously staring at it.

"I'm waiting for you to give me a high five," she replied. I smiled and high-fived her. After she started to lean in, her beautiful blue eyes trapping me in a trance, I started to lean in too, but before I could kiss her, her flowers brushed in front of our faces.

"I was grabbing my flowers," she said, her smug smile reappearing. "Did you think I was going to kiss you?"

"You're mean," I said. Her smug smile changed into a very large tight-lipped smile as she shrugged her shoulders. "Right. I have to go to work now. I'm not lucky enough to have Fridays off like you."

"Enjoy your day at work," she said as she opened the door and exited the car.

"Thanks, I'll try." And then she closed the car door and walked up to her apartment block. I hoped she would turn around and wave, but she didn't. I made sure she got inside ok and then began my journey to work.

I arrived at the office fifteen minutes late because I got stuck behind an impassable tractor for seventy-five percent of the way there.

Ted was waiting for me in reception as I arrived. "You're late," he said, jumping up from the sofa.

"I got stuck behind a tractor."

"Was it a nice tractor?"

"It was an ordinary tractor. Nothing special."

"What colour was it?"

"It was red. Why does that matter?"

"I'm making conversation as we walk upstairs, Will. And you know I love a good tractor."

"It was an ordinary red tractor. A very slow ordinary red tractor."

"Thank you for clarifying." Ted quickened his pace up the last part of the second flight of stairs and opened the door for me. I thanked him and walked through it to see everyone calmly sat at their desks. But they were all wearing party hats, and there were four or five banners up that said "Congratulations!" on them.

"What's going on?" I asked.

"We've all been sent an email so go check your computer," Ted answered.

I frowned. "Why can't you tell me?"

"Because the email is funnier," Ted answered again.

The room was so silent. Suspiciously silent. Everyone was focusing on their screens. The only sound you could hear was from the fans in the computer hard drives. I wanted to say hello as I would normally do, but maybe the email would explain why everyone was acting so weird?

"Is it for your dad, Ted?"

"Just read the email, Will."

I frowned as I walked into our office, and on my desk were two or three balloons, all saying "Congratulations!" I then realised what was going on. I stepped out of my office to see Ted sniggering at me with a party hat on like everyone else, and everyone else's faces in the offices turning red from holding back their laughter.

"You're such an arse hole," I said to Ted.

He brought his hands from behind his back and put a party blower into his mouth and blew it. "Congratulations on getting laid, Will!"

And then everyone else in the office stuck a party blower in their mouth and blew on theirs, creating a deafening sound of horn-like noises. And then they all started clapping.

Once they'd stopped, I didn't know whether to punch Ted or laugh or lock myself in my office. Ted then passed me an envelope. "We all signed it for you."

I took the envelope from him in disbelief. "Thanks, everyone," I muttered. I opened the envelope to see another "congratulations" in big bold letters with an exclamation mark. The card felt thicker than it should have done, and for a second, I thought they'd all put some money in it. But instead I found four condoms.

"Those are from Jeremy," Ted said.

"You're welcome," Jeremy shouted. The card said:

To Will,
Congratulations on bringing a female home.
Love from everyone x

And then everyone in the office had signed it. Even Ted's dad had signed it. It was such a nice confidence-boosting gift.

"You're such a dick," I said to Ted as he closed our office door.

"Do you have any idea how difficult it was to carry everything to the office by myself? Only Ellie was in reception so I had to set everything up myself."

"I feel really sorry for you," I replied.

"Can you not see the funny side to this, please? I thought this would be the funniest thing. I invested a lot of my time and money into this idea."

I sighed and decided to humour him. "Thank you, Ted. For making me feel so special about my evening with Zac, and for taking so much time out of your schedule to do this for me. It means so much to me."

He smiled and nodded. "Thank you. You're welcome, Will. Could you maybe send me that in an email, too?"

"No, I'm not sending it to you in an email."

"Fair enough. That's understandable."

I thought that was it. It was over. I stuck my earphones in to distract myself from thinking about throwing an item from my desk at Ted. But after I'd read the long list of useless emails in my inbox, lunch was soon approaching. Ted went to the bathroom as I logged off my computer and put on my suit jacket. And as I stepped out Ted was standing in the same spot as he was before when he blew the party blower. But this time, he was holding a cake, with a lit candle in the middle of it.

"You've got to be kidding me," I said.

"Just blow out the candle so we can all go for lunch. You don't appreciate anything I do for you," he replied, moving the cake forward.

"I swear if you push my face into it, I will launch you through our office window." I stepped forward and closed my eyes and blew out the candle.

"Don't tell me what you wished for," Ted whispered, "otherwise it won't come true."

"Shut up. You can buy lunch since you're in such a generous gift-giving mood." Ted's happiness dimmed, as he couldn't think of an excuse or a comeback.

NEW MESSAGE FROM ZACHARY WILLIAMS III
Hi.

NEW MESSAGE FROM WILL EVANS
Hello. Is this you maybe texting me?

NEW MESSAGE FROM ZACHARY WILLIAMS III
Maybe.

NEW MESSAGE FROM ZACHARY WILLIAMS III
What are you doing later?

NEW MESSAGE FROM WILL EVANS
Nothing, yourself?

NEW MESSAGE FROM ZACHARY WILLIAMS III
Nothing.

NEW MESSAGE FROM ZACHARY WILLIAMS III
I could come over.

NEW MESSAGE FROM WILL EVANS
Could you now?

NEW MESSAGE FROM ZACHARY WILLIAMS III
Yes.

NEW MESSAGE FROM WILL EVANS
Your breasts are breathtaking (.)(.)

NEW MESSAGE FROM ZACHARY WILLIAMS III
What?

NEW MESSAGE FROM WILL EVANS
Sorry. I can pick you up after work if you like. I may
need your help removing and burying the body of my
dead best friend though.

NEW MESSAGE FROM ZACHARY WILLIAMS III
Haha. Text me when you're on your way.

NEW MESSAGE FROM WILL EVANS
I shall. Sometimes we leave early on Fridays so I'll
probably be there between 4:30 and 5:00.

NEW MESSAGE FROM ZACHARY WILLIAMS III
Ok.

"Can you for one second, please, stop being an annoying
idiot?" I said to Ted as I punched his shoulder as we waited
for our fish and chips.

"Have you asked me if it's ok for you to have a guest
around this evening?" he replied.

"Oh God, Ted. How many guests have you had around
without asking for my consent?"

"Excellent point, Will. Fine, she can come over."

"You were ecstatic for me a couple of hours ago. You
got me banners and cards and a cake."

"I know I did. But it's the weekend. It's me and you and
whatever we do time. Don't forget pizza time, too."

"If we order pizza and she wants some pizza she can
share mine or have her own. You don't need to get all
worried about your pizza consumption."

JANUARY 24ᵀᴴ

Ted and I were eating a bowl of cereal on our sofas while Zac was showering. We decided to watch SpongeBob. We didn't even know we had that channel until Zac found it yesterday.

"So, what do you think of Zac?" I asked while I heard my hair dryer being used in my bedroom. Ted entered the kitchen and washed his cereal bowl before returning. He was about to answer my question upon his return to his seat, but then Zac emerged from my bedroom. But I couldn't see her as my sofa faces away from my bedroom. She walked to the fridge and grabbed herself a bottle of water.

I then saw Ted's face. He was watching Zac as if she were a unicorn. He looked that fascinated and amazed. For a moment I thought she might have walked in in her underwear or naked or something. And I felt scared to turn and look at her in case she was looking at me.

She then walked behind me and sat beside me on my sofa. And that was when I saw the fascinating and amazing sight that Ted had witnessed only moments ago. Zac was wearing my Star Wars pyjamas. Well, it's a T-shirt that has Darth Vader on them and it says Star Wars underneath, and then a pair of shorts. My look had now matched Ted's. Zac hadn't washed her hair. Although the back of her hair was slightly wet from where the water must have splashed up, so that explains why she'd used my hair dryer.

She tied up her hair and then saw us both gawing over her. Her eyes were weary as she flicked between us both. "What?" she asked. "Have I got something on me?"

"It's just how ten-year-old me pictured it," Ted said.

"Pictured what?" she asked with a frown.

"That one day we would have a girl sat here wearing something with Star Wars on it."

Zac's frown increased, as if to say "Are you being serious?"

"You look really hot," I said.

She laughed. "You two are acting very weird."

"This is a rare phenomenon, Zac. Don't take this moment away from us," Ted responded.

"So because I'm wearing Will's pyjamas, you're going to stare at me all day?"

"Well, Will would during the night, too. Although I feel like he'll want to take them off."

"Ted!" I said. "You don't always have to be so inappropriate. Show some respect."

"Sorry, Zac. It sounded like a compliment in my head."

She smiled. "That's ok, Ted. You're forgiven."

JANUARY 25ᵀᴴ

Sundiscussion Topic:
Who is the coolest person dead or alive?

Ted and I were both stood in the kitchen talking.

"Interesting choice, Ted. Haven't we done this one before? It got a little heated up last time I believe," I said.

"Yes, we have. But since Zac is new to Sundiscussions, I thought we could re-use some previous topics to see what her opinion is," Ted replied.

We changed our attention to Zac, who was biting her nails on my sofa. "What?" she said, her eyebrows rising.

I sat next to her and explained what a Sundiscussion is, and the story behind it.

"So, what is today's topic?" she asked once I'd finished.

"Today's topic is who is the coolest person dead or alive?" Ted answered.

"Do you need some time to think it over?" I asked.

"No, it's ok. I have someone in mind." she replied.

"Ok. So Ted is going to say Denzel Washington, who is one very cool guy. But he isn't as cool as Sir Sean Connery," I said.

"Is he the guy who played James Bond in the seventies and they asked for like fifty thousand pounds otherwise they would blow up the world?" she asked.

"His first James Bond film was in 1962 and his last James Bond film was in 1983. And yes, they did ask for those kind of amounts, I can't remember how much it was exactly, but back then that was a large amount of money," I answered.

"Sean Connery doesn't even come close to Denzel Washington," Ted said.

"Do you want this to turn into another fight?" I asked. "Because you know I will kick your ass again."

"You didn't kick my ass," Ted said before he took a sip from his mug.

"We had to go to the hospital because you thought you broke your arm," I said.

"It was only a sprain," he mumbled.

"Exactly my point. I kicked your ass." Zac must have been watching our exchange with a considerable amount of questioning.

"Anyway," I said. "Let's move on and see what Zac's suggestion is." I shuffled around and faced Zac.

"I'm going to say Angelina Jolie. Because she's amazing in real life and in her films. If you say she isn't a badass in the Tomb Raider movies, then there's no point me ever taking part in one of these Sun...discussions ever again."

"I think Zac has won," Ted said out of the blue. "She's had an outstanding debut Sundiscussion. Congratulations, Zac," he added.

"Thanks," she replied.

"I wish I had thought of Angelina Jolie," Ted mumbled as her stood and wandered into the kitchen.

To celebrate her debut victory, Zac took a nap on my sofa while Ted and I spent our day watching football or soccer, depending on your preference. When I say nap, it was basically another eight hours of sleeping. It is possible that Zac could be a human sloth or koala, because she had been awake for no more than two hours before taking her long nap on the sofa. And by the time she woke up, it was time for me to drive her home.

When we pulled up outside her apartment I said, "So if you're free next weekend we could do the same again." She went all shy and didn't know what to say. I think I've figured out when she's shy. If she has her arms crossed, and tucks her hands under her armpits, then that's the sign that she's being shy. And if she's super shy she will hunch up her shoulders and rest her chin on the top of her chest.

"We can maybe text and see?" she said, her hair almost blocking my view of her.

"Ok, I'll maybe text you during the week."

JANUARY 29TH

"Will you do me a huge favour?" Ted asked, walking into our office not long after lunch. It's not very often Ted asks for a favour so when he does, I know it's genuine. So before I heard his favour I knew I could trust him to not prank me. Ted does actually take his work seriously and he is very good at his job. We both do and are.

"What's this favour you require?" I asked, placing the tips of my fingers together and leaning back on my chair.

"I completely forgot that I booked a private tour around the factory with this girl and her little sister on the phone before Christmas. But I'm having a meeting with my dad right now and was wondering if you could help me out?"

I hummed for a moment and spun around on my chair.

"Please," he added.

"Is it full VIP treatment? Put them in the funny sanitary suits and make the ice cream? And then do the work shop afterwards?"

"Yes, hit them with everything you can think of. Take good care of them. She paid a lot of money, and I think she's rich or famous or both or something."

I didn't pay attention to the rich or famous part. I was more interested in having the rest of the afternoon to leisurely watch the ice cream being made, which I haven't done in months. "Ok, I'll do it," I said.

"Thank you. They're waiting in reception for you."

"What?" I said.

He said goodbye and shut the door behind him, leaving me no time at all to prepare myself. But I wasn't too worried. Jim, the main man who runs the factory and makes sure nobody steps a foot out of line, loves explaining to anyone what procedures take place in the factory when he gets the chance. The factory is like his child.

I got up from my chair and walked into reception and saw that the sofa in front of the reception desk was unoccupied, which meant that they had to be sat on the one around the corner, not viewable as you walk down the stairs. I walked around the corner and there she was, the girl from the film. I couldn't remember her name, something to do with a month of the year. June or July or August! August! She was sitting next to some guy, and a little girl with ginger hair and freckles was sat on his knee.

"Hello," I said cautiously.

The little girl's head shot up. "Are you the ice cream man?" she asked, her eyes widening.

"No, but I get to take you to the ice cream man. He's called Jim."

"Does he wear a superhero costume if he's the ice cream man?"

I sulked. "I guess you could say he does, but it's not as cool as Batman's."

The little girl nodded in agreement, "Ok."

August smiled and then she stood and held out her hand. She and the little girl were wearing matching purple Ron's Ice Cream hoodies. August said something, but I didn't hear what she said, it sounded like mumbling; I was too busy taking in her beauty and the fact that she's a global superstar. I figured she was introducing herself and asking my name, but I said, "I saw your film the other day with Zac."

She raised an eyebrow. "That's an interesting name. Do you have like a nickname or a shorter version of it that people call you?" she joked.

I grinned, but didn't laugh. "Sorry, I'm finding it hard to believe that you're actually here. My name's not that, it's Will."

"Ok, Will. Nice to meet you. I'm August, the adorable ginger girl is my little sister, Madeline, and the lap she is sitting on is my fiancée, Ethan Knight."

"Fiancée?" I blurted, immediately regretting my inconsiderateness.

"Yes," she replied. "Is that so hard to believe?" she asked, turning back to him.

"Sorry. No, not at all." I reassured her. "It's just, I thought you were really young." I looked down at her left hand and then noticed the huge ring on her finger. I know nothing about rings, but I figured this one must have been a rather good and expensive one.

Ethan startled to chuckle. "Don't you start," August said to him.

"Sorry, dear," he replied.

"How old did you think I was?" she asked me as she crossed her arms.

"I thought you were sixteen or seventeen. Clearly that assumption was incorrect."

"I'm nineteen!" she pleaded, once again turning toward Ethan, who was chuckling.

"You're quite small, dear, maybe that's what confuses everyone?" He popped Madeline off his knee and onto her feet. He walked over and shook my hand. "Nice to meet you," he said.

"Nice to meet you, too," I replied.

He put his arm around August and kissed the top of her head. Ethan was only just shorter than me and he had a very fresh face. I thought he was dressed a bit too smart to be touring around a factory. Through his open coat I could see he was wearing a white shirt and a turquoise tie that had a pattern of ice cream cones on it.

"Can we go see the ice cream now?" Madeline said, appearing from behind them both and standing in front of them. She'd put the hood up on her hoodie and tightened the strings so only a small part of her face was visible.

I laughed. "Of course. Follow me. The entrance you came through is to our office. The entrance to the tour of the factory is on the other side. But there is a secret door that we can go through to take us there."

We walked past Ellie and the reception desk and I scanned my card that opened the door. We entered another room with a door to the factory that can only be opened by very few people because of hygiene rules, and a staircase that leads up to the museum, or history of Ron's Ice Cream room.

We walked up the staircase and I allowed them to go through first. "This is the history of Ron's Ice Cream room. This is where you can find out how Ron began his journey and how it has developed. We're actually starting in the middle of the tour. If you look down that corridor in front of us with the large glass windows, you can see into the factory and watch the ice cream production. So the real entrance is down there, you walk along the corridor and look into the factory for as long as you like, and then you come in here and see all the old tubs and cartons that the ice cream used to be kept in from twenty, thirty, or sixty years ago. And after you've been in here you go through the door to the left of the corridor we just saw, and that takes you into the room where you get to make your own tubs of ice cream."

August and Ethan didn't seem too interested; I'm sure the main reason they came was to bring Madeline, whose face was getting redder by the second with excitement. She sprinted to the corridor and placed her hands on the window as she peered into the factory with such joy that it could have been mistaken for someone discovering the lost city of Atlantis.

August, Ethan, and I walked over and joined her. "Wow," August said. "I didn't think it would be this big!"

Ethan immediately started laughing and couldn't stop himself. August didn't look too pleased with his immaturity. She rolled her eyes and punched his arm. "Will you grow up for a second, please!"

"I'm sorry, dear, but it was funny!" I must admit I did find it hard to contain myself, too. It's been a while since I've done the tour, but that is pretty much what everyone says when they first see the factory, and it never gets old. I suppose I may need to grow up, too.

"I thought we could start in the history room first. I know it may seem a little boring, but most people find it surprisingly interesting. Then I can take you into the factory and we can all make some ice cream together. And after that we can come back up here and we can go into the other room where you can make some tubs of ice cream that you can take home with you!"

"Right, Maddie, if you want to go down there, we'd best go and read about all the boring—I mean, interesting history first," Ethan joked. Madeline sighed and they walked back into the history room and perused around the displays. I stood by the wall and allowed them to wander freely since I've seen the displays many, many times.

"Is there anything about the bubblegum flavour in here?" Madeline asked. I walked over and found a piece about our bubblegum flavour. It was originally made twenty years ago and it stopped being sold after being in production for four years. It hadn't sold as well as planned. And then they brought it back two years ago to give it another go and it sold well so we kept it.

Ethan had to pick Madeline up and hold her so she could read the display. She read it aloud so everyone could hear. I glanced over at August and she had a small smile on her face. She looked so proud of her little sister being able to read the text. When Madeline struggled on a word, she helped her, and then once she'd finished August said, "Well done, that was great!" And they high-fived. It was so nice to see. It made me think about the relationship I had with my older sister when we were younger. She didn't used to do things with me like that. She'd just trip me up or throw things at me. She was nice like that.

After no longer than five minutes Madeline's patience could withhold no more and she insisted we go to the factory. So, we walked back along the corridor where you could see the factory and we entered the reception for the tour, where fifteen to twenty people were waiting for the next tour. One boy, who looked about ten or eleven, walked up to Ethan and asked for an autograph while I radioed down to Jim to come up and meet us so he could take us into the factory.

While Ethan had a photo with the young boy, I whispered to August, "Sorry. Is he famous, too?"

"He's a magician," she whispered in reply.

"Ah," I said. "Stage magician or..."

"He has his own street magic TV show. The second series just started. We were also on Patrick Miller's show on Christmas Eve. He performed a magic trick on there, too. That's also where we had our first kiss."

It made me think back to New Year's Eve where the girls were talking about the magician and the actress on Patrick

Miller's show on Christmas Eve. Now I realised that August and Ethan were who they were talking about. "Ah," I said again. "I'll make sure I watch it."

"He's really good," she said, still whispering. "I'm not just saying that because he's my fiancée. I'm saying it because I've been the one watching him for nearly thirteen years now."

"Wow," I said. "So you were friends before you two got engaged?"

"Yes, we were."

"Wow," I said again. "He must be extremely patient." I added.

She laughed. "Yeah, I guess you could say that." The door behind us then made a beeping noise as it unlocked. Jim appeared in his Ron's Ice Cream overalls, like ones a mechanic would wear. Jim is fifty-five. He took charge of the factory after his dad retired twenty-five years ago. Yes, Ron's Ice Cream is a very family-take-over-based company.

Jim and I greeted and shook hands, and then I introduced him to August, Ethan, and Madeline. I didn't bother telling him that they were famous because even after explaining he'd still not fully understand who they were. He's very old-fashioned I guess you could say. I just told him that they were our VIPs today and if he would happily show us around his factory. He held out his hand and I led the way downstairs to our first stop.

"The people who were waiting in reception will be watching you make the ice cream from the window on the corridor," I told Madeline.

She grinned. "Really?"

"Really," I replied.

"Cool!"

At the bottom of the stairs was a bench and some lockers. "Because we have the strictest rules about cleanliness and hygiene, everyone has to wear one of these suits," Jim explained as he walked over to a big locker, even bigger than me, and opened it with a set of keys. Inside were the white suits I've worn countless times. The best way to describe them is if there were ever an alien spaceship that crash-landed, these would be the suits the scientists would wear as they examined and recovered the wreckage.

"Don't worry, these suits are new. We throw them out once someone has worn them," I said. Jim passed everyone the package they needed to enter the next stage of the factory. Shoe protectors, the suit overall, gloves, and a hat, similar to what you would wear in the shower to prevent your hair from getting wet.

"This is even worse than the time I visited the hotel you were bringing down on yourself," August muttered.

"What do you mean?" Ethan replied.

"When I had to wear that stupid builders hat and the high visibility vest that didn't fit."

Ethan smirked. "Oh yeah, that's still my screensaver on my phone."

"No, it isn't," August said with a sigh.

"Yes, it is." He removed his phone from his pocket and the screen lit up; I could see out of the corner of my eye August wearing a bright orange helmet and vest with a huge sulk on her face.

"Oh, Ethan, change it!" she said, trying to grab it from him.

"No! I like it! Leave me alone!" he whined.

August's eyes then started to bulge and her nostrils began to flare. Meanwhile everyone else was almost fully dressed apart from those two.

"Are you ok?" I asked her.

"Oh, she's fine," Ethan said. "That's her poop stare. She just really needs a poo." He and Madeline giggled.

"I do not!" August cried. "This is my super-serious I'll-kick-the-poop-out-of-you look." Jim and I kept to ourselves in case this was actually developing into an argument or if they were actually joking.

August maintained her gaze and Ethan's face became more and more concerned. "Guys, she's not blinking, why isn't she blinking?" But no one said anything. Jim and I certainly couldn't say anything, and Madeline was too busy swinging her legs on the bench. "Fine, I'll change it later!" Ethan said, accepting defeat.

August held her stare for a little longer and then she smiled. "Thank you, babe," she said, kissing him. "If I hold it long enough, it starts to scare him," she said to us. Jim and I laughed and then he locked up the giant locker.

Ethan walked to August and squeezed her cheeks and then he kissed her again. They smiled at one another after. But Madeline and I looked at each other and made gross faces. "Will?" Ethan said.

"Yes?" I replied.

"Would you mind taking a photo of us all in our suits, please?"

"Of course." He unzipped his suit slightly and grabbed his phone and passed it to me. I took the photo and gave Ethan his phone back, and then Jim asked, "Is everyone ready?" as he stood beside the next door.

"Yep!" we all said.

"Ladies, if you could make sure all your hair is tucked into your hats, please. And if everyone could please refrain from coughing or sneezing or spitting, that would be great. But if you need to, please make sure you use your hand to contain it," Jim said, scanning his card and opening the next door.

"The next room is slightly colder, so when we go through the next door into the factory, the temperature isn't affected. The factory isn't that cold to say we make ice cream, but it's not exactly warm. We're making ice cream after all. Grab yourselves a pair of goggles and those ear protector radio things. I can still remember the day we got those, best day of my life," Jim said, admiring *those ear protector radio things* like they were the greatest things on Earth. "Because the machinery is quite loud in the factory, ear protection must be worn. It's not like if you take them off and expose your ears to the noise it will cause your head to explode, but say you worked in those conditions for a long period of time, it would definitely damage your hearing. So they're just like call centre headphones, but much thicker and bigger and better. There's a switch on the right ear, you'll be able to feel it. Push and hold it in for a second and it will turn itself on. Then we should connect to one another within a few seconds and we'll be able to talk through these. Otherwise we'd have to shout without them!" We each said hello to test that they were working and then we were ready to enter the factory.

"Welcome to the factory!" Jim said, opening the final door and allowing us all to pass. We took our first steps onto the spotless white floor. I glanced down at Madeline, who was scanning the factory in amazement. "Did you know there are three Ron's Ice Cream factories around the world? The first one is the one we're standing in that has been open for over fifty years. And then fifteen years ago we opened another in America because we couldn't make enough over here to send to them, and transporting it over there was very difficult and expensive. And then five years ago we opened a huge factory in China because we sell millions and millions of tubs over there now.

"Right then, I'm going to need your help making some ice cream," he said to Madeline. "We're making chocolate today, do you think you'll be able to help me with that?"

She fiddled with her hat and nodded. "Follow me," Jim said, pacing into the heart of the factory.

I was given the specifics of the factory before I'd even started working at Ron's Ice Cream because Ted's dad arranged for Ted and me to come and make the ice cream with Jim on my fourteenth birthday. We made chocolate that day, too. As you walk along to the first mixing tank you can see the different stages the ice cream tubs go through. You can see the empty ones being stacked and separated in one section and then farther along they're being filled with ice cream and capped. And then they run along a conveyer belt ready to be stacked by robotic arms and placed into a freezer for a few hours. When we reached the first mixing tank, two employees were already waiting for us with the ingredients we'd need to firstly make the ice cream. They'd also provided a small stepladder so Madeline would be able to reach and see into the mixer.

"Right, although Madeline is super strong, she may need some help pouring the ingredients into the mixer as they're so awkward to handle. Ethan, if you wouldn't mind assisting Madeline on this first tank since this mixer is taller than the next one, and then August, you can help her on the next mixer. That's not me trying to be funny by the way."

August smiled. "No, it's fine, don't worry."

"So if you look over there at those six big tanks or silos, those are filled with cream, and the cream is going to come along here into this mixer and you're going to add these ingredients to it."

Madeline and Ethan poured five or six bags in together, and then they had these canisters of syrups and natural flavourings to pour in. Like I said, the fifteen to twenty people on the next tour were watching Madeline add the ingredients into the mixer, and she enthusiastically waved up to them and they waved back while she made the ice cream.

"You'd normally have to wait thirty minutes to an hour before we were ready to move onto the next stage, but we have a of batch of what you just made already waiting for us. So now we can move on to the next mixer and make some chocolate," Jim explained, directing us to the next mixer. "This is a different mixer," he began. "I call this the hot pot. The hot pot is where we melt all the chocolate and add some extra ingredients to make it taste even chocolatier."

I have no idea how many times Jim has taken people around the factory. It must be more than a hundred times. But watching him now, he's still showing the same amount of excitement and devotion as he did when I first took my tour around here more than six years ago. And of course it's his job so he has to, but you can see on his face and the way he talks that he really loves it. And it's nice to see that after so many years of working here. Without him it could mean the fall of Ron's Ice Cream.

"So, we have two big boxes full of chunky chocolate pieces here. I need you to pour them into the hot pot for me. August, it's your turn to assist Madeline this time, so I need you to step up to the plate." Madeline's stepladder had been placed in front of the hot pot, ready for her to pour in the chunky pieces of chocolate.

"Can I try a piece of chocolate before I pour it in?" Madeline asked.

"Of course!" Jim replied. Her face lit up and she reached into one of the boxes and picked a small chunky chocolate piece and placed it into her mouth. She chewed it and then she hummed.

"Is it good?" August asked.

Madeline nodded. "Yep, it's great!"

Jim reached into the box and passed August and Ethan a piece, too. "We can't have you two feeling left out, now can we?" He tossed a piece to me, too, which I happily consumed, enjoying the rich taste I had forgotten.

Jim lifted the large square lid of the hot pot and placed the metal arm underneath it so it wouldn't fall. "If you two could drag one of those boxes onto the grate here and then you just need to lift it up and tip them in. Some of the pieces may get stuck between the grate, but you can poke them through after with your fingers."

August and Madeline did as instructed and poured the first lot of chunky chocolate pieces in. As they did so Ethan said, "Try not to drop your phone in there, dear." We laughed, and then they poured in the second box. Afterwards they added a few small bags of cocoa powder to make it even chocolatier.

"So, that's it for the ingredient adding and mixing. We're going to stack the ice cream tubs now, and then we can watch them rub along the track and be filled up with chocolate ice cream."

We strolled over to the other side of the factory where there were many boxes of tubs waiting to be stacked and filled with ice cream. "Don't worry, I don't want you to empty every box. We'll do one box and then we can move along to the filler."

The employee who was currently stacking them stepped back and allowed Madeline to take charge. She grabbed as many stacked tubs as she could in her hands and then Ethan lifted her up and she placed them on top of the ones already waiting. There are two piles of tubs stacked up, dropping down onto the machine that shoots them along the track, sending them across to the filler. By the time Madeline had added her first amount, they'd already half gone, the process works that fast.

Once she'd emptied the box, she and Ethan had become quite tired. "You have to be quick," Jim said. "It's a good workout stacking tubs."

He then escorted us over to the filler. You can't really see a large section of the filler. There's a small window, I'd say the same size as a DVD case. So the tubs are spun around by a rotating piece of metal that looks similar to the inside of a cowboy's gun where the bullets are kept. I think Madeline could have watched it all day. She loved it. After that we watched a robotic arm organise the tubs into blocks of eight and push them into a box, and then another robotic arm placed them onto a wooden pallet. They're then moved into the freezer where they're left for a few hours and then they'll be boxed and shipped either tonight or tomorrow morning.

"So that concludes all we're able to do in the factory today I'm afraid," Jim said, taking us back to the door we entered the factory from. "Thank you for your help, Madeline. It's so nice to take a break sometimes."

Madeline had a small sulk on her face because she didn't want her experience to end, but she managed to say, "You're welcome, Jimmy," and then returned to sulking.

"If you place your headsets and goggles back onto the side, and then leave your suits on the bench, that would be wonderful. We will take care of those later." He opened the door and we all stepped inside. "It was lovely meeting you all and I hope you enjoyed seeing a glimpse of what we make here. I wish I could come and make some more ice cream with you upstairs, but I have to get back to work, so much more ice cream needs to be made!"

"What do you say?" August said, looking at Madeline after she took off her headset.

"Thank you, Jim," she said with a large grin.

"You're very welcome, Madeline." He opened the door

back into the room with the bench. I shook his hand and thanked him, and then he returned to what he does best, making ice cream.

The tour had left the do-it-yourself room no longer than a few minutes ago, and Mel, the lady who helps during the do-it-yourself part, was finishing tidying up. She smiled and said, "All ready for you, Will."

I thanked her and asked August, Ethan, and Madeline to take a seat on one of the dining benches. They're similar to the ones that they'd have in school dining halls or cafeterias. I grabbed four large metal mixing bowls, one for each of us. I thought I'd make one for Zac for when I next saw her. At the back of the room is a large shelf unit. Each tub on the shelf is labelled with what's inside it. There's various types of biscuits and cookies and chocolates. There's about twenty or thirty tubs. And then on the table to the side we have fresh bananas that can be mixed in, too.

"You just unclip the lid and grab a packet of whatever you want. I'd advise grabbing three or four packets," I said as we wandered over and began our selections. I grabbed myself a packet of small chocolate chunks and a packet of cookies. August selected bananas and white chocolate. I've never tried that combination before, but I'm guessing it must have an interesting taste. Ethan chose some cherries and fudge. Madeline couldn't reach the top shelves so Ethan had to lift her up so she could examine and make her choice. In the end Madeline chose nearly every biscuit possible from the shelf. But she'd been clever with her over choosing because she decided she was going to add one or two biscuits from each packet. Meaning every biscuit would be in her ice cream.

"Before you empty your packets into your bowls, you need to decide what ice cream you're going to use for your base." Behind the counter are eight flavours of ice cream in a fridge/freezer like what you would find in an ice cream shop where they scoop some up and pop it into a cone for you. This ice cream is soft. If it was frozen solid, then you'd have to wait ages for it to soften so you could mix your packets in with it.

I went first so it gave them time to consult over their selections. I scooped myself some vanilla into a bowl. August chose vanilla, too. Ethan chose strawberry. And Madeline chose bubblegum. I scooped some ice cream into everyone's bowl and then we returned to the bench and began adding our packets and mixing them into the ice cream with a spatula.

"So what did you think of the film?" August asked as we all mixed.

"I thought it was great. The girl I went to see it with works at the cinema. She had a small crush on you after the film," I replied.

August smirked. "Aw, how cute. Is that the Zac person you mentioned earlier?"

"Yes, it is. I know it's a guy's name, but it's a family name, she's actually Zachary Williams the third. But you can't tell her I told you that."

She laughed this time. "It's a pretty cool name though. So is she your girlfriend or is she a friend?"

"I'm not sure how to put it," I said. "We're sort of...seeing each other, but she doesn't want a relationship or a title."

August quickly replied, "So you're sleeping together?"

"August," Ethan interrupted, nodding his head over to Madeline.

"A train could pass through this room and she wouldn't notice, Ethan. Have you seen how much fun she's having?" I glanced over at Madeline; her tongue stuck out as she dropped tiny bits of biscuits into her ice cream and then sang quietly as she stirred them in.

"Maybe," I answered August's question shyly, which we all knew translated into yes.

"Ethan, can I have a playing card and your marker, please?" August asked Ethan as she held out her hand.

"What makes you think I have one?" Ethan replied.

August didn't reply, she just raised her eyebrow marginally. Ethan leant forward and said, "I don't have any on me because they're behind your ear!" And then he pulled a deck of cards and a marker from behind August's ear. August raised her other eyebrow marginally this time. She took the deck and marker from Ethan and found the queen of hearts, and then started writing on the back of it.

"What are you doing?" I asked.

"I'm guessing she's writing an autograph to Zac. So you can take it to her and it'll gain you the biggest amount of brownie points ever. Good idea, August," Ethan said.

"Thank you, babe," she replied as she wrote on the back of the card. After she signed it she told me to pass Ethan my phone, which I cautiously did in case he made it disappear and couldn't bring it back.

"Why does he need my phone?" I asked wearily.

"Because we're going to take a photo together to prove the authenticity of my autograph for Zac."

"Ah, good idea," I replied.

"Thank you."

Ethan held up my phone and said, "I might as well quit being a magician and become a full-time photographer for August's fans."

We smiled as the flash went off and then she replied, "I've taken plenty of photos for you and your fans!"

"I bet if we counted how many photos we've taken, I would have taken ten times the amount you have."

She smirked. "Yeah, that's probably true."

"So what are you going to call your ice cream flavours?" I asked everyone.

"I'm calling mine Madeline's Mayhem," Madeline answered.

"I'm thinking something like Bashful Bananas," August answered.

"I was just gonna call mine Cherry And Fudge," Ethan answered.

"You've got to call it something a little more interesting than Cherry And Fudge, Ethan."

"I didn't criticise your ice cream name selection, August."

"That's because Bashful Bananas sounds amazing."

"Fine. I don't know why I need to think of a name for it because either you or Madeline will have eaten it before I've even had a spoonful."

August smirked. "Yeah, that's true."

Ethan pondered for a moment before saying, "Ok, how does Ferry Chudge sound?"

"I mean, you've only swapped the beginning letters around, but I suppose it will do."

"Thank you for your support, dear."

"You're welcome, babe."

Mel then reentered the room. "Hey, what's up?" I said.

"I came to let you know that we're closing in fifteen minutes."

"Already?" I asked, glancing down at my watch and realising it was nearly 4:45 p.m. "That went quickly." I added.

"Do we have to go?" Madeline whined.

"Yes, Madeline, otherwise the ice cream factory monster will eat us all," August said.

Madeline's face didn't budge. She blankly stared at August. "I'm eight, August, not four." Madeline then turned to me. "Please can we stay?"

"I'm sorry, it's not my decision. I think the only way you'd be able to stay was if you bought the factory, then you could live here."

Ethan's eyes then lit up. "No!" August commanded.

"Aw, but why?" Ethan whined similar to Madeline.

"Because we came here to make ice cream, not to leave here owning the ice cream company."

Ethan frowned down at his ice cream. "I hate you."

August threw a cookie at him. "You love me. Now let's finish our ice cream and go home so Mum and Dad can try it before we have to leave."

"Fine," Ethan replied, stirring his ice cream with the spatula.

"If you love Ron's Ice Cream so much, we could always look into you becoming an ambassador," I suggested.

"Don't they fight bulls?" Madeline asked.

"No, that's a matador, Madeline. You were kind of close," August answered.

"So what's an ambassador?" Madeline asked.

"An ambassador is someone who endorses, I mean promotes, certain things depending on what they are."

"If August did it, would that mean I'd get free ice cream?" Madeline asked, clearly putting her priorities first.

"I would think so," I replied.

"August, you should do it!"

August laughed. "I'll see."

I put my hand inside my suit jacket and removed a business card. "Here's my card if it sounds like something you'd be interested in. I'm sure we'll be able to do something together." She took the card and placed it in her back pocket. "Right, we'd best hurry up and get these into some tubs otherwise none of us will be going home with some ice cream," I said. "The next step once the ice cream is mixed in the bowls is to scoop it all up and place them into these bags similar to what you would put your sandwiches in for your packed lunch. Then you cut a small hole on the corner of the bag, and squeeze the ice cream into your tub."

We filled our bags with our ice cream and lined up our tubs. "Don't spill it everywhere, Madeline, I'm not sharing mine," Ethan said, nudging her with his foot.

"Although my hands are frozen, Ethan. I won't be dropping any of my ice cream as its deliciousness is too precious for the floor," she said, licking some ice cream off the tip of her finger. I paused for a moment. I couldn't believe how well-spoken this little girl had just sounded. I think it caught August and Ethan off guard, too. And they must spend a lot of time with her.

Madeline counted us down from three, and then we all squeezed the contents of our bags into our tubs. "It's so cold and weird," Ethan said.

"I think my fingers are frostbitten," August added.

"You two are such an old couple," Madeline said, squeezing her ice cream neatly into her tub like a pro. August and Ethan both looked at each other and laughed; maybe it's because it was a little true. I suppose there's nothing wrong with that.

Once we'd filled our tubs with ice cream, I passed everyone a lid to pop on top of their tubs. And then we placed each tub in a small box so they're easier to carry and won't roll around.

"Make sure you put it in the freezer when you get home," I said, passing Madeline her box.

"Oh, she will. You should see the collection of ice cream she has at home," August said, crouching beside her and kissing her cheek.

I quickly rinsed the mixing bowls in the sink and then

took them back to the reception. "Have you guys enjoyed your day?" I asked as I opened the door to the reception.

"I enjoyed it more than I thought I would actually," Ethan replied.

"Yeah, me too," August said, linking her arm with his.

"I loved it!" Madeline growled like an angry bear.

"Good," I said. They signed out at the reception desk and I walked them to the exit.

"What do you say, Madeline?" August said.

"Thank you, Will," Madeline said with a cheesy grin.

"You're more than welcome, Madeline. I'm glad you enjoyed yourself. Thank you for visiting."

"Thank you," August said. "Don't forget to give Zac that card."

"I won't," I said, patting my jacket where the card was. And then just like that they walked out and left. I'd spent my afternoon with one of the most famous actresses in the world. How on earth did that happen? I stood there for a moment or two as I sunk back into reality. I was about to walk back up to the office to see if Ted was still there, but as I started walking up the stairs, he was walking down them.

"Hey, I was wondering where you were. How did it go?" he asked.

"You're not going to believe who I just spent the afternoon with."

Ted was very disappointed that he missed out on meeting August Bishop, as you can imagine. He told me not to tell him any more, as he was angry with himself for missing out on such an opportunity.

"All the boring and shit private tours I've done," he said as he drove us home, "and you're the one who gets the smoking hot world-famous actress. Was she single?"

"No, she was with her fiancée."

"Fiancée?"

"Yes."

"I thought she was like eighteen?"

"Nineteen," I corrected.

"And she's engaged already?"

"Yes. I think they've been in a relationship for a long time, though. He's that magician guy that was on Patrick Miller's show that everyone was talking about on New Year's Eve."

"Was he a good-looking dude?" he asked.

"Yeah I guess so, I don't know."

"What do you mean you don't know?"

"I'm not into guys, am I?"

"Doesn't mean you can't comment on a guy's looks. Like me, you think I'm stunning, right?"

"I don't believe I've ever been quoted saying that before."

"Well, as a best friend it is your obligation to find your other best friend attractive for moral support. Even if they look like a donkey or they allow you to insult their ugliness."

"I disagree, but fair enough."

We pulled up to a set of lights at the bottom of our road. Our apartment was in sight. I then remembered the photo August and I had together. I took my phone out of my pocket and put it in front of Ted's face.

He snatched my phone from my hand and after staring at it for a couple of seconds he threw it onto my lap. "She's not that good-looking," he said.

"You're only saying that to make yourself feel better."

"Will, be quiet and let me comfort myself, ok?"

"Ok."

The lights changed and we moved forward again. The car was silent as we drove up the hill to our apartment. And then I remembered the card August had signed for Zac.

"August signed a playing card for Zac as well. I think I might drive over to hers later and surprise her with it."

Ted's face twitched, but instead of being frustrated with himself or annoyed with me, he decided to change the subject. "You like her," he said childishly.

"Who, August? She was nice, friendly."

"No, not August, Zac."

"Oh, yeah, she's great."

"You know what I mean. You *really* like her."

"We're keeping it casual."

"Ah, casual. That explains why you're going to drive over there later to drop off the signed playing card from August."

"Ok, I *really* like her. But she doesn't want anything serious so I guess we'll see how it goes. I don't know what else to say."

"If she wanted something serious, would you want to be with her?"

"We've spent four days together, so it would be a bit soon. But yeah, I can see myself in a relationship with her. But she doesn't want one, which is why I said we shall see how it goes."

I was only at the apartment for five minutes before I was driving over to Zac's apartment. I bought her some more flowers on the way, too. And while I was there I bought a gift bag and a frame to put the card in from August. I also brought the ice cream I made for her, too.

I knocked on her apartment door, and Zac's head poked around the corner of the door a few seconds later. "What are you doing here?" she asked, not seeming very happy to see me.

"I bought you flowers." I said.

"Aw, you bought me flowers," she said, all cute. But then her mood snapped back. "What are you doing here?"

"I'm sorry to show up unexpected. I bought you flowers, and I got you a present," I replied, holding up the flowers and the gift bag.

"Why?"

"Because it's a great present." She stared at me blankly and I don't think she knew what to do or say. "Is this a bad time?" I asked.

She opened her mouth, but she didn't say anything. She made like an umm sound.

"Is there another... guy here?" I asked.

"No!" she quickly replied. "My friend, Natalie, is here and I haven't told her about you yet."

"Ah I see, but we're not a title, remember? So why would you have?"

"I know, but we've spent some time together. So she'll get suspicious. And you brought me flowers and a present. That's very implicative."

"Yes, but it's a very good present, you'll want to see this."

"Zac, what are you doing?" I heard Natalie ask inside the apartment.

"Nothing," she replied, turning her head back into the apartment.

"Then who are you talking to at the door?"

"No one." Footsteps then approached the door. Zac went back inside and shut it. Then I could hear talking and then little knockings against the door. The door opened a small amount and then it shut. And then it opened a small amount again and then it shut. Meanwhile I stood there with the flowers and the gift bag wondering what the hell was going on. I then heard someone say, "Ouch, why did you do that?" And the door fully opened this time.

Zac was stood behind the most unattractive girl I'd ever seen in my entire life. That's a lie, but I have to find every other girl that Zac knows unattractive because that's just the rules. If I show any slight interest or Zac gets suspicious, then my life is at risk. Even though we're nothing serious. Don't pretend you don't know what I'm talking about. But the thing is, I'm not interested in any other girls anyway.

Natalie had brownish red hair. And she was a couple of inches taller than Zac. She had very big eyelashes, and her eyes were a dark brown. And she had quite a noticeable jawline.

"Zac...why is there a really cute guy at our door holding flowers and a little red bag?" she whispered out of the corner of her mouth.

"Natalie, this is my friend, Will," Zac replied. I looked back at her with a slight puzzled look that meant *friend?* But she tilted her head and glared at me for a moment as if to say *Just go with it.*

Natalie folded her arms and scanned me from head to toe. "So this is the guy you've been spending time with?" she said smugly. Once again I had no idea what to say so I stood there quietly.

"How did you know?" Zac said loudly.

"I didn't," Natalie began, "but you confirmed it for me just then." Zac seemed to get angry with herself for falling into such an easy trap. "Is he coming in?" Natalie asked.

I shrugged my shoulders. "No, he has to leave," Zac said, raising her eyebrows very suggestively to me.

"Come on in, Will," Natalie said, stepping aside and allowing me entry to their apartment.

"What? No! He has to leave!" Zac said, standing in the way on my entry. I therefore stopped and thought I'd better wait.

"Zachary, stop being an arse and let the hot tall guy with the flowers into the apartment, you silly child."

"He has to leave!" Zac yelled. I took a step forward and whispered between them, "I think I'm just gonna go."

"No!" Zac blurted. She closed her eyes and took a deep breath. And we all stood there in silence.

"So you want me to leave, but you don't want me to leave?" I asked with a small squint.

"He's coming in for dinner," Natalie said.

Zac opened her eyes and looked at Natalie and then at me. "Fine."

They stepped aside and I gave Zac her flowers and gift bag as I walked in. "Take a seat on the sofa, Will," Natalie said. I did as she asked and sat on the sofa facing the back wall. She sat on the one across from me. "How tall are you?" she asked.

"He's six foot one or two," Zac answered as she dashed around the kitchen to replace the previous vase of flowers I had bought her with the new ones I had bought her.

"Ah," Natalie said. "And are you at university or do you work or both?"

I opened to my mouth to respond, but Zac once again spoke on my behalf. "He works at Ron's Ice Cream. His best friend is the great-grandson of Ron."

"Ah," Natalie said again. "So you're her new boyfriend that she is trying to keep from me, I presume?"

"No!" Zac yelled.

"She's so amusing when she gets all worked up like this," Natalie whispered.

"I heard that!" Zac replied.

"Please say something, Will, you look very uncomfortable," Natalie expressed with a wince on her face.

"Am I allowed to speak, Zac?" I asked, turning towards her direction.

Her head poked up from behind the corner. "Of course you can, why wouldn't you be able to?"

"No reason," I replied. "What would you like to ask me next?" I asked Natalie.

She ran a hand through her hair and then asked, "Have you two had sex?"

Zac then jumped up from behind the counter and head flicked between the both of us like she was watching a Ping-Pong match.

"So that's a yes..." Natalie joked. "How many times?"

Zac grunted, "Really, Natalie?"

"I'm only trying to find out how well you two know each other."

"Well, ask how we met or something more appropriate," Zac suggested.

"Eleven times," I answered.

"Will!" Zac shouted.

"What?" I replied.

"You counted?!"

"Am I not allowed to?"

Zac placed her flowers onto the kitchen side and then walked over and sat beside me with her gift bag.

"Hi," I said to her.

"Hi," she replied, all flustered. She started brushing her hair with her hand and then she got annoyed with that and decided to tie it up.

As she took the bobble off her wrist I said, "Stop worrying about your hair, it looks lovely." She looked at me out of the corner of her eye and continued to tie up her hair. And then she looked over at Natalie.

"I like him," Natalie whispered to her. "Open your present then," she added. Zac placed the bag and her knee and peered into the bag. She looked at me before pulling out the frame with the card inside.

"What is it?" Natalie asked.

"Dear Zachary Williams the third," Zac began to read

aloud. She gave me an unamused look after reading that. "Will told me you liked my film. Just wanted to say thanks. Lots of love, August. And she put a kiss at the end."

"She came into the factory for a private tour with her fiancée and little sister, and I was the one who showed them around," I said.

Zac shook her head. "No, I'm not buying it. This is fake, you used it as an excuse to come over, didn't you?"

I smugly removed my phone from my pocket and showed her the photo of August and me making ice cream. "No way!" Zac whispered, snatching my phone from me.

"Is she the girl from the film you were telling me about last week?" Natalie asked.

Zac nodded, still staring at the photo. "I can't believe you got to meet her."

"Spent most of the afternoon with her. We made ice cream together."

"I want to make ice cream with her," Zac moaned. She placed a hand on my knee and said, "Thank you, Will."

There was a slight pause and then Natalie said, "And I can't even get a text back." Zac and I smirked.

"This was nice of you do to do," Zac said, hiding away and going back into shy mode.

I stayed with them for dinner. We had pasta. Zac prepared it in the kitchen whilst Natalie continued to question me about who I am and what I do. But I didn't want to interrupt their evening, and I had work tomorrow so I said I was going to leave after my pasta. I asked to use their bathroom before I left, and when I returned to the living room, Zac was sat with her coat and her beanie and her shoes on.

"Are you coming with me?" I asked.

"Of course she is," Natalie said. "Unless you want you'd rather I came back instead?" she added smugly.

"Let's go then, Zac," I said.

JANUARY 30TH

Since Zac had the day off work, but I was working, I gave her a key to our apartment in case she needed to go anywhere. She could stay in bed all morning or watch TV all day. Whatever her preference was. I trusted her to not steal anything, and if we did come back and everything had been stolen, then we knew who it was, and where they lived. But I doubted highly that would happen.

After work, Ted and I stopped by the store to pick up some food and other essentials. "You should buy some things for Zac," Ted said, stopping at the toiletries isle.

"What do you mean?" I asked.

"If Zac is going to be staying over more frequently, you should buy some feminine hygiene products."

I sighed. "I'm not going to do that."

"Why not?"

"Because it will be weird and awkward."

"Oh, Will, grow up." He began to walk down the isle then stood next to a lady who was looking at the shelf. "Which ones do you want?" he asked, nodding to the shelf. The woman stood next to him frowned, probably questioning why two guys were buying things from this section.

"I don't know," I said. "What are we even staring at?"

"Tampons, Will," Ted replied, blank-faced.

I sighed. "I've no idea. Buying tampons isn't my specialty."

Ted tutted. "Just pick some!"

I sighed again and reached out and grabbed something from the shelf. "Just get these ones," I said.

"Those are nappies, Will."

"Are they?" I asked, frowning down at the package in my hands. Ted took it from me and placed it onto its original spot on the shelf. Then he grabbed a box of tampons from the shelf and placed them into the trolley.

"You worry me sometimes," he said, shaking his head as he walked down the isle and grabbed several other items and then placed them into the trolley.

When we got home, I placed the shopping onto the kitchen side and began to place the items into their designated areas. Zac appeared from my bedroom and sat on the sofa with the television already on.

"Will got you some things," Ted said as he took off his coat.

Zac lifted her head and seemed surprised. I walked over and passed her the bag we had packed for her. She peered into the bag and a small smirk appeared on her face. "Thanks, guys," she said.

"Will almost bought you nappies instead of tampons." Zac laughed and then glanced over at me to see if that was true.

"They all look the same to me," I said, moodily stacking the fridge.

JANUARY 31ST

"I've been thinking," Zac said as we lay in bed.

I rolled over. "Been thinking about what?"

"Our situation." Her expression indicated that I should have known what she had been thinking about.

"Ok, what about it?"

"If we're going to continue to sleep together, I think we need to establish some rules or laws."

I frowned. "Ok?"

"The way I want to put it is that our situation is the ship, you're the crew, and I am the captain."

"Are we casual sailors or are we pirates?"

She smiled. "We're pirates obviously."

"I just wanted to clarify."

"Since I'm the captain, I decide what rules we shall have. I will listen to your recommendations, as I am a humble although brutal pirate captain. So do not mistake my humbleness as weakness or I shall strike you where you stand."

"Right... Have you made any rules up yet or is that what we need to do now?" I asked.

"I have thought of some already. Once I have finished announcing them, you may comment afterwards."

"Ok, can we make pirate names first? I feel like that will help a lot with my character. He needs an identity."

Zac frowned. "Why can't we use our own names?"

"Because that's no fun."

Her jaw clenched. "Fine. I'll be Captain Panda."

"Excellent choice, Captain Panda. I shall be Horatio."

"Horatio?"

"Yes, like the guy from *Hamlet*."

"That's a bit silly, don't you think?"

"Sillier than Captain Panda?"

She paused. "Ok fine. Horatio and Captain Panda."

"Now let's hear these rules."

"No affectionate physical activities outside of the bedroom. Examples: kissing, cuddling, holding hands etc....

"No cuddling at all. (Want to make that very clear.)

"If people ask what we are our response shall be 'Pirates or friends' and no further explanation shall be given.

"Cannot see each other more than four times a week.

"Finally, if feelings start to develop then the ship must be sunk. (Which means stop seeing each other.)

"Is there anything you would like to add?" Zac asked after she had finished her list of rules.

"Are we seeing other people?" I asked. It's not that I wanted to see other people. I only wanted to see if she did.

"I'm going to say no, for now, and then we shall see in the future. How does that sound?"

"Fine by me," I replied.

"Do you want to see other people?" she asked, her eyes looking as beautiful and innocent as I've ever seen them.

And I knew if I even joked about wanting to see other people, it would hurt her feelings and her confidence. So I said, "Absolutely not."

She smiled her usual tight-lipped smile and then started twiddling with her thumbs all shy like.

"Can I still buy you flowers?" I asked.

She looked up and squinted at me. "I'll allow flowers.

But you can't buy them all the time."

"Ok, noted." I leant forward and kissed her.

"Just because we can kiss in here doesn't mean we have to."

"I disagree," I said, kissing her again.

"I really... want to... watch... *Pirates Of The Caribbean* now," she said during each break between kisses.

"I have all three of them on DVD. We can watch them today if you like."

She pounced on me and said, "Good idea. We shall do that later."

FEBRUARY 1ST

"Who the hell is Rosie?" Zac yelled as she woke me in a rather vigorous manner.

"What?" I asked, still asleep. It must have still been early because I don't normally feel this groggy when I wake.

"I can't believe it. You already have a girlfriend. I'm some chick on the side for you while she's away, aren't I?" she continued to yell. I instantly shot up, realising what she was accusing me of. Zac was rushing around the room, filling up her bag with her things.

"No, I don't have a girlfriend—" I tried to say, but Zac wouldn't allow me to say anything.

"Oh, save it, Will! I don't need to hear your bullshit!"

"Rosie—" I tried to say again, but once again Zac wouldn't let me talk. She threw my phone at me and it showed I had a missed call, voice mail, and text from Rosie. And then she threw the beanie that I bought her at me.

"I thought you were a nice guy, Will. You're just another fucking arse hole!"

"Rosie is my sister!" I yelled.

Zac froze. Her face looked all colourless and shocked. But then her anger regained control. "No, you're lying!"

I shouted for Ted, thinking hearing it from him might help her believe me.

Ted poked his head around my door as Zac continued to stuff things into her bag. "What's up?" he asked, pretending he was oblivious to our loud discussion.

"Will you please tell Zac what my relation to Rosie is?" I asked, getting off the bed and standing beside Zac, who was knelt beside her bag.

"Rosie is Will's smoking hot older sister," he answered helpfully.

"Older sister would have done just fine. No need for the smoking hot," I added.

Zac's eyes met mine and then she peered over her shoulder at Ted, but she still didn't believe any of it. "You're lying, too! You're just covering for your mate."

I flapped my arms; I couldn't think of another way to make her understand. I'd barely been awake for longer than a minute. Ted pulled a funny face as if to say "good luck" and then he vanished from behind the door and shut it.

I thought for a moment as Zac pushed down on her bag to try to fit everything into it. I dropped my phone beside her. "Call her," I said calmly.

"What?" she barked.

"Rosie. Call her. Hear it from her yourself. I really think if you ask my sister if she's my girlfriend, she will definitely say otherwise."

Zac must have thought I was bluffing. She grabbed my phone. "All right, I will." She opened the bedroom door and exited my room and sat on my sofa across from Ted, who was watching TV with a bowl of cereal. She pressed call, and then put the phone on speaker. It rang twice and then Rosie's voice answered.

"Hey, Will."

"Hi, Rosie. Will is...busy right now. I'm Zac, a friend of his."

"Are you a guy or a girl?"

"I'm a girl..."

"Why do you have a guy's name?"

I shook my head at Rosie's indiscreet directness. I glanced over at Ted. He had a mouth full of cereal, but you could see in his eyes that he was enjoying this little drama set before him.

"It's a long story." Zac continued, "I was just wondering, how do you know Will?"

"Oh, well, I'm his girlfriend. How do you know Will, Zac?"

Zac's eyes glared up at me as if she had just been possessed by the devil. I wanted to run away, but I felt paralysed. Her beautiful innocent blue eyes had now turned into molten lava.

"I think the last thing I will be known as is the girl who beat Will to death."

Zac's voice had turned into a deep rumble. I glanced over at Ted again. The delight on his face was indescribable. Zac was three seconds away from ending the call. But then Rosie came through.

"Do a favour for me before you do?"

"Name it."

"Please tell my brother, who's probably stood there shitting himself, that I'm back from America and now I'm back at Mum's house."

"What?!" Zac squeaked.

"Will, my brother, your boyfriend, the guy stood somewhere near you. Tell him I'm back from America and I'm at Mum's house."

"Rosie, that really wasn't funny," I said.

"Oh, I don't know about that. For you, it wasn't. But for me, it was."

"I'll text you."

"Ok, bye, love you."

"Love you, too, bye."

I picked up the phone from the table and ended the call. The room was silent. Zac stared forward emptily. I didn't know what to say. But then she stood and ran off into my bedroom and slammed the door behind her. I sighed and thought Ted would have something comforting to say, but all he said was, "Am I allowed to find that funny, too, or not?"

"No, you're not allowed to find that funny. Zac is really upset by this. I'm going to see if she's ok."

A second later my phone began to ring, and it read that Mum was calling me.

"Hello."

"Rosie has told me that you have a girlfriend. How come you haven't told me?"

"I got off the phone with Rosie about twelve seconds ago. How can you have already been gossiping about this? No, I don't have a girlfriend."

"So who is this Zac girl?"

"Mum, I'm busy right now. Can I call you later?"

"I want to know who this girl is."

"Right, I will call you later."

"Are you coming for dinner with us soon?"

"You're not seeming to understand the phrase 'I will call you later,' Mum."

"Is Zac hot?"

"She's smoking hot, there, will that do for now? I'll call you later."

"Interesting. Ok, love you, bye."

"I love you, too. Bye."

"God, I hate Rosie sometimes," I groaned to Ted.

"If it's ok with you, I would have to disagree. She's the best," he replied.

I shook my head at him and then entered my bedroom and found Zac huddled in a ball underneath my quilt. "Are you ok?" I asked, sitting beside her. I kept the covers on her, but pulled them down a little so her head was visible.

She was crying. "I'm so sorry," she whispered, wincing her face and squeezing out more tears.

I put my hand on her back and rubbed it. "It was a simple misunderstanding," I said to her. I looked down at her beanie in my hand and decided to wear it. After I had put it on I hopped over her and lay beside her. I aligned myself so our eyes were at the same level. Her hair had fallen over her face so I brushed it aside so she became visible. Her watery eyes opened and looked into mine, and then she saw the beanie on my head. She giggled and then snatched it off my head.

"Another rule I want to add is you can't wear my beanie," she said.

"Ok, deal, but only if you stop being upset. Can we pretend this didn't happen or laugh it off, please?" I asked. "Why don't you have a bath?" I added.

"Do I smell?" she said, lifting her arm and smelling her armpits.

"I've been trying not to say anything, but the smell has become unbearable." Then I added, "Na, I'm kidding. I thought it would be nice for you to a nice hot bath and relax."

Zac nodded and she looked down at her beanie as she fiddled with it. "Are you... are you taking one with me?" Her eyes flicked up to meet mine now.

"How about I make us some breakfast?"

"I'm not hungry."

"How about I make you a cup of tea then?"

"Ok."

I got up and walked into the bathroom and set the hot

water running in the bath. And then I exited my bedroom and walked to the kitchen and turned on the kettle.

"Have you got a Sundiscussion topic?" Ted asked.

"Are you not going to ask if she is ok?" I replied as I grabbed some mugs.

"I didn't know how delicate the situation was so I thought I would stay out of it. Is she ok?"

"Yeah, she's ok. Today's topic is: What's the saddest film of all time? Zac is having a bath so we'll wait for her until we start. It'll give you plenty of time to think it over."

"Ok, cool."

Zac had sat up when I returned to the bedroom. "Do you want bubbles in your bath?" I asked.

"Of course I wants bubbles in my bath," she replied, sniffling her nose. I reentered the bathroom and grabbed one of the bubble bath bottles from the shelf. It was one of those that I got in a bathroom pack for Christmas that I had no intention of ever using. I poured a small amount in and watched the bubbles begin to form.

"Are you sure you don't want anything to eat?"

Zac stretched up her arms. "No, thank you."

Once she'd got into her very bubbly bath I brought her tea to her. Her head was barely visible. There was just a huge pile of bubbles and then her head poking out of it. Maybe I poured too much in.

"Feeling better?" I asked, placing her tea onto the small high table I had moved in so we could place our mugs onto it. I sat on the wooden chair that I had also brought in so I could sit and talk to her.

"Yes, thank you," she replied.

"Good. So today's Sundiscussion is: What is the saddest film of all time?"

"Like what makes you cry?" she asked.

"Yes."

"Ok, I know mine already."

"Once you've finished your bath we can sit down on the sofa and you can tell us."

"Ok."

Sundiscussion Topic:
What is the saddest film of all time?

After Zac had finished her bath and dressed in my/her spare Star Wars T-shirt and shorts, and dried her hair (which took about an hour by the way, even with the hair dryer), we sat down and got onto today's Sundiscussion. Zac and I sat on my sofa while Ted sat on his.

"Ok, Ted, you start us off," I said.

"There's so many," he said, placing his fist in front of his mouth and trying to compose himself. Zac and I glanced at each other. We thought he might break down in front of us before he even named his film. "There's *Peter Pan*. *Field of Dreams*. *Iron Giant*. *Fox and the Hound*. *Forrest Gump*. All of those films make me cry."

"I thought we only had to say one? Did you just say three cartoon films?" I said.

"They're all very sad, ok?" he said, biting his lip afterwards.

"Right...well, can you narrow those down to one?" I asked.

"How is *Peter Pan* sad?" Zac shouted not long after.

"It's in *Return To Never Land*, when Wendy's all grown up and he *Peter Pan* says good-bye to Wendy." Ted was clearly letting his emotions get the better of him, but Zac didn't seem too interested.

"What's your sad film, Will?" she asked me.

"Mine is *Dead Poets Society*," I answered.

"That's sad, too," Ted added, his voice cracking.

"I've never seen that," Zac said.

Ted shot up like a meerkat watching out for lions. "What? How can you have never seen *Dead Poets Society*?"

"I just haven't," she said. Ted's ajar mouth turned to me, and then back to her, and then back to me. "I bet you both haven't seen my sad film, and it's the saddest film of all time, you will see your own heart be ripped out of your chest."

Ted didn't look that bothered. He thought nothing could beat his or my suggestion. "What's this film called?" he asked.

"*The Bridge To Terabithia*," Zac answered.

"That sounds crap," Ted muttered.

"Why don't you say that after you've watched it?"

"Is that a challenge?"

"I don't know. If you sob over *Peter Pan*, maybe this will be a little too much for you."

I suddenly found myself between a brutal confrontation between Zac and Ted, which led to Zac and I going to a store to pick up DVDs of *The Bridge To Terabithia* and *Dead Poets Society*. Ted only agreed to watch *The Bridge To Terabithia* if she agreed to watch *Dead Poets Society*, so then we had a clearer perspective of what films were being represented in our Sundiscussion.

We watched *Dead Poets Society* first, and at the end Ted and I had slight tears in our eyes. But Zac produced slightly more tears since it was her first time watching it.

After it had finished Ted said, "So?"

She wiped her eyes and responded, "It was good, really good, and it was sad. But it's still not as sad as my film."

"You're talking a big game, Zac. Let's take a short break and have something to eat, and then after we will watch your film."

"Whatever feeds your panda," she replied. We prepared some noodles, as they're quick and easy to make, and Ted and I ate them. Zac wasn't hungry, so she got a chocolate milkshake from the fridge. Then we sat down and watched Zac's film suggestion, *The Bridge To Terabithia*.

At first we thought it was a kids' movie, and it kinda was. But as the film progressed it then decided to rip your heart out, just as she described. I believe it would have hurt less for someone to punch me throughout the entire length of the film than it would to watch it. I couldn't stop crying, and there was no way to cover it up. Zac was sat on the edge of the sofa and her hair was covering her face so I couldn't see if she was crying or not. When I checked on Ted, you would have thought someone had poured a bucket of water over his head he had been crying so much.

After the film finished Zac casually said in a cheerful manner, "So what did you think, Ted?"

Ted rose from his sofa and said, "I can't believe you made us watch that, you cruel bastard."

"You said you wanted a sad film."

"Not one that was going to destroy my life!" He stormed away and headed towards his bedroom.

"Where are you going?" Zac asked.

"To sit and cry in my room alone!" he yelled.

Zac giggled and then she turned to me. "Aw, Will. Are you ok?"

I shook my head and just managed to say, "No."

She patted my knee and said, "Will you be ok to drive me home? I can see you're in an emotional state at this present moment."

After about three or four attempts of me trying to talk I said, "Thirty minutes. Maybe thirty years. I'm not sure."

FEBRUARY 2ND

"So who's Zac, Will?"

"Hello, Mum. How are you?"

"I'm good. Who is this Zac girl? Is she your new girl-friend?"

"No, she isn't my girlfriend. She is just a friend."

"Ah, friend. So you're just friends, if you know what I mean. Wink, wink."

"No! And don't ever say wink, wink again."

"Hm. Rosie has evidence that says you're more than just friends. Why else would Zac call her and ask if she's your girlfriend?"

"When are we having dinner?"

"Aha, got you. Rosie is going to her friends up north somewhere for a week or two, and then when she gets back we were going to go to the coast for a few days. I was thinking we could all have dinner together on the twenty-eighth?"

"You haven't got me. I'm ignoring what you're saying about her. And ok, the twenty-eighth is fine with me. How long is Rosie staying for before she returns to America?"

"I'm not sure. She said she might go at the beginning of April. So you have plenty of time to see her before she leaves."

"Ok. I'll speak to you soon, Mum."

"Ok. Love you. Bye."

"Love you too. Bye."

FEBRUARY 8TH

Sundiscussion Topic:
Who would win in a fight between a T-Rex and Darth
Vader?

"I've been meaning to ask this one for a while," Ted
said, and then he kicked us off with his opinion.
"I'm going to go straight in and say the T-Rex. I don't have
an explanation as to why. It is just a gut feeling."

I sulked as I pictured an actual fight between a T-Rex
and Darth Vader. "I'd say Darth Vader," I said. "His
powers and his lightsaber would be no match for the T-
Rex."

"Ok. So it's a tie. Zac, you're the deciding vote," Ted
said, his focus moving onto Zac.

"I think they'd both die," she said. Ted flapped his arms
and sighed.

"Hold on," I said. "Allow the lady to explain her theory."

"Thanks, Will," Zac said. She sat up and said, "I think
before Darth Vader can react the T-Rex will just eat him,
but while he's being eaten he uses his lightsaber and swings
frantically, tearing the inside of the T-Rex. And you may
think he'll climb out of the decapitated T-Rex or whatever,
but I think he would die moments later because he will have

been badly damaged by the T-Rex's powerful jaws and huge-ass teeth." Her beautiful blue eyes flicked over to me as she finished. She blinked a couple of times with a blank expression on her face.

Ted slapped his knee and sighed. "I think Zac has won this one, too."

FEBRUARY 14ᵀᴴ

"**A**re you getting Zac anything for Valentine's Day?" Ted asked as we sat and ate our lunch on our sofas. We were having chicken nuggets.

"I'm sending some flowers to her apartment. I know we agreed that we wouldn't be doing things like that, but she can't not have at least some flowers sent to her on Valentine's Day. She's working, too, so I thought it might cheer her up."

"Aw, little Willy is in love," Ted teased.

"And here I was thinking we were going to have a sensible conversation," I said.

"You should send her some lingerie."

"I'm not sending her lingerie."

"I knew you would say that, which is why I took the liberty of sending her some from you."

I sat upright and stared across at Ted. "Please, tell me you're joking," I said, closing my eyes and hoping he was.

"Where is your wallet, Will?" he asked. My eyes immediately flicked over to my bedroom. I got up and walked over to it. I felt my jacket pockets, and my wallet was nowhere to be found. As I reentered the living room, Ted was holding up my wallet.

"Please, tell me you're joking," I said again.

"What is a number between thirty-one and thirty-three, Will? And what is the second letter of the alphabet?"

"Thirty-two and b," I replied. And as I did so I shut my eyes and realised this definitely wasn't a joke.

"Doesn't 32B happen to be Zac's bra size, Will?"

"Maybe," I answered.

He picked up his laptop from the table and opened it to show me the order he had placed. "Did you know they do same-day delivery now? How amazing is that?"

"Oh, Ted, why?" I moaned.

"I'm doing you a very big favour here. You will be thanking me later."

"Give me my wallet," I said, snatching it from him. "What did you order?" I asked.

"Just four pairs of bras and panties, relax. Black, blue, green, and red. I think the red one will look nice."

"This isn't funny. She's going to think I'm a lunatic."

"I don't know. I think it's funny. But like I said, you shall be thanking me later."

I threw numerous cushions at him before spending the rest of my day cautiously watching my phone, expecting her to ring me any second to yell at me for how weird this was in case Natalie called her and told her what had arrived for her. It got to about 8:00 p.m. She would be due home any minute according to the timetable she told me. And then at 8:17 p.m., as I lay on my bed, watching my phone charge, it started to ring.

"Hello."

"Hello. It's Zac."

"I know. How are you?"

"I'm good. I just got home from work not long ago."

"I see. How was work?"

"It was ok. So I got your flowers."

"Oh good. Do you like them?"

"Yes, thank you. I also got your other gift."

"Ah. Do you like those...?"

"They're very nice. I've been meaning to buy some actually, but you know, I need money to do that."

"Oh really? Well, it worked out conveniently then."

"It did. So what are you doing right now?"

"I'm in my bedroom. How about you?"

"I'm outside your apartment door."

"Are you?"

"Yep."

I hung up the phone and exited my room to open my front door. And there she was, in her beanie, with her phone in her hands.

"Hi," I said.

"Hello," she said, walking past me and into my bedroom. "Although I am wearing your gift, I'm not here because you bought me underwear. Let's make that very clear. Natalie has a guy around for dinner so instead of hiding away in my bedroom, I thought I would come here," she said, poking her head from behind my bedroom door. I closed the apartment door and turned around in puzzlement. Ted was still sat on his sofa.

"Hi, how are ya?" he asked smugly.

"She just said she's not here because of the bras and whatever else you bought her, so I'm not thanking you," I replied as I walked into my bedroom and shut the door behind me.

FEBRUARY 20TH

"**I**'m going to stay behind today. I have some other things that I need to do," Ted said as I was putting my coat on, about to leave the office.

"Ok, man. Do you need me to stay behind with you or?"

"No, it's fine. I was hoping you would leave me the car, though."

"Ok, sure. I can walk home. Zac is at the apartment already as you know so she doesn't need picking up."

"Ok, thanks, Will."

"So what is it that you need to stay behind and work on?" I asked.

He shrugged. "Bits of crap."

I nodded. "Ok. Well, if you need me, call me, otherwise I'll see you when you get back."

"I will. See you later."

I closed our office door behind me and then began to walk to the stairs. Jeremy was still sat at his desk as I did.

"Any plans for the weekend, Jeremy?" I asked.

"I have a date," he replied.

"Who's the lucky guy?"

"Some guy from the new gym I found. He's an instructor there."

"Nice! I hope it goes better than the last date you had with someone from the gym."

"Thank you, Will. What are your plans for the weekend?"

"I'm just going to go home and put my feet up."

"I wish I could do that, but my quest for true love prevents me from doing that without a man beside me."

I smirked. "I understand. You can tell me if the instructor is that man on Monday."

"I can. See you later, Will."

"Bye, Jeremy." I opened the doors and began to walk downstairs. When I reached the bottom of the staircase, my phone buzzed in my pocket. The screen flashed to show me that I had a missed call from Zac. So I called her back.

"Hey."

"Hi. It's Zac."

"I know it is, I have your number saved."

"Ok. Are you still working?"

"I'm about to walk back now. Ted is staying behind so he is keeping the car."

"Ok. Could you pick me up a milkshake?"

"A milkshake?

"Yes."

"What flavour?"

"Chocolate."

"Ok. Chocolate milkshake, got it. Anything else?"

"No. That's it, thanks."

"Ok. I'll see you soon with your milkshake."

"Ok. Bye."

"Bye."

I picked up a couple bottles of chocolate milkshake for Zac and then returned to the apartment. I passed Zac a milkshake and then placed the other in the fridge.

"Thank you," she said, opening it and taking a sip. I sat on the sofa after making some chicken and rice. Zac said she had already eaten. We watched a reality television show she insisted on watching. And during the final minutes of the fourth episode of the same show, two hours later, Ted entered the apartment and dropped onto his sofa with an ice pack on his right eye without saying a word.

Zac and I faced each other and frowned. "Did somebody punch you?" I asked him. He sighed and lowered the ice pack. His eye wasn't black or bruised; his eye and cheek were just very red and flushed.

"Guys, I think I'm in love," he said.

"With the guy who punched you?" Zac asked with a small smirk.

"No, of course not, you fool. With the girl who punched me. Well, it was more of a backhanded slap than a punch."

"Why don't you explain what happened to us? Before we think you're weirder than you already are," I said.

Ted sat up. "So, I was at the museum—"

"Wait, why were you at the museum? I thought you were staying behind to do some extra work?" I interrupted.

"I did, for like five minutes. But I thought I would give you two some space so you could have dinner together or whatever. So I decided to check out the museum. I got there at like five-ish and it was closing at six thirty, so that gave me plenty of time to have a wander around. I don't know if you saw the article, but two guys went into the museum one time to examine an old pirate gun that they had on display there. And it's rumoured that it led them to some form of treasure. So I thought I would go see this gun since the story sounded pretty cool. I also wanted to see the dinosaur section with all the fossils, but that was the farthest away section, meaning I had to walk through all the other sections anyway. The first couple of sections were about trains and old timepieces and other boring things so

I quickly scanned them. And then the next section was much more interesting, it was a jungle, like the whole theme of the room was a jungle, apart from the floor. And it had sound effects playing, too, so you could hear rainfall and frogs and monkeys. In there it was talking about global warming, and how if we don't act now then soon it will be too late and we'll all die. As I was leaving that section, they have this automated monkey that senses your movement and screams and jumps towards you, and I nearly physically shit myself. Thankfully, there was no one around to see me freak out. Maybe the security man on the surveillance was laughing his head off watching me—"

"Ted, can you skip to the part where you were punched?" I interrupted again.

"Backhand slapped," he corrected. "I found the gun and took a look at it. It appeared to be an ordinary old-fashioned gun. It didn't seem anything special, but you know I couldn't collect further information because it was in a glass display. I was pretty disappointed—"

"Ted."

"Right, I'm in the dinosaur section, admiring a Diplodocus skeleton. No idea if it was real or not, but it appeared real. It wasn't full scale, so I'm guessing it was the remains of a younger Diplodocus." I nodded, and I could see Zac watching me and then turning her head to nod as if she knew what he was talking about. I was going to laugh at her, but Ted carried on talking. "And as I'm admiring the Diplodocus skeleton I can hear a tour guide explaining something about the foundations of the museum or whatever. She came from the opposite section I had come from, which means I must have walked around the museum the wrong way. Not that it really matters. She had her back to me and she was talking about one of the exhibits, but she wasn't talking to anyone. Nobody. She was alone and going on about this exhibit. So she was either crazy or she worked there and was rehearsing her speech during the tour. I decided to guess the second option. But I kept my attention on the skeleton and decided to stay there and let her pass through. Anyway she stopped not that far away from me so I still don't understand how she didn't see me. Although I'm glad she didn't. She was talking about the Diplodocus remains, and mentioned that the main person who discovered these remains was called Theodore. And obviously I'm stood there like 'Hey, that's my name!' so I turn around naturally out of curiosity, to see the side of her goddess face, and two seconds later she backhand slaps me straight in the face." He replicated the backhand as he spoke. "She was clearly trying to offer her hand to the skeleton, and she obviously had no idea I was stood there. Total accident. I took it well, though. I only said 'Ouch' and then placed a hand over my face."

Zac and I glanced each other and began to snigger. "Hey, it bloody hurt! I could feel my eyes watering! She must have apologised three hundred times within the first minute to me. And I kept reassuring her that I was fine and she didn't need to apologise, but she took me to the first aid room of the museum. She kept apologising as she frantically searched for some wipes or something for my eye. She seemed to be more distressed than me. But she was explaining about how she had only been working there for two months and was about to take over the tour because the girl who did it before quit recently and unexpectedly. That was her third time around rehearsing and now she'd whacked someone in the face. She was in such a state of panic that she couldn't open the wipe packet. I put my hand on her shoulder and told her to relax and take a deep breath because it was an accident. And then she told me her name was Autumn. And then I introduced myself. But she was unreal. Without question the hottest girl I've ever met. I think she must have been on holiday recently because her skin was tan. And it looked so soft and smooth. She had short brown hair, down to her chin, maybe a bit longer, I don't know how to judge hair length. All I know is that it was short. But it was her eyes." Ted wandered off for a moment as he gazed past Zac and me. "Her eyes. I can't describe them. They were so... I don't know—"

"I know what you're trying to say, Ted," I said, looking into Zac's eyes, which made me feel the exact same way.

He rubbed his eye and continued, "She joked about the Theodore previously mentioned, which gained my attention in the first place, and I had to pretend that I hadn't heard her. Anyway while I was heroically sat there with her lightly dabbing my eye with this wipe, I was thinking of a way to ask her out or see her again. Then I remembered I came in the car. So, I left it there and got a taxi home, which means I can go back there again tomorrow and see her. But she also gave me her number to call her tomorrow so she knew I was ok."

I watched Zac as she pouted and pondered over Ted's story. "Are you feeling ok then?" I asked.

"I'm fine! My eye stings, that's it, no need to worry."

"Ok good. We can go and pick up the car tomorrow."

"Actually, no, Will. I was hoping Zac would come with me."

"What? Why?"

"Because I'm going to take her on Autumn's tour around the museum and then afterwards we can all chat and Zac can tell Autumn how amazing I am and that she should have dinner with me sometime. And then Will and I can go the day after if that doesn't work."

I paused for a moment and nodded to his well-thought-out plan.

"Don't judge me, I did the same for you when you wanted to ask out Zac."

"I'm not judging you," I replied, "I'm admiring your well-thought-out plan."

Zac was still childishly grinning over at me because of Ted's comment about us going to the cinema just for her, but I pretended to not notice her. "I'd be delighted to go with you, Ted. Tell me more about her," Zac said as she sat up and shuffled over to edge of the sofa so she could gossip with Ted about Autumn.

And for the next thirty minutes, Ted went into greater detail about Autumn's appearance. It was weird listening to Ted talk about a girl this way. He's always hooked up with girls and then moved on to the next. I think what I'm trying to say is he's never gone into detail about a girl the way he did with Autumn. Normally he would say she was smoking hot and then that was it. Maybe Autumn slapped him a lot harder than he thought.

FEBRUARY 21ST

Ted called Autumn the next morning and told her that his eye was much better, and then he asked if she was doing the tour today and if he could bring a friend to go on it with him. And she was, so he booked himself and Zac a spot on it. He was so excited. I felt like telling Zac to hold his hand during the tour so he didn't run off.

So they left at lunchtime and got a taxi to the museum because it closes earlier on the weekends. I sat and watched some television, waiting for their return. But there wasn't much on so I visited the shops and bought some food and cooked us all dinner upon their return. I decided to make some spaghetti and meatballs. I thought it would be nice to eat dinner and talk about how it went. And then the door flew open, as I was mixing everything. Perfect timing really. I didn't even hear the key in the lock.

"Will, you have to meet Autumn! She is amazing!" Zac yelled, skipping and jumping over to me like an excited child.

Ted walked in and sat on his sofa without saying a word.

"Ok..." I said. "So how did it go?"

"The tour was so good. Some of the bits were a bit boring and uninteresting. But she wasn't boring. She was amazing. I could have watched and listened to her all day.

She's super clever and spoke so well. She's very funny, too, but I didn't understand the jokes she was telling, but people laughed, so that means she's funny! And her face, her face looks like a thousand angels carved it. If Ted doesn't ask her out, then I'm asking her out!"

"I can ask her out myself, Zac. I'm going to do it tomorrow when I go with Will," Ted said.

"I wasn't talking about you asking her out. I was talking about me asking her out," she replied.

"Excuse me," I said. "You're already the captain of my ship." Zac placed a hand on the small of my back and sulked.

"Yeah, Zac," Ted added. "You have Will. You can't have Autumn, too."

Zac dismissed Ted. She hopped onto the kitchen side, beside the stove, so she could look and talk to me. She took off her beanie. "Ok, so imagine the most beautiful girl ever to have existed, ever," she said.

I stopped stirring for a moment and I looked into Zac's beautiful blue eyes and said, "Ok."

"Are you imagining her?" she asked, her perfect smile visible.

"I'm looking at her."

Zac looked at me silently for a moment, and then she produced her adorable blush. And then she hid herself behind her hands. She looked unbelievably cute, as always. I so wanted to kiss her. But, you know, rules, so I smiled and watched her.

"Will," Ted said.

"Yes?" I said, not moving my sight from Zac.

"That was the smoothest thing I may have had the pleasure of witnessing since my existence began."

"Thanks, Ted. You were saying, Zac?" I said, leaning forward and poking her shoulder.

She rubbed her face and ran her hands through her hair. "Yes. I was going to say then times her by ten."

"I don't think that's possible, Zac. But thank you for trying to help me out. I'll see Autumn tomorrow anyway. Right, Ted?"

"Yes, you shall." Ted replied.

"I made dinner for us all," I then said, beginning to stir again.

"What did you make?" Ted asked as he rose from his sofa and wandered over.

"Spaghetti and meatballs."

"Yummy." He grabbed three plates and placed them onto the kitchen side.

"I'm not hungry, thank you," Zac said.

I glanced up and asked her, "Are you sure? There is more than enough for everyone."

"Yes, I'm sure. I might have some later. I'm not hungry right now."

"Ok, that's fine. I'll plate mine and Ted's food up and then you can tell me more about meeting Autumn."

Ted and Zac went on for the entire evening about how amazing Autumn and the museum were. They got to the museum a little early so they inspected the pirate gun that Ted had previously mentioned. And Zac agreed that they couldn't see anything of significance that could lead them to a secret hidden pirate treasure.

FEBRUARY 22ND

I woke up this morning to feel a light breeze on my face. I thought it was Zac trying to wake me up. So I smiled and said good morning and then I got a reply of good morning in return, but it wasn't from Zac. Unless her voice had severely changed during the night.

I opened my eyes to see Ted lying on her side of the bed with his head on the pillow. "Hey handsome," he said. "Ready to meet Autumn?"

I groaned. "We're not meeting Autumn for another four or five hours," I replied as I rolled over.

"Still, it's exciting."

"Where's Zac?" I muttered.

"She's making toast." As I thought over what he said I heard the familiar sound of something being spread onto toast. And the familiar smell of toast. The radio was on, too. I could hear Elton John singing "Bennie and the Jets."

Zac entered the bedroom moments later with two slices of toast on a plate. "Good morning," she said. "I made you toast."

"I've never had breakfast in bed before."

"Me neither," Ted said. I turned to him and gave him an unamused "get out" look. He raised his hands and exited. I took the plate from Zac as she sat beside me.

"Erm, Zac."

"Yes?"

"I think you've given me the wrong toast, these slices have a bite taken out of each of them."

She shook her head. "No, that's my thing. I always take a bite out of each slice. I've done it since I was a kid if I ever made toast for my family."

I smiled. "That's adorable."

"No, it isn't."

"Yes, it is."

"It isn't." She fiddled with her hair and then slumped into the cushions.

"Thank you for my part missing toast, Zac," I said, biting into a slice.

"You're welcome, Will."

Sundiscussion Topic:
What is Harrison Ford's best movie role?

"I've only seen *Indiana Jones*, and small bits of *Star Wars*. So I'll take *Indiana Jones*," Zac started.

"And Will and I will be defending *Star Wars*," Ted added.

"I'm saying *Blade Runner*. As much as I love *Star Wars* I think *Blade Runner* is Harrison Ford's best film. I love *Blade Runner*. It's one of my favourite films." I responded.

"Will, why?" Ted whined. "*Star Wars* is Harrison Ford's best film. How can you not agree with that?"

"I think I'd choose *Indiana Jones* over *Star Wars*, too. Don't get me wrong, you know I love *Star Wars* more than anything in the world. But he's one of three plus main characters, where as in the other films, he's the leading role."

Ted nodded and accepted my defence. "That is a fair point, Will."

"Can I ask a relevant, but also nonrelevant question?"

Zac then asked.

"Of course," I replied.

"How come when Indiana Jones throws his whip around a branch or whatever, it stays there until he swings across to wherever he needs to go. But when he arrives there, he just simply tugs the whip and it unravels the knot. How does that work? Surely if it was that simple it would unravel while he swung and he would fall?"

Ted and I both started to smile and we opened our mouths to reply, but then we looked at each other unable to provide an explanation or an answer to her question.

"I actually have no idea," I said.

"I've never thought about that," Ted added.

Zac made Ted and me a ham sandwich before our trip to see Autumn at the museum, while we tried to figure out how Indiana Jones was able to swing on his whip without falling and then was able pull it free afterwards for her.

"So the whip is pretty thick and strong. If he can make a knot around a log or whatever, it should hold his weight," Ted said with his fingers on his chin. He was in a similar posture to that of a Greek statue.

"But Zac didn't ask about it supporting his weight, she wants to know how the knot is unravelled once he reaches the other side," I replied.

Ted pouted for a moment and then he slapped his knee. "I've no idea, maybe tugging the rope from a different angle undoes the knot somehow. That's all I'm going to think about when I watch Indiana Jones from now on. Thanks, Zac. You've ruined it for me."

"You're welcome," she replied, with her usual tight-lipped smile. She walked over and placed a plate in front of Ted and me with our ham sandwiches.

"Are you not having a sandwich?" I asked.

"No, I'm not hungry," she replied.

"You know, apart from the time you had a small amount of pasta at your place, I don't think I've ever seen you eat anything. I mean taking a bite out of each slice of toast doesn't count. Even when we're here and I ask what you want for tea you say you're not hungry or you don't want anything eat," I replied. I didn't say it in a mean or angry way. I just said it as an observation.

After I said that, Zac looked really uncomfortable and upset. She stood up and walked into my bedroom without another word being said. I looked over at Ted, unsure if it was something I did that upset her.

"Was it something I said?" I whispered. I became really concerned that it was something I said and I felt so guilty and stupid.

Ted shrugged. "I didn't think you said anything offensive. You were only commenting on her not having anything to eat."

I turned and stared at my closed bedroom door. I placed my sandwich back onto its plate and walked to the bedroom to see if she was ok. Zac was sat on the edge of my bed, fiddling with her hands. I closed my bedroom door and sat beside her and put my arm around and kissed her cheek.

"I'm sorry," I whispered.

"It's nothing you did," she quickly whispered back.

"Then what's wrong? You can talk to me. You could say anything and I wouldn't judge you, and it definitely won't change how I feel about you. Unless you're going to tell me you don't like puppies, because everyone likes puppies."

I heard her laugh a little, but I couldn't see her that much because her hair was covering my view of her. "That's why I left my parents' house," she began to say. "My ex cheated on me with three girls. It could have been more. I'm not sure. But Natalie showed me some pictures of the girls he had been with, since she found out, and they were all…they were all…thin. And then when I looked at myself, I thought that's why he did it. I became depressed and stopped eating, and made a habit of it. And maybe after a month, my mum noticed and told my dad. And he was furious with me. When I got home one day, he and my mum sat me down. But he wasn't trying to be supportive or trying to help, he just yelled at me. Told me how stupid I was acting over a boy. And then he said I wasn't allowed to live with them until I started behaving properly. So I moved in with Natalie. My wages from the cinema just about covered everything. I've tried to start eating more and be more like myself, but it's hard, I can't help myself, I don't know what to do."

I could feel my eyes filling with tears. I rubbed them and then sniffled. "Thank you for telling me. I can't imagine how difficult it was for you to tell me that," I said.

"That's why I got so mad with you when I thought Rosie was your girlfriend. I know how horrible it is to be cheated on. And I don't want to be one of those girls that causes another girl pain like that… I'm sorry." She started to cry, and I put my arms around her and rested her head on my chest. "No cuddling," she mumbled.

"Oh, shut up. Your rules can be put aside for a moment," I replied. As I rubbed my hand up and down her back, I thought about her mentioning Rosie as I did so. What Zac didn't know, what Ted doesn't even know, is that Rosie had a severe eating disorder. It's been longer than a decade ago now since. I was nine or ten and she was fifteen or sixteen. And I don't remember much from that time, as I was only young.

But one thing that I haven't forgotten, and will never forget, was the one time I was in school and my grandfather took me out of class early to take me to the hospital because the doctors didn't think Rosie was going to make it. And I remember walking up to the hospital bed she was in, all my family was gathered around. My mum was sitting in a chair beside her bed and she picked me up and put me on her lap so I could see Rosie. And I can't describe the girl I saw in the hospital bed. All I can say is that it looked nothing like my sister. The heartbreaking thing was that I thought she was already dead. She looked so lifeless. I hadn't seen her for a month or two because my mum sent me to live with my grandparents. And I don't know what the doctors did, but over the next couple of days and weeks, she started showing unbelievable signs of change. And somewhere between the next six to twelve months she was Rosie again.

I barely saw her during that time as I continued to stay with my grandparents. But Mum would always visit and sometimes she would bring Rosie with her. And when Rosie visited it always made me so happy.

I lifted Zac's head and wiped her eyes and brushed her hair back. "I'm not going to try to tell you to do something or force you into anything. I will do whatever you want and be whatever you need. But may I suggest something?" I said, looking at her beautiful blue eyes looking back at me.

"Yes, ok," she replied.

"My sister, Rosie, had an eating disorder when she was younger. I was very young at the time so I can't remember a lot. But like you said about knowing how horrible it is to be cheated on and you don't want to be one of those girls that causes another girl pain like that because you know that pain. I think if Rosie knew you were going through something similar to what she has, she wouldn't want you to deal with that pain, too. And I'm going to my mum's next weekend for dinner, and Rosie will be there. If you would like to come, you could maybe talk to her or you could text her or call. Whatever you feel comfortable with. I'm not expecting you to make a decision now, and you don't have to come if you don't want to. Ted and I have to go see Autumn soon, so you can relax here and then I'll drive you home later."

Zac sniffled her nose and took a deep breath. "Thank you."

I was about to stand and kiss the top of her hand, but I took a deep breath myself and remained seated. "I just want you to know, I think you're perfect, I do. And you shouldn't have to change for anyone, ever, no matter what. And yesterday, when you told me to imagine the most beautiful girl ever to have existed, ever, and I said I was looking at her...I meant it. I meant it."

"You better not be falling in love with me, Will. That's not what we agreed," she joked.

I laughed and then said, "I'm going to run you a bath."

"Do I smell again?" she asked with a smirk.

"I'm nearly throwing up, you smell that bad," I replied.

"Don't forget my bubbles."

"Roger that, Captain Panda."

I got a chair and sat beside Zac in the bath to keep her company.

"So does your sister work in America or was she there on holiday?" Zac asked.

"She has been over there for a few years now. She originally went there to study at university. But after she finished, she decided to stay and she got herself a job. She comes back during the holidays sometimes, or she'll surprise my mum for Mother's Day or me for my birthday. But over the past five years I bet I've not even seen her for a full month if you added all the days together."

"That must be hard," Zac said. "I'm guessing you two were always close before she left?"

"Yeah," I said. "We always used to annoy each other and

get on each other's back. But we loved one another really. Do you not have any siblings?" I asked.

"Nope...just me," she replied. She poked her feet out of the bubbles rubbed them together. "What... what about your mum? What does she do?" Zac asked.

"My mum is a gardener. She doesn't mow the lawn. If that needs doing, she has a guy who goes with her to do that. She works on all sorts of scales though. Sometimes she does work for her neighbours, and then she maintains gardens for companies and retirement homes as well. If she's not gardening for somebody else, she's in her own garden. She's always happiest when she's gardening. You should see her garden. It's like a magical wonderland. You'd like my mum. She's lovely."

"She sounds nice."

"What about your dad?" she asked.

"Oh, I don't see my dad. He cheated on my mum and they got divorced when I was three. Rosie was eight. I used to see him when I was younger, but then I stopped seeing him. Rosie and I didn't particularly like him that much. He lives in Scotland now. He got remarried about ten years ago and they had two kids together, too."

"I'm sorry," Zac said. Every strand of her hair was wet. So her hair above the water was clinging to the side of her face. And her hair below the water was very flowing and fluffy and free. It was odd seeing her hair with its less than normal volume.

"That's ok," I said. "So tell me about your parents?"

"My mum works in a library, and my dad is a police-man."

"Oh."

"Oh?"

"Don't think inviting me around for dinner with your dad would be fun."

"Yeah, a lot of people find him a bit intimidating."

"And what about your mum? Is she a mean old librarian?" I asked.

"Na, my mum is lovely. If you met my parents, you wouldn't believe they were a couple. They're just completely different people."

"Opposites attract," I said. "Well, in magnetic cases anyway."

She smirked and then submerged underneath the large quantity of bubbles. She returned ten seconds later, her face covered in bubbles, giving her a bubble beard. I laughed and told her about the bubble formation on her face then said, "I'm going to get changed. I want to look nice for Autumn."

I've visited the museum before, but it was a couple of years ago, so I was expecting its appearance to have changed slightly. And the museum was as grand as I remembered it when we parked the car. I had forgotten how huge it was. The car park was at the back of it so we had a nice walk around to the front entrance through a lovely garden. Everything was so precise and bright coloured. My mum would be proud of the job they had done here.

Ted wouldn't let me admire the garden though. He kept dragging me towards the entrance. He was a bit eager as you can imagine.

"You're not allowed to say anything apart from hello, ok?" Ted said with a very serious face.

"Hello," I replied.

"Excellent."

"Look how magnificent this entrance is—" I started to say.

"What did I just say?" Ted whispered in an angry tone.

"I'm sorry."

So we walked through the magnificent entrance that I was unable to comment on, and then we passed a couple of security guards who were checking people who were carrying bags. But we didn't have any so we went straight through.

The museum wasn't as busy as I expected. I mean, it would be closing soon-ish, but I still expected it to have a larger quantity of people wandering around. Maybe it's because it was a Sunday. Ted walked up to the reception desk, leaving me, and started having a friendly conversation with a young man behind it.

I walked over and stood beside him and said, "*Hello.*"

"Here," Ted said, passing me a lanyard. "That's your tour pass, so don't lose it."

"*Hello,*" I said quietly back to him. He shook his head, unamused. I followed Ted as he joined a queue of people standing behind a sign that said WAIT HERE.

"I'm nervous," Ted said.

"Hello," I replied.

His eyes beamed onto me.

"Why are you nervous?" I asked.

"Because I didn't speak to her when I phoned up and booked our place on the tour. She isn't expecting us."

"So how do you know she is here?"

"Because there isn't anybody else to do the tour I think, and I also asked if she was taking it just to be sure."

"Ok."

"There she is," Ted said, his face looking like a prince in a fairytale when he sees the princess for the first time. I had my back to where he was facing so I had to turn around to view Autumn. I was actually really anxious. Ted and Zac had built Autumn up so much. So here is what I was thinking, *Right, turn around, one step, and another and anothe—holy bloody shit.*

Ted shuffled beside me and nudged me with his hand. "I know right?" he said. That was it. He didn't say anything else.

Ted and Zac hadn't exaggerated her appearance at all. If anything, they had under-exaggerated her appearance. She wasn't beautiful. Beautiful is the top complimentary word of a girl. And that word is reserved for Zac. Autumn was stunning. Maybe that's still too good. Zac would get mad at me if I said that even though she's not my girlfriend. I can just picture the patient look she would be giving me if she were here and asking me what I thought of Autumn. I think if I had to name that face it would be "Go on, I dare you to say she's beautiful so I can kick the shit out of you." I think that suits the face I am picturing nicely.

I'll use handsome. Autumn was very, very, very handsome. Ted and she shared a look but didn't exchange conversation. Autumn walked past us and up to the front of the queue and began the tour.

I didn't need to go on the tour. Ted and Zac had already repeated the description of the displays and exactly what Autumn says at each one. And when I say exactly, I mean it. I almost started laughing at one point because I remember Zac reenacting one point where she's describing this statue of some dude with his balls out. And she said whatever it is Autumn said, and then she pauses, and she replicated the face Autumn made as she paused, too, and I don't know, it doesn't make much sense, but I found it hilarious. And I started coughing from trying to prevent myself from laughing. Ted was repetitively nudging me to stop it.

We then stayed behind for a moment and Ted showed me the pirate gun in the large glass display case. "If you were going to hide a clue to a secret pirate treasure in a gun. Where would you hide it?" he asked.

"In the barrel," I answered. Ted's eyes lit up. He was at the side farthest away from the barrel. I stepped to the side of the display case with the barrel closest to it. I crouched and shut one eye and peered down the barrel.

"Oh my God," I said. "You're not going to believe this."

"What?!" he squeaked. He rushed to my side and pushed me away and replicated my actions. "I don't see anything," he said.

"That's because I was joking," I replied.

His head slowly turned to me and he looked so angry. "Do you realise how excited I was for ten seconds then?" he said.

"If they're going to hide a secret clue in a secret gun that leads to a secret treasure, they're not going to make the clue so obvious to see, are they?"

Ted lifted himself and then we left the glass display with the pirate gun in to rejoin the tour. It didn't go on for much longer, and Autumn was talking about soap from the Victorian times. It was very boring. She wasn't boring. But the soap was boring. Ted obviously couldn't take his eyes off her, and he would remind me to pay attention every few minutes.

Once the tour had finished, Autumn was bombarded by people from the tour asking her extra questions. So Ted and I sat down on a bench in the main entranceway and waited for her. She'd noticed Ted so we assumed she would come over and say hello afterwards. But once she'd answered everyone's questions, she disappeared back into the museum. But Ted and I continued to wait for a few more minutes. The museum was due to close in five minutes so we figured she would leave then and we could catch her.

"I need to pee so bad," Ted said, fidgeting next to me.

"Go pee then."

"But what if she comes and I'm peeing?"

"But what if she comes and you're stood there fidgeting like a weirdo."

"Excellent point, I'm going to go pee. If you see her stall for me, please."

"Don't worry," I said, "I've got your back."

Ted rushed to the nearest bathroom, leaving me sitting in the entranceway of the museum. And then I started to hear the sound of high heels gradually become louder and closer. And then Autumn appeared from one of the corridors, and I thought I was going to panic, but I remained surprisingly calm. She noticed me after she'd visited the reception desk and walked over.

"Hello," I said, following Ted's orders.

"Hi," she replied. "So are you Ted's friend or brother or boyfriend?"

Don't make jokes about being in a relationship with him. Don't make jokes about being in a relationship with him. I repeated to myself. "We've been best buds since we played with our dinosaurs in the sandpit when we were four. I'm Will."

She smirked. "How cute. It's nice to meet you, Will, I'm Autumn." We shook hands and then she asked, "Where is Ted?"

"I'm not sure. He told me to wait here for him." I thought it would be better to say that instead of he went to pee.

"Right," she said. And I could sense either one of two things were going to happen. 1) There would be an awkward silence as we waited for Ted. Or 2) she was going to leave and tell me to tell Ted that she had to go. So I decided I would boldly act to help my friend out.

"I don't know if you've noticed after his third visit in three days, and bringing two friends on your tour. But he really likes you, a lot. I didn't need to take your tour because he'd told me every single detail about it. And every single detail about you. And Ted is normally always full of confidence and shows no sign of embarrassment, but he seems to be struggling a little when it comes to you. So, like a kid would do at school to cause embarrassment and denial, I would like to ask you out for my friend." Her face went blank and then she looked out of the corner of her eye, and I looked out the corner of mine to see Ted was walking over.

Autumn's eyes and mine met. "Is this the part where you tell me you're already in a happy relationship?" I whispered.

But before she could answer, Ted had rejoined us.

"Hey, guys, I see you've met."

"Hello," I replied. His eyes flicked over to me for a moment and he dead-eyed me before returning his sight to Autumn.

"Yes, we have," she said. "You have my number, don't you, Ted?" she asked straight after.

"Yes, I do," he replied.

"I have to go now, but you should text or call me sometime. I'll buy you dinner. I think that would only be fair since I did hit you in the face." Her eyes glanced over to me and then back to Ted.

"Ok," he said, completely taken by surprise.

"Cool. I'll see you later. It was nice to meet you, Will."

"You too, Autumn," I replied.

Ted and I watched her leave and then he grinned and starting nodding for a few seconds. And then he stopped and said, "I love you," to me.

I paused and soaked it in before saying, "I know."

FEBRUARY 24TH

"Hello."

"Hi. It's Zac. How are you?"

"You don't have to identify yourself every time you call, you know. I have your number saved. I'm good. How are you?"

"I'm ok...."

"Good."

"I was calling to see if it would be ok to come with you this weekend?"

"To meet my mum and Rosie?"

"Yes."

"Yeah, of course that's ok. I'll let them know that you will be joining us."

"Ok. Thank you."

"You're welcome. What are you doing right now?"

"I'm just in my bedroom. What are you doing?"

"I'm in my bedroom, too."

"I was thinking..."

"Yes?"

"Natalie is away Friday."

"Ok?"

"You could stay with me and then we could go to see your mum and Rosie the day after. Since my place is kinda closer."

"Ok, yeah. Sounds good."

"Come at seven?"

"I'll see you Friday at seven."

"Ok... so what are you doing?"

"We just asked this ten seconds ago. I'm in my bed-room..."

"Ok..."

"Are you ok?"

"Yes..."

"Are you sure?"

"Yes... I was just seeing if you were busy."

"Hold on. Are you booty calling me?"

"Erm..."

"You are! This is the first time this has ever happened to me. I don't know how to feel."

"Ok. So what are you doing?"

"I'm in my bedroom for the third time."

"You know what I mean."

"I'm afraid I don't. You're going to have to tell me."

"Are you... Are you coming over?"

"Hmm."

"Ok, never mind."

"I'm kidding. I'll come over. Do you want to come back to mine or are we staying there?"

"It's up to you. Natalie isn't here right now. I think she might be staying at some guy's house."

"Ok. I'll see you soon."

"Ok."

She hung up and then I hopped off my bed to get changed. I called my mum as I did to make sure that it was ok that Zac came Saturday, too.

"Hello, love. How are you?"

"I'm fine, Mum. How are you? Are you and Rosie en-joying your trip at the coast?"

"I'm good. We're having a lovely time. It's not very warm. The sun is out, but the wind is still cold. We're sat in a pub now having a drink."

"Sounds delightful. I quickly wanted to call you to see if it would be ok if Zac joined us for dinner Saturday?"

"Of course she can come."

"Ok, good, because I told her she could."

"I figured you would have."

"I was wondering if you and Rosie could speak to her? She...ugh..."

"She's not pregnant, is she?"

"No, she isn't pregnant! She...ugh..."

"C'mon, Will, spit it out. I don't have all evening."

"Zac is going through a difficult time at the moment. She is going through something similar to what Rosie went through. I didn't know if you could help at all."

"Do you know how long or how bad it is? Is she forcing herself to be sick at all?"

"She's spent a fair amount of time with me and I haven't seen or heard her throwing up. She just doesn't eat a lot or at all. She has a bite out of each slice of my toast on a Sunday, and then that's all she may eat that day. But that's one day. And I don't know exactly how long, but I think it has been a few months. I care about her that's all and want to try to help."

"Ok, love. Rosie and I will talk to her Saturday."

"Thanks, Mum. I love you and we'll see you Saturday."

"I love you, too."

"Bye."

"Will's girlfriend is coming Saturday."

"Mum, hang up the phone. And she isn't my girl-friend."

"I hope he doesn't bring home a girl who is exactly like me. Apparently some boys do that, they find a girl identical to their mum."

"Mum, hang up the phone!"

"Can you remember the first girl he brought home? Becky or Betty. She was hilarious."

"Oh, for the love of god! Mum! Mum!"

"Hello?"

"Zac isn't my girlfriend and she is nothing like you and her name was Bethany, and I was fifteen, now hang up the phone."

"Ok. Here, speak to Rosie, you haven't spoken to her properly since she got back."

"Ok."

"Hey, bro."

"Hey, Rosie. How are you?"

"I'm good. We were just talking about your new girlfriend and old girlfriend."

"I know, I heard."

"Aha, you admitted it!"

"Rosie, if I had a girlfriend, do you not think I would tell you? If I had a girlfriend, I'd make sure everyone knew. I get teased enough for being single."

"Oh, I am going to have so much fun when I meet her Saturday."

"Ok. I'll see you then. Love you. Make sure you hang up the phone this time."

"Love you too. I shall. Bye."

Ted was sitting on his sofa as I came out of my bedroom. He was holding a mug and had a disturbing smile on his face already poised.

"Are you being booty called?" he asked.

"No," I replied, sitting on my sofa and putting on my shoes.

"Ah. So where are you going at 9:12 p.m. on a Tuesday, Will?"

"To Zac's," I answered.

"So you're being booty called."

"No," I replied, opening the apartment door.

"Have fun. Behave yourself."

"I will."

FEBRUARY 25ᵀᴴ

"Have you spoken to Autumn since Sunday?" I asked Ted as we sat in our office. He didn't reply so I threw a pen onto his desk.

"What?" he asked.

"Have you spoken to Autumn since Sunday?" I asked again.

"Oh, yeah. We've texted a few times." He seemed relaxed about it. Which was not his normal emotion when Autumn was mentioned.

I paused and waited to see if he had anything else to say, but he didn't say anything. "*So*, what is she saying?" I asked.

"Not much. We're chatting," he replied.

"Is it going well? Do you think you'll be seeing her anytime soon?"

He shrugged. "I dunno."

I frowned. "Why are you acting so odd? Normally you're like an ecstatic schoolchild whenever her name is mentioned."

"I'm trying to keep my cool. I don't want to scare her off. So I'm in play it cool phase."

"Ok. Let me know how it goes."

"I will. Don't worry."

"I'm staying at Zac's Friday night, by the way, and then we're going to see my mum and Rosie Saturday."

"Can I come and see Rosie, too?" he asked.

"No, you can't."

"Why not?"

"Because Zac and I are going to see them. I'll take you to see them another time. Or just ask Rosie out, and then you can be turned down for the thousandth time."

"I only asked her out seven times," Ted corrected.

"And how many times did she go out with you?"

"Zero, but that was before she went to America, and I was still at school."

"You hadn't hit puberty either. You were ugly as hell."

He chuckled before saying, "I'll pay her a visit soon. Get her some flowers, make a scene, pour my heart out. I'm sure that will work."

"She's never going to go out with you, and I would normally convince you otherwise to not do it, but it'll be funny hearing that you failed again."

FEBRUARY 27TH

I asked Ted if he needed the car at all on Friday and Saturday, and he said no, he was only staying in the apartment. We left work, earlier than usual, and went to eat a cheeseburger. We'd been craving one all day so we drove to the nearest burger place and got seated in a booth. We had a delicious cheeseburger with fries each and found ourselves in cheeseburger paradise.

We returned to the apartment afterwards, and I got showered and changed and packed a little toiletry bag with my toothbrush, and deodorant. By the time I had done that it was time to drive over to Zac's. Ted was snoring on the sofa as I came out of my room. He knew my plans already so I left without waking him.

I was really excited to spend the night at Zac's. I've been there before, but never slept over.

Zac was wearing denim short dungarees. I think that is what they're called. Whatever they were, she looked so hot in them when she opened the door. I found myself gawing at her.

"Will?" she said with a frown.

"You look so hot," I said.

She smiled her tight-lipped smile and her eyes wandered around. "Thanks." We didn't say anything for a few seconds. She didn't stand aside to let me in. She looked unbelievable. "Will, will you stop staring at me, please. You're freaking me out."

"You look really hot." I stepped forward and kissed her, and then picked her up.

"Wait," she said. "The door." I took a couple of steps backward and then she swung her arm and shut it. I laid Zac on her back onto the sofa and continued to make out with her.

I don't know how long we were kissing for, but her apartment door opening suddenly interrupted us. We stopped kissing and froze. Zac brushed aside her hair as we stared at her front entrance, waiting to see who it was. And then Natalie appeared from behind the wall. She jumped a little to see us both lying on the sofa. I only had my shirt off so it wasn't the worst sight she could have found herself walking into.

Zac and I stood and waited to see if she had anything to say. Natalie smirked and she didn't seem to take her eyes off me. "I was feeling bad about ending things with Jordan, but this has definitely brightened my mood. Thank you, Will." She continued to stand there watching me.

"Natalie," Zac whispered.

"Yep. I'll go in a minute. I'm going to listen to some loud music so don't let me interrupt your evening." She tilted her head as she continued to stare at me, and I was becoming a little self-conscious now. Because for the past thirty seconds everyone was silently staring at me.

"Ok, Natalie," Zac said, standing in front of me.

"Sorry," she said, shaking herself and venturing into her bedroom. I put on my shirt and then Zac and I went and lay on her bed. Her bed is only small. We just about fit on it widthwise, but lengthwise my feet hang off the end of the bed.

Zac shut her eyes for a moment and rolled over so her back was facing me and she was facing the wall. I shut my eyes, too. And I woke up an hour or so later to see her resting her head on my chest. She looked so peaceful. It was nice. No cuddling was one of her rules so this was a rare moment.

I wasn't really tired. So I lay there and watched her sleep. She woke up not long after and she jolted and sat up. It freaked me out and I thought something was wrong.

"Are you ok?" I asked her.

"Why were we cuddling?" she asked as she pulled her legs to her chest and rubbed her eyes.

"I fell asleep and when I woke up, you were lying like that, I didn't want to disturb you."

She continued to rub her eyes and then she mumbled, "Ok." And then she rested her head on my chest again and returned to her peaceful slumber.

February 28th

Zac was sat in her underwear on the floor in front of her large mirror in her bedroom when I returned from the kitchen to bring her a cup of tea in bed. I stopped at the doorframe and watched her as she put some hot device through her hair. It could have been a hair straightener or curler or something else. All I know is that it was hot.

She glanced up at me and then placed down whatever it was. She covered herself with her arms and said, "What?"

"Nothing," I said. "Just watching you. You look beautiful."

She blushed and then grabbed her dressing gown from off the edge of her bed and dressed into it.

"Tea?" I asked, holding the mug out towards her.

"Thank you," she said, taking it from me.

"I'm sorry about last night," she said.

"What do you mean?"

"The whole cuddling thing. I was exhausted."

"There's no need to apologise. You're the only one who doesn't want to cuddle here. I'm only following your rules."

She smirked down at her mug. "What do you think I should wear today?" she then asked, looking up at me and tilting her head.

"We're only going to my mum's, you don't need to worry about what you're wearing that much."

"I know. But I always like to make a good first impression."

"How about, since I know what I am wearing, I sit on the bed and you show me some clothes?"

Zac grinned. "Like one of those cheesy movies?"

"Like one of those cheesy movies," I replied.

So Zac spent maybe ten to fifteen minutes holding up different types of shirts and dresses and then t-shirts with jackets. She showed me a lot of clothes. It was hard to believe that she could fit it all in her small wardroabe. In the end she decided she was going to wear her Timberlands and ripped black jeans. Then she chose this tartan-style red and black long-sleeved shirt to go with it.

"I'm just going to wear this flannel," she said. "I think that would look nice."

"I thought a flannel was a small towel?" I asked.

"What?" she replied with a small giggle.

"You know, a small towel that you would wash your face with. They're called flannels, aren't they?"

Zac frowned and continued to giggle at me. "I don't know what you're talking about, but this type of shirt is called a flannel."

"Ok," I said, feeling like I was receiving an education about clothing. She put on a blue jacket accompanied with the blue beanie I bought her, and she was ready to go.

"Before we go in, what am I telling my mum and Rosie about us? They're not believing the whole 'just friends' thing. And I can hardly tell them you're Panda, the captain of my ship," I said as we drove from Zac's apartment to my mum's house. My mum lives out in the countryside, which isn't a surprise since she's a gardener. But it's only a thirty-minute drive; depending on the traffic it can be less.

"Why not?" Zac asked, flipping down the sun visor and checking that her blue beanie was in its correct position in the mirror. She ruffled or fluffed, I've never had long hair so describing the actions you do with it is new to me.

"Because she'll think we're seeing each other or we're in a relationship."

"You can introduce me as anything, but your mum will still think we're something more than that."

"That's true," I said. "I'll just introduce you as Zac, and leave it as that."

"Ok."

Zac's shyness rating was increasing as we parked up in the courtyard outside my mum's house. There are three cottages surrounding the small courtyard. Two on one side, and one on the other. Mum's cottage is the one by itself. It's been a while since I last visited. The cottage looked like how you would expect it to. The courtyard has a waist-high wall running around it. But along the wall in front of Mum's cottage was a gate, providing entrance into the garden and leading up to the front door. The garden wasn't fully visible from the car, but you could seem some lovely colourful flowers blooming in some of the hanging baskets that were visible.

Zac was waddling behind me as I made my way towards the gate. I tried to stop and let her walk beside or in front of me, but her beautiful blue eyes flicked up at me as if to say she was happy where she was. We'd not even crossed the halfway point of the courtyard and she must have stood on the heel of my shoes three times. I could actually feel her nose pushing into my back, she was that close.

"What are you doing?" I asked, stopping and turning to face her.

"I'm nervous," she replied.

"So why do you keep standing on my shoes?"

She smirked. "I don't know."

"Right, well, walk in front of me or beside me."

Zac's eyes flicked up at me and then to the brick court-yard ground. She wasn't going to budge.

"Fine. You leave me no choice." Without warning I picked her up and flung her over my shoulder, and decided carrying her would be the more efficient option. She screamed and then she covered her mouth and the scream dimmed.

"Put me down!" she squeaked.

"No," I said. "It would take us an hour to get inside otherwise." She wiggled around and tried kicking, but my right hand was on her ankles so her heavy boots couldn't kick me.

"This is unacceptable. I command you to put me down," she said.

"Sorry, Captain. A mutiny has taken place."

"What the hell is a mutiny?" she asked.

"When the crew overpower the captain and take control of the ship."

"That's not a thing!"

"Yes, it is, look it up online!"

I opened the gate once we came to it. I maintained my forward position otherwise Zac would hit her head on something.

"Will, you're going to ruin my hair!" she yelled. I ignored her and carefully rotated so I could close the gate, and then walked along the small winding path through the garden to the front door of Mum's cottage.

"Aw, this is such a nice garden," she then said all child-ish. "I like the tulips over there."

I quickly perused the garden as we walked. It looked even

more spectacular than when I last saw it. The sunflowers I had planted with her a couple of months ago were looking all tall and yellow now. They looked great. I don't know where she finds the space. There's only so much garden she can work with, and somehow she manages to plant something new every time I visit.

"Oh wait, Will, I dropped my beanie!" Zac said, patting my bum. I sighed and took a step backwards.

"Can you reach it?" I asked.

She made a weird noise, I think that was her stretch, reach for something noise. She then started laughing. "No, I can't!"

I sighed again and turned around. I crouched down and picked up her beanie. It wasn't so easy to do so since I had Zac resting on my shoulder. I held the beanie behind me so she could grab it.

"Thank you," she said. "Will you put me down now, please?"

"Nope." There are three stone steps up to the front entrance, which I walked up with ease; the difficult part was making sure I didn't let Zac bump into any wooden posts or hanging baskets. It's like being in an obstacle course if you're not familiar with the garden. You never know what you can and can't stand on.

I knocked on the door and heard a voice start to yell inside.

"Will, put me down or I will get very angry," Zac growled. Her angry should really be her cute.

"Be quiet you," I replied.

"I can't meet your family like this!"

The door then opened, and Rosie stood there with the happiest look on her face, her brown hair tied up and her rosy cheeks as rosy as ever. Rosie has dark brown eyes and really straight white teeth. And she is five foot ten and a half. I know this because her height was often mentioned as a teenager. And she measured herself frequently so she could tell everyone when they asked.

"Freckles," I said. Freckles is the nickname I gave her when we were younger. She still has them now, but they're not as distinctive.

"Will!" she screeched. "And...someone's ass," she said, not so excited.

"This is Zac. She was a little shy to come in so I thought I would give her a hand."

"I see... Come on in then." She stood inside and allowed us entry. Rosie shut the door behind us. I placed Zac onto her feet. She pushed me with an angry look on her face.

"That wasn't nice, Will," she said.

"You liked it really," I replied. A smirk broke through her frown. She fiddled with her hair and then placed her beanie on. "Zac, this is my sister, Rosie," I said. Zac turned to look at my sister and she seemed a little shocked. Rosie's height always seems to catch people off guard.

"Hello," Rosie said, stepping forward and hugging Zac.

"Hi," Zac said, hugging her back. "You're really tall." Rosie and I laughed. "Was that rude?" Zac asked. "I thought it sounded like a compliment."

"It's fine," Rosie said. "It's nice to meet you, Zac." She then stamped her feet and rushed to me to hug me.

"How were or are things in America?" I asked as we firmly embraced.

"Good," she said. "I broke up with Mike. Can't be bothered with relationships at the moment. I don't think I like American guys either. They're super enthusiastic, but at the same time dull."

"Ted is available. He's made that very clear. I'm sure he'd fly out there to be with you in a heartbeat."

"Aw, Ted. How is he? How are you?"

"We're good. We're working and stuff, and it's going well. Where's Mum?"

"She's on the phone. Let's go sit down."

We took off our shoes, and then walked down the step into the living room. The stairs to the bedrooms are to the left of the entrance, and then to the right and kind of behind them is the living room. The living room is the biggest room in the house. It's shaped like a square. The TV is on the back wall, so it is facing you as you walk into the cottage. And then the step down to the living room is the bottom of the square. It has the comfiest sofas in the world, too. They're on the right and left side of the square. Rosie jumped onto the left one while Zac and I occupied the right one.

"So, Zac, what do you do?" Rosie asked, spreading herself across the sofa and then leaning on her hand to lift up her head.

"I work in a cinema. I sometimes give people popcorn and hot dogs or I check people's tickets," Zac replied.

"That sounds cool. Are you studying at university as well?"

"No, just working in the cinema at the moment. I haven't decided if I want to go to university yet."

"Ok. And if you did go to university, what would you study?"

"I'm not sure."

Rosie glanced over at me. I think all of her questions that she had thought of asking had been asked. "Does anyone want a cup of tea?" I asked, rising from the sofa.

Zac gripped my arm. "Where are you going?"

"To make tea," I replied.

"I'll have one, Will," Rosie said.

"Do you want one?" I asked Zac. She nodded. "Talk to

Rosie, she won't bite," I said, signalling over to her. Rosie pulled a funny face and stuck out her tongue. "She's not really twenty-five," I said. "She's still fifteen in her head."

"I'm actually sixteen!" she corrected. I smiled at them both and then walked back up the step and to the left into the kitchen to make some tea. When I returned, Zac and Rosie were sitting on Rosie's sofa together, looking at an old photo album.

"Rosie!" I said, placing their mugs in front of them on Mum's special rose coasters. If you didn't put your drink on a coaster, you're basically asking for death. Mum will burn a hole into your soul with her terrifying glare.

"What!" she said.

"Don't you play dumb! You had that beside the sofa, didn't you? So you could show Zac once I'd left the room."

"You know how much everyone loves to see your baby photos and see you running around on the beach with your tiny penis. Believe me, this is the least embarrassing thing I could have shown her."

I took a deep breath. Zac and I made eye contact. She tried to fold in her lips to prevent herself from sniggering.

"Aw, look at this one," Rosie said as I returned to my sofa and kept a wary eye on them. "He used to love running around naked. We could never get him into clothes. I used to call him No-Pants Peter. He was so mischievous." Zac laughed and looked over to me. I didn't share the same amusement as her. "His penis hasn't grown a lot since then. Has it, Zac?" Rosie then asked. She's never been considerate. She and Ted have always teased me. This was why I avoided bringing a girl home. Not that I have any to bring.

I choked on my tea and almost spat it all over Mum's carpet, which would have been even worse than not putting your mug on a coaster.

"I wouldn't know," Zac said. "I've not seen it."

Rosie leant back and laughed once. A very, very, very emphatic fake laugh. "She can play the cover-up well, though," Rosie said, nudging Zac.

Before the situation could get any worse, Mum's stomping footsteps were then heard above us. She gradually then became visible on the stairs as she descended them. When she reached the bottom of the stairs, she and Zac instantly made eye contact. It was like Mum knew where she was before she even came downstairs.

My mum is only small. She is maybe five foot one or two. And my dad wasn't much taller either. So that doesn't explain why Rosie and I are so tall. Mum has long blonde hair, and she has green/brown-coloured eyes. Mum turned fifty—I mean, thirty-seven in December.

"Holy shit, Will, she's beautiful," Mum said. She held out her arms as if she was an Italian opera singer singing to his love.

Zac looked over at me, unsure what to do.

"Thanks, Mum," Rosie said.

"Not you," Mum quickly responded. "I'm talking about Zac." Mum sat beside Zac and gave her a hug, which Zac returned. "Sit next to Will, let me take a look at you," Mum then said afterwards. I closed my eyes and accepted that no matter what I tried to say or do, my mum would still get her way. Zac looked at me again, and then wandered over and sat next to me.

"Aw, don't they make a lovely couple," Mum said, sitting next to Rosie and then staring at Zac and me.

Zac and I faced each other and then we frowned. "We're not a couple, Mum." I assured.

Mum completely dismissed what I said and started making conversation with Zac. "Hi, I'm Will's mother. My name is Mandy."

"I'm Zac," Zac replied, her shyness increasing once again.

"So you're sleeping with my son?"

"Mum!" I said. "We're friends."

"Oh, please," Mum said. "I'm not an idiot. And I called Ted the other day and he told me all about you two."

I gritted my teeth and thought of the beating I would give Ted upon my return to the apartment. "What's new with you, Mum?" I asked.

"You know, gardening and more gardening. I'm maintaining the garden for the museum now, the one twenty minutes away from here."

"Oh, we've been there," I said. "Ted likes a girl who works there so he took Zac one day, and then he took me the day after. I saw the garden. It looks lovely."

"Thank you, my baby. So, Zac..." Mum said. My attempt at creating a conversation topic about something else had failed. "Do you want anything to eat or drink?"

"No, thank you. I'm ok with tea."

"Ok, love. Will, you can begin to make our food then," Mum said, signalling to the kitchen.

"I thought you were making food?" Mum didn't take to kindly to my assumption. She just gave me her glare. I stood and made my way towards the kitchen.

"The recipe and ingredients are in the kitchen. I'll come and check on how you're doing later."

"Ok," I grumbled.

Mum came to check up on me five minutes later. "How is the lasagna coming along?" she asked.

"Good," I said. "I'm starting on the base now."

"Good work," Mum said, hugging me from behind. "I miss you. You're too old and tall now. Can't you become a baby again?"

"I'm not sure that's how it works, Mum," I replied.

"You'll always be my baby," she said, squeezing her arms around me tighter. "There's a brand new boxed blender over there in the bag," Mum said.

"Ok. Why is that relevant?"

"It's a present for you."

"I don't need a blender."

"It's for Zac, you dumbass."

"Oh. Why does she need one?"

"Can't you remember the plan that Rosie and I created together? And you used to complain about the noise of the blender all the time."

I thought back to my ten-year-old self living here. Then I remembered Rosie's stupid blender used to wake me up every morning. "I remember now," I said.

"We'll sit down later with her and we can talk about it. But what you might not remember is that I only used to eat whatever and whenever Rosie did. So I thought you could do that with Zac if you really want to support her through this."

"Of course. We can talk about that later with her."

"Good." Mum released her grip from around me and then exited the kitchen. She poked her head around the kitchen corner moments later. "By the way, I took twenty pounds from your wallet in your coat earlier so you paid for the blender."

I laughed. "Ok, Mum. No problem. But how did you know I didn't have one already?" Mum laughed and then vanished again without saying another word.

Once I'd prepared the lasagna, and also preheated the oven, I placed the lasagna in the oven and set the timer for thirty minutes. I made my way into the living room afterwards. Mum was reading a book about flowers, and Rosie was sat painting Zac's nails.

"What are you two up to?" I asked.

"I'm painting Zac's nails," Rosie replied, not breaking her concentration on stroking the brush along Zac's nail.

"Sounds fun. What colour?"

"Since her beanie and eyes are the same colour, we thought we would make her nails the same colour, too."

Zac smiled and held up the hand that Rosie wasn't painting to show me the same colour nail polish as her eyes and her beanie.

"I bought her that beanie on our first…meeting," I said. "She wears it all the time now."

"That's nice," Rosie said. "So how did you two meet?"

I waved my hand to Zac to allow her to answer Rosie instead of me. I also thought it would be interesting to see if she mentioned anything about what she thought during the times that we met at the cinema.

"We met at the cinema that I work at. He came a couple of times in a couple of days and then we saw a film together."

Rosie lifted her head and looked at Zac and then me. "I'm sure you've missed out a lot of the details there, but fair enough."

Mum dropped her book onto the table and then saw me. "Oh hello, love. I didn't notice you were finished in the kitchen."

"It should be ready in thirty minutes or so," I replied.

"Finished!" Rosie then said, placing the brush back into the bottle.

"Why don't I show you around the garden, Zac? They'll dry much quicker outside," Mum said.

Zac looked at Rosie and then me. "She won't hurt you," I said. "She stopped burying her murder victims in the garden a long time ago. She doesn't murder family or friends either so you're safe."

"That's the story I used to tell him," Mum said. "He used to ask me why my flowers grew better than everyone else's, and I told him it was because I used dead bodies in the soil."

Zac laughed, but you could tell that she was a bit scared. She slowly got to her feet and she and Mum went outside to view the garden.

I sat on the sofa beside Rosie. She shuffled over and rested her head on my leg. "Tell me the truth, Will," she said all soft and innocent.

"Truth about what?" I asked.

"About Zac." I smirked and leant my head back.

"Aw, c'mon, Will. I'm being serious. I know I tease you about things, but I honestly want to know what the deal is between you two."

I sighed and took a deep breath. "She doesn't want anything serious. We've been seeing each other nearly every weekend since we met. And she created these rules that we have to follow if we were going to sleep together and keep it that way."

Rosie nodded her head. "Ok. But you want to be with her, don't you?"

I wobbled my jaw and thought about lying, but I knew Rosie would see right through that. "Yeah, I want to be with her. But she doesn't want anything serious like I said. So, I don't know. I guess I'm hoping she will change her mind the longer we spend together."

Rosie smiled before saying, "She might change her mind, Will. But I haven't spent long enough with her to figure out if that would be possible. The one thing I can say to you is that ninety-nine percent of the time, this ends with you being left hurt or heartbroken. And I don't want to see or hear that happen to you."

I smiled. "We'll be ok. Don't worry."

"Ok," she said, sitting up. "I love you, little brother, I've missed you so much." She wrapped her arms around me and rested her head on my shoulder.

"You too, Freckles." She rubbed my back and tightened her grip. "Is everything ok in America then?" I asked.

"I don't know," she said. "It feels like home, and then sometimes it feels nothing like home. And I have so much fun there, but at the same time, I have some bad times there."

"That's life," I said.

"I know. I just don't know whether to stay there or come home."

"Either way, we will love and support you no matter what, Rosie."

She leant back and said, "Thank you, little brother."

"I am taller than you, Rosie. It should be younger brother now."

"I know, but that doesn't sound as good. Can you remember when I was seventeen and I had stopped growing, and you were about to turn eleven and still hadn't had your growth spurt? You barely went past my hip."

She started to laugh, but I didn't find it as amusing. "It's not my fault I was a slow grower! Not everyone becomes a big tree like you immediately."

"You'll always be my little brother! No matter what."

Mum and Zac then came through the front door from outside. "Hey! How was it? What do you think about Mum's garden? Or did she just take you outside to quiz you about me?" I asked Zac.

"A bit of both," Mum replied.

"Did she give you the break my son's heart I'll kill you speech?"

"No!" Mum responded. As she sat back down on the opposite sofa, Zac and I quickly made eye contact and she smiled and she nodded. I grinned, and then Rosie went to sit beside Mum, allowing Zac to sit beside me. "I spoke to Zac outside about how Rosie had an eating disorder, too." Mum grabbed Rosie and locked her arms around Rosie's neck, trapping her in Mum's loving death grip. "Rosie and I created this plan together. We would have three meals a day. Breakfast, lunch, and dinner. To show her that she wasn't alone in this, I followed the same plan. If she ate, I ate. If she didn't, I didn't. But she always ate. My baby never skipped a meal again after those terrible days in the hospital. We would have a smoothie in the morning, soup for lunch, and soup for dinner. When we first started. We started with smaller quantities. We calculated how many calories each meal was, and then how many calories that would be per day. And we gradually increased the quantity as time progressed until we made it to the calorie intake that we should be having per day. We used a blender. And we put all sorts of fruits and vegetables in so we were eating healthily and got lots of nutrients and vitamins and the other ones, I can't remember them all. Like I said outside, Will has bought you one, it's in the kitchen."

Zac's eyes flicked over to me and she smiled her tight-lipped smile. Mum leant over the back of the sofa she was sitting on and grabbed a journal from behind it. "This is the journal that Rosie and I kept a log in. I think you should have it. You can see what we ate each day, and how we progressed." Mum stood and leant over to hand the journal to Zac. She sat with it on her lap and ran her fingers over the black cover.

"Zac," Rosie said as Mum recaptured her into her loving death grip. "I know you're scared. I do. Because I almost died. I can't describe what it felt like, thinking I was going to die." She tried to sit up, but Mum's grip was too tight. "Mum," she said. "Release me from your grasp for a second, please." Mum slowly opened her arms and allowed Rosie to sit up, but she took her hand afterwards and held it.

Rosie regained her attention to Zac. "And I decided to accept it when I was in the hospital. If that's what the doctors and nurses thought, and they're experts, then I thought there would be no way I could survive. But then I remember waking up one time, and looked around my bed to see nobody. Until I looked to my right and saw my little brother sat holding my hand. I figured everyone else must have been busy talking to the doctors. And he said to me, 'Please don't die, Rosie.' I've never told this to anyone before, and I don't know if he remembers or not. I just thought about what he must have been thinking. How scared and confused he must have been. But I told myself if I recovered, and didn't die, I would do everything I could to be myself again. Because my little brother needed me; otherwise, he wouldn't have anyone else to tease him."

I smirked as I was looking down at my hands. I was trying very hard not to cry, because I didn't want Zac to see me cry. I glanced up and saw my mum. She was gone already, she was continuously wiping away her tears.

"I know you don't have a brother or sister," Rosie continued after she kissed my mum's cheek. "But you have a mum and dad, and I know things have been difficult between the three of you recently. And I'm sorry about that. But they care about you. However, if you feel like things are too difficult between the three of you at the moment, then remember you have Will. He will do anything and everything he can to help. I know you two have an unusual...relationship. But all I wish you would do is give it a chance, and give him a chance, and let him be whatever you need him to be whenever you need him to be it. Because he'll do it. Because he cares about you. You're a beautiful girl, Zac. And if you ever need to talk to me, you can always contact me."

Zac nodded. "Thank you, Rosie."

Zac sat and read through the journal whilst Rosie, Mum, and I ate my pretty surprisingly delicious lasagna, and then she asked if she could make one of the soups from the journal. Mum got up and showed her where everything was. And then a couple of minutes later, the blender was buzzing around. I'm not sure what ingredients she used, but it looked delicious. She heated the blended mixture in the microwave, and then sat with us at the kitchen table. After lunch Mum told us that Rosie had bought her the *Mamma Mia!* movie on DVD. I remember when she made us go to the cinema with her last year to watch it. She kept dragging different people along to go and see it with her so she ended up watching it about five times.

So Mum made a big pot of tea while we all sat in the living room, and then we watched the film. Mum sat on her sofa with all her blankets and cushions while Zac, Rosie, and I sat together. Rosie placed a cushion across my lap and rested her head on it.

"She's just a really tall baby," Mum said from across the room. Zac just sat beside me with a bit of space between us because that was what her rules permitted. Towards the end of the film she shuffled up to me and put her head on my shoulder. I think she was a bit tired, even though she slept all evening and all last night.

We didn't stay much longer after the film had finished. Zac was sleeping, so I thought I'd wake her and drive home before Mum forced us to stay there. Because then we would never leave. She'd trap us there. Zac hugged Mum and Rosie and thanked them both, and then she dawdled into the garden towards the front gate.

I hugged my mum and said, "Thank you, Mum. I love you."

"You best come and visit me again soon," she said. "Your room is still the same if you ever want to stay."

"I know," I said. "I'll come back soon, I promise."

I hugged Rosie after and she said, "I love you, bro. Let's do something soon?"

And I said, "I love you, too. Text me and we'll do something next week." When I tried to end the hug and step away, she tightened her grip around me. "Are you going to let me go?" I asked.

"Nope. We're stuck like this forever now."

"I've got to take Zac home," I said.

"Oh Will, we all know you're going back to yours for sex," Mum said.

"Ok, I'm going now," I said, breaking free from Rosie's grasp and grabbing Zac's blender off the table.

"Use protection!" Mum shouted as I walked towards the gate.

"Please shut up, Mum!" I yelled. I shuddered as I approached the gate and shut it behind me. This was why I didn't talk to Mum or Rosie about girls. Because they always say things that I don't particularly want to hear them say.

Zac was leaning against the passenger side of the car as I walked over. "I have some condoms in my bag," she joked.

"Don't you start," I replied. "They're bad enough."

She giggled as she opened the door and slid inside. I placed her blender on the backseat and then got into the driver's seat.

"Thank you," she said as I sighed and fastened my seatbelt.

I looked into her beautiful blue eyes and said, "No thanks necessary, ma'am. Just remember whatever you need whenever you need it, I'll try my best to make it happen."

She smiled her tight-lipped smile, and then I placed the car key into the ignition. She leant over and started to kiss my neck. I flinched my shoulder and leant away.

"What?" she said.

"Wait until we're home," I said. "My mum has probably set up surveillance cameras around here, and she'll be spying on us right now." Zac frowned. "I'm not kidding! I wouldn't be surprised if my phone started ringing now and it was her calling to tell us to knock it off."

She laughed and returned to her normal seating position. "You're too cute sometimes," she said.

I raised an eyebrow and peered over at her. "You better not be falling in love with me, Zac. That's not what we agreed." She pulled a funny face and sarcastically laughed. "Right," I said. "Let's go home."

MARCH 1ST

Ted was nowhere to be seen when we returned to the apartment yesterday. So we figured he was chilling in his room. I sat down on the bed and Zac didn't even let me take off my shoes before she continued to kiss my neck.

When I woke up this morning, I heard Zac talking to someone, but I assumed that it was Ted, although I couldn't hear his voice. Then I heard quick thumping footsteps and Zac suddenly sprinted back into the bedroom and jumped onto me.

"Will, Will, Will, Will, Will, Will, Will, Will, Will," she whispered no farther than an inch away from my face.

"Oh, I'm sorry, were you talking to me?" I asked, opening my eyes to find hers looking directly into them. She looked extremely happy and excited. "What's up?" I grumbled.

"Autumn is here."

"No, it can't be. It's still March."

She sighed. "No, Autumn, the girl from the museum, is here, you idiot."

My eyes opened and I sat up, my mood matching hers. "Where is she?" I asked.

"In the kitchen. I can't believe it!" Zac whispered.

"Did she say anything to you?" I asked.

"Not really, we said hello and asked how each other was, that's when I came to tell you she was here."

Zac and I both rose from the bed and poked our heads around the bedroom door to peer into the kitchen. And there she was, wearing a T-shirt and pair of jogging bottoms of Ted's, making herself some toast with Ted, and they were smooching.

"How did this happen?" I whispered.

Zac hummed. "The sex we had last night must have been so amazing that we entered an alternate universe, and in this universe, this Ted and Autumn are already in a relationship."

I frowned down at Zac, as she seemed pretty pleased with her explanation as she watched Ted and Autumn. Her focus changed to me, and her happiness faded when she saw my frown. "What?" she whispered.

"Our sex must have been so amazing that we entered an alternate universe?"

"I don't know the science behind it."

We returned to watching Ted and Autumn. And then Ted turned towards us. "Are you two going to come and say hello or are you going to stand there watching us and thinking that your presence and whispering is going unnoticed?"

Zac nudged me with her arm and we walked through the living room to the kitchen. "Hey Autumn," we both said in unison.

"Hi," she replied.

"Sorry we didn't come over sooner. Zac was explaining to me that our sex last night was that amazing it has sent us into an alternate universe where you two are in a relationship," I said. Zac nudged me. "What?" I said.

"Shut up," she whispered. "You could tear open the timeline and destroy everyone."

I sighed and apologised.

"This isn't an alternate universe, Zac," Ted said. Zac folded her arms, awaiting an explanation. She looked so adorable. "When I heard that Will was spending Friday and Saturday with you, I thought I would ask Autumn out for dinner. And if she wanted to come back to the apartment then you two wouldn't be here spectating or quizzing her."

"That makes sense," Zac replied. "So this isn't an alternate universe," she said, seeming disappointed.

"No, Zac," Ted confirmed. "And obviously it went very well and we spent the weekend together. And now we're going to get a dog together."

"We're going to see how it goes," Autumn corrected.

"Are you staying for the rest of the day?" I asked.

Autumn smiled. "We hadn't discussed what are plans were for today." Her focus changed to Ted to see what his thoughts were.

"Stay as long as you like," he said. "Don't leave. Stay forever."

"I don't know about forever, but I might stay until after lunch." Ted pulled her close and they kissed again.

I glanced down at Zac and she had a smile on her face. "I knew she'd be a good kisser," she whispered to me.

"She's a fantastic kisser," Ted replied.

"What's today's Sundiscussion?" I asked Ted.

"What's what?" Autumn questioned. "My apologies, I've never heard that reference before."

It was at this moment that I realised how slightly posh and well-mannered Autumn was. I know she works in a museum and escorts people around the tour. So that job requires her to be. But I've not had that long of a conversation with her to notice. She's just so polite and lovely. Ted will probably say she's like a ray of sunshine or she brightens his day. Even though they're currently entering the third day they have spent together.

"Sundiscussions are discussions that take place between Will and me every Sunday. So if you combine Sunday and discussion together, you get Sundiscussion."

"*Ah...* So do you talk about politics and stuff?" Autumn asked. I bit my bottom lip to prevent myself from laughing. The thought of Ted and I talking about politics on a Sunday, never mind any other day, was a humorous vision.

Ted's eyes quickly met mine and then he said, "We talk about less boring matters. So today, the topic was going to be: If you could go back to one part in time, where would you go?"

"That's a good one," I said.

"Thank you, Will," Ted replied. "So, let's all think it over and then we can talk about it on our sofas."

Sundiscussion Topic:
If you could go back to one part of time, where would you go?

Zac and I set up her blender and looked through the journal that Mum and Rosie had given to her. We were going to follow it exactly as they recommended. She asked me last night if I would follow it with her, like Mum did with Rosie. And I said I would. We're going to build our way up and progress onto consuming more each week or each couple of weeks like they did.

They had a list of different types of smoothies that they drank, and the amount of calories in each amount of grams. So we made a strawberry smoothie since we didn't have any other fruit or vegetables to include. Since this blender is Zac's, but she has another blender at her apartment, she is going to leave this one here. But when I take her home later, we're going to stop and buy some fruit and any other ingredients she would like to make her smoothies with.

"This doesn't taste too bad," I said as we slumped onto my sofa with our smoothies.

"It's the first time we've made one as well. Surely over time they will taste even better."

"You got some on you," I said. Zac wiped her mouth in order to wipe away what she thought she had on her. She didn't have any on her. I was just trying to be funny, because, you know, I'm utterly hilarious. I told her she hadn't got it three times. Each time she became more and more frustrated.

"Will you get it then please, Will?" she then snapped. I smirked and then wiped her eyebrow with my thumb. She whacked my hand away, realising she had fallen for my excellent joke. She punched my leg, but then she hurt her wrist in doing so.

"You two are so cute. How long have you been together?" Autumn asked as she was lying on Ted on his sofa.

"He's not my boyfriend," Zac quickly responded.

"I am not her boyfriend," I added.

"Sorry, I thought with how flirty and close you are that you were," Autumn replied.

I pushed Zac to the edge of my sofa with my foot. "We're not flirty," I insisted. Zac pushed away my foot and threw a cushion at me, which I caught and placed neatly beside me.

"I don't flirt with Will, he flirts with me," Zac then said, budging back over into her original seating spot.

"I do not!"

"So you didn't just joke about me having some smoothie on me and then wipe my eyebrow to try to be funny? That's flirting, Will."

I pointed and opened my mouth to provide a substantial explanation for that, but I couldn't think of anything to support my case. I turned to Ted and Autumn, and they both marginally raised their eyebrows to show that Zac was right.

I sat up and budged up next to Zac so we were touching. I looked down at her as she stirred her smoothie and was waiting for her to make eye contact with me. Seconds later she did and I had her trapped in my gaze.

Her eyes may be my weakness, but I knew I could do this if I didn't take too long. I slowly began to lean in to kiss her, ever so slowly, and she did the same. And I stopped when our noses were beside each other, just to intensify the moment before the kiss, and I waited for her to close her eyes just before our lips met. And then I leant away, leaving her with her eyes closed and lips slightly parted. She opened her eyes two seconds later, realising that we should have kissed by now, and she saw me, sat back with a grin on my face.

She smirked and then she became funnily angry. "You did not just do that. You best kiss me right now," she said.

"But your rules state—"

Zac put down her smoothie and then dove onto me and planted her hands on either side of my face. I was now flat on my back on my sofa with Zac on top of me.

"She's flirting with me, guys. Tell her to stop," I said to Ted and Autumn.

"In Zac's defence, Will, you started it and you're still being the more flirtatious one now," Ted replied.

I sighed and then kissed Zac. To claim that Zac was still in charge she didn't move off me and sit on the sofa. Instead she shuffled around and sat on my stomach. I didn't say anything or try to move; I just remained there.

"Does everyone have an idea for today's Sundiscussion?" Ted then asked.

"I'd go and visit the dinosaurs," I said. "I'd like to see either a T-Rex or a megalodon." (A megalodon is like a huge great white shark from millions of years ago.)

"Of course," Ted said. "I'm stuck between visiting the dinosaurs or finding out what really happened in Area 51, or to a time when aliens did land on this planet." He turned to Autumn. "Where would you go?"

Autumn leant her head backwards so she could view Ted. "Working in a museum means that I know a lot of history. So it's difficult to decide. I've always wanted to find out what the real story of Robin Hood is. Or pirates like Blackbeard. Or visit the Egyptian times to see Tutankhamun and Cleopatra."

"Speaking of pirates," Ted said, "I've been meaning to ask you about that pirate gun in your museum."

Autumn sighed. "You're going to ask me if I saw the guys who came in and inspected it and somehow found a pirate treasure or something?"

Ted bit his lip. "Well, not those exact words, but yeah."

"You're like the ten thousandth person to ask me. I always tell people I don't know anything. But the truth is one of the girls who worked there, literally two days after I started. She apparently knew one of them. I think the guys were brothers or good friends, I don't know. They entered the museum in the morning and they asked me where she was and I told them, and escorted them to her. I think she may have dated one of them because there was definitely some friction between them when they met. But I left right away and got back to work. She was still talking to them in the afternoon, and they were still staring in the gun's display box as I was leaving. And she quit that evening. That's all I know."

Ted's inner child started to rise. "Imagine doing that, though. Imagine finding a clue on a however-many-hundreds-year-old gun that leads you to a pirate treasure or whatever they found!"

"No one really knows the truth. Apart from them. No one knows if they did find anything, and if they did find anything, no one knows what it was. Some rumours were written in the papers. But they didn't have any proper evidence to support the articles. It was all kept quite secretive. It's all very mysterious."

Ted leant over Autumn. "You know something, don't you?"

"I just told you everything I know."

Ted squinted. "I think you're bluffing. You definitely know something."

Autumn gasped. "Are you claiming I had some involvement in helping them?"

"I don't know. Did you?"

"No!"

Ted kissed her. "Did you?"

"No!"

He kissed her again. "Tell the truth, Autumn."

"I am!" Then they started kissing and being all playful. Zac and I faced each other and grimaced at their unbearable cuteness.

After they'd finished making out, Ted asked Zac about where she would go if she could travel through time.

"I'd find out if anybody escaped from Alcatraz," Zac answered.

Ted's eyes and mine met. "That's a great answer, Zac! We love that film *The Rock* that is based on Alcatraz."

"I haven't seen it," she replied.

"We should watch it together sometime," I said.

"Am I invited?" Autumn asked.

Ted ran his hand through her hair. "Autumn, you're great, but I don't know if I'm ready for this kind of commitment so soon. I think this isn't going to work out between us two."

"Yeah, ok, so text me when you guys want to watch it and we should all do dinner," Autumn replied. She had called

Ted's bluff. They kissed again and Zac and I grimaced again. I don't know why I was grimacing because what they're doing is what I wish Zac and I could be like. But, you know, we have rules to follow.

"Does your dad have anything to do with you wanting to know about Alcatraz? You know, since he's a policeman."

She nodded. "He always said that no one ever escaped alive, but I think he's wrong." She hopped off my stomach and ventured into the kitchen. She returned moments later with a bottle of water for us both. Autumn said she had to return home an hour later. She'd told her mum she would be home Friday night and now it's Sunday at midday. She would have stayed for longer, but her mum and dad were going to have dinner with some friends, and they wanted Autumn to join them. Ted walked her down to her car, giving us a break from their kissing, while Zac and I made our lunch, which was vegetable soup. Mum had noted in the journal that you could have canned soup as long as you counted the calorie intake and amount. And since our fridge didn't have any vegetables in, we had soup from the cans we had in a cupboard.

We were sat on my sofa with our bowls when Ted came through the door. Zac held up her hand and Ted high-fived it. He then jumped onto his sofa and let out a long sigh. "Guys, I'm definitely in love," he said, gazing up at the ceiling.

"I love her, too," Zac said. "She's so amazing and wonderful and beautiful."

Ted spun around and leant on his elbow. "I know right! And I had sex with her," he whispered. I don't know why he whispered. It seemed unnecessary.

"Does she have nice boobs?" Zac asked.

"Zac!" I said.

"What?" she replied, hiding behind her bowl of soup.

"Little bit inappropriate."

"Sorry." I continued to consume my soup. And then she whispered, "Does she though?" I rolled my eyes and decided to leave her be.

"Every inch of her is perfect," Ted replied. "I think even if she murdered people with chainsaws I'd still wanna be with her."

"So are you going to see her again?" Zac asked.

"Of course! We're having dinner together tomorrow. She's going to pick me up from work."

Zac didn't stay much longer either. Natalie had texted her and asked her if she wanted to do something. She didn't say what it was, but I didn't need to know. I drove Zac home and we stopped to pick up some fruit and vegetables for her smoothies and soup. We also picked up some cans of soup in case she didn't have time to blend and create her own soup. She kept the journal that Mum and Rosie gave her. I took some photos on my phone so I had copies of what to do during this week. We also agreed that we would send each other photos of our smoothies and soups three times a day so we both knew that we were following the plan. It's only the beginning, so I'm not sure how it is going to go. I just want Zac to be happy. And I feel like I may be helping with that.

MARCH 2ND

My normal "So listen here right" conversation with Jeremy was taken over by Ted today. He pretty much sprinted up the stairs and told Jeremy about his weekend with Autumn. And then told everybody else in the office. It was like he acting out a number from a musical. He even ran into his dad's office and told him. I thought he was going to start throwing paper into the air and glide down the office corridor. Then he called me on my office phone on my desk from his office phone on his desk.

"Did I tell you I spent the weekend with that gorgeous lady from the museum?"

"You did. I happened to have spent Sunday morning with you both."

"Oh yes, my bad. As you were."

I'm happy for Ted. I'm glad he's met someone he likes. I only hope that this doesn't wear off after a couple of days. Autumn is great, and she likes him, which is a bonus, so we shall how things progress. They're going to be seeing each other for the fourth time in four days so their relationship is off to a good start!

Ted left work fifteen minutes earlier than usual, as Autumn was outside to pick him up for their dinner that evening. He asked me if his tie was ok, and if he looked ok, and if he smelt ok. And I said, "You look great, babe. You go have fun."

So after work I went home to chill out. I had my soup and texted it to Zac. Then I went and had a shower. I'd been out of the shower for two seconds and I was in the process of wrapping the towel around my waist when Ted burst into my bathroom, uninvited, scaring the hell out of me.

"I'm calling it," he shouted.

"Calling what?" I asked, feeling like throwing a punch at him.

"Autumn is the girl I'm going to marry."

"If you say so. Time will tell," I said.

"My odds are better than yours. Autumn likes me. Zac's only sleeping with you."

"Ok! No need to make it so personal."

"Do you know what it feels like?" Ted said. "It feels like I've known her for four years, not four days. We get along so well."

I nodded. "Ok. I'm happy for you. Now can I get dry in my own bathroom, please?"

"Need a hand?" he asked, stepping forward.

"No! Get out, you weirdo!"

He sulked and shrugged. "Fine. Just being nice." He shut the door behind him and I locked it. It's the first time I've locked it in forever. I've never needed to lock it before because I didn't expect my best friend to burst in and then offer to dry me.

You know how people are supposed to mature when they get older? I think Ted may be the opposite of that.

MARCH 9TH

Once again, Ted took my "So listen here right" conversation with Jeremy. Which is fair because he had a lot to say since he'd spent every day of the week with Autumn. Each day he or they returned to the apartment they brought with them a different souvenir from what they had been doing. One day it was stuffed teddies that they had made for each other. The next it was a stream of photos from a photo booth. Then one day they came home with this trophy because they got a hole in one at this crazy golf place. It was nice and annoying at the same time.

Zac had taken on some extra shifts at work, too. So she was working Friday to Sunday, meaning I couldn't see her until next week. Ted told Autumn that he couldn't cook Friday evening when we were all sat watching TV. So she dragged him straight into our kitchen, and said they were going to cook something together. Autumn told me I had to stay so I could judge the meal that they prepared together. I'd not had my soup yet so I thought it would be ok to replace it with whatever they made. They didn't have some of the ingredients needed so they left and walked to the shops to buy them. I called Zac while they did so. It was late so I knew she would have finished work by now.

"Hello."

"Hey, Zac. How are you?"

"I'm good. How are you?"

"I'm ok. I've been told I have to wait on the sofa as Ted and Autumn are cooking for me. Ted can't cook, as you already know, so Autumn's teaching him. I've not had my soup yet so I thought I'd ask if it was ok if I replaced it with whatever they made?"

"They're so cute. And yeah, of course. Permission granted."

"Thank you, Captain. How are things? How's work?"

"Things are fine. I keep going to make my smoothies or soup to find that my ingredients keep decreasing. Natalie has started making them, too. And work is fine. It's boring that I'm not going to have this week off, but I'm getting extra money so I can't complain."

"Aw. Do you have enough ingredients left? Surely you must be running low now? And Ted and Autumn were talking about going to see a film so you might have some visitors soon."

"Yeah, Natalie bought some more yesterday so there's plenty. And, oh really? Are you coming as well if they do?"

"I don't think so. I don't want to get in the way and also I'll have to entertain myself most of the time as they'll be smooching."

"Ah, ok."

"Why, did you want to see me?"

"No. I was just seeing if you were going to come, too."

"Do you miss me?"

"Nope."

"I think you do."

"Whatever feeds your panda."

"Aw, c'mon. You don't miss me a little bit?"

"Nope. Do you miss me?"

"Of course I do."

"What?"

"I'm used to seeing you. It's not the same when you're not here."

"Ok. I'll see you next Thursday."

"Ok."

"Bye."

"Bye."

Ted and Autumn returned five minutes later and made fajitas. They were so delicious.

"Exactly what did you make, Ted?" I asked as I munched on one.

"I technically made everything, but I was controlled by Autumn like that rat controls the dude in *Ratatouille*. She didn't pull my hair, though. She held my arms, very, very firmly." He glanced over to Autumn and she blew him a kiss and smiled smugly afterwards.

"I spoke to Zac while you two went shopping," I said.

"What did she say?" Autumn asked.

"Not much. I asked how she was and I told her you two were cooking, and I mentioned that you might go and see a film so she may have some visitors at work." Ted dropped his head into his hands and sighed. "What's wrong with you?" I asked him.

I glanced over at Autumn and her smug smile had reappeared. "I wanted to go and see this film. I think he was hoping I'd forgotten." She placed her hand in his and gave it a squeeze. "Are you ok, darling?" she whispered.

Ted raised his head and nodded. "Of course I am, babe. I was hoping you would be reminded about our trip to the cinema."

"What film are you going to see?" I asked, matching Autumn's smug smile.

"*Confessions of a Shopaholic*," Ted muttered.

"Ah, well, I hope you two enjoy yourselves."

Autumn rose from her seat. She kissed Ted and then said, "Excuse me. I need to use the bathroom." She kissed Ted again and then went into his bedroom.

Ted returned his attention to his plate and ate his final piece of fajita. "Thanks for that," he said.

"You can knock off the act now," I said. "You love this really."

"I know I do," he replied. "I love how she bosses me around. It's great. I've always wanted someone to boss me around."

"I can boss you around if you like," I said.

"No, I mean a girl, silly."

"I know you did."

"I just love her. I'm happier and happier every second I'm with her."

"You've only known her for a week."

"Did you not hear the whole 'it feels like I've known her four years not four days' speech?"

"I did."

"I really do love her. I really do." His eyes slowly moved over to me, and I knew what he was going to say and do.

"Don't do it," I said.

"I'm going to tell her," he replied.

"Don't do it. You will scare her."

Ted's bedroom door then reopened. Ted spun around on his chair to see her. Autumn was looking down at her phone and then she raised her head and saw Ted and I both staring her.

She tucked her hair behind her ear and said, "What are you two staring at?"

Ted turned back to me and for I second I thought he was going to go through with it and tell her. Instead he said, "You're just so beautiful, Autumn. I'm a very lucky guy."

She smiled, walked over, and kissed him before reclaiming her seat.

MARCH 13TH

Ted and Autumn went for dinner with her parents on Wednesday. Autumn wanted him to meet them. Something else Ted would never normally do when he was seeing a girl. Instead he went and they had a big fancy meal. Autumn even helped him pick out a suit and chose his tie. I must admit it was cute listening to Autumn picking a suit out for him.

Ted arrived at the office just after lunch today because he stayed over at Autumn's parents' house with her, and they live in the middle of nowhere apparently. Rosie and I had just had lunch together. She texted me, and I asked if she could quickly see the factory, too, since she had never seen it. So she came in, I showed her around the factory, but we didn't put all the suits on and stuff. We just stood on the glass corridor. Then she sat at Ted's desk while she had a sandwich and I had a bowl of soup. We talked about Zac, and how the blender plan is going well so far. And then she gave me a hug and left.

And two minutes later Ted entered our office and slumped into his chair. He didn't say hello or ask how I was or mention Autumn or anything. And even when I told him about Rosie or asked if he saw her, he didn't reply. I thought it was bit strange. He opened his phone and started texting.

"If I went on holiday, would you be ok here on your own?" Ted then asked.

I frowned. "Of course I would. I've worked on my own before when you've been sick."

"I know, but a day or two isn't the same as a week or two."

"I'll be fine. Where are you going anyway? Is your dad planning something?"

"No. Autumn has asked if I want to go to Spain with her."

I was a bit shocked when I heard what he said and I remained quiet.

"Will?"

"Yeah, sorry. It just seems a bit soon, doesn't it? Are you sure you're not moving way too fast?"

"We don't think so. It's something to do with Autumn's work. Her museum got invited to this event at a Spanish museum. And the guys at Autumn's museum decided to send her because nobody could be bothered apparently, which sounds stupid. Everyone thinks it sounds super boring, but Autumn has convinced me that it is going to be the complete opposite. We'd be away for ten days. I think for the first few days, Autumn or Autumn and I do museum stuff, and then after that we can sunbathe and swim. Have a holiday, you know."

"I want to do that," I said with a sulk.

Ted laughed. "I wanted to ask you first before I agreed to go, and then it catches you off guard and you can't really cope by yourself."

"Don't be silly. I'll be fine! I can't believe nobody else from the museum would want to go."

"The manager woman said Autumn could take a person of her choice or one of the fifty-year-old assistant managers would have to go. I think a holiday with her boyfriend would be a little more pleasant."

"Boyfriend, eh? Is it official?"

"I've been her boyfriend since like the fifth day we met."

"You didn't tell me."

"Will, I'm Autumn's boyfriend since the fifth day she and I met."

"Thanks for letting me know."

"You're welcome."

"Call her now and tell her you'll go. When is it? Like, when would you leave for Spain?"

"Monday," he answered. Before I could ask him if it was the Monday that was just a couple of days away, he removed his phone from his pocket and exited our office to call Autumn.

I sat back in my chair and thought about how fast and well things were going between them. I only wished that things between Zac and me were working out that well. Instead, I've got to refer to her as Captain Panda and follow rules. I still love spending time with Zac. I just think things between us are a tiny bit strange. I know I agreed to them, but I just want to be more couple-like, I guess. And take pictures in photo booths or make teddies for each other or play crazy golf. I don't think there are many other people on the planet who do what we do. Whatever it is that we're doing.

NEW MESSAGE FROM WILL EVANS
Ted and Autumn are going to Spain.

NEW MESSAGE FROM ZACHARY WILLIAMS III
I know.

NEW MESSAGE FROM WILL EVANS
How did you know?

NEW MESSAGE FROM ZACHARY WILLIAMS III
She told me.

NEW MESSAGE FROM WILL EVANS
When?

NEW MESSAGE FROM ZACHARY WILLIAMS III
Earlier today. We had lunch together.

NEW MESSAGE FROM WILL EVANS
Oh, why didn't you tell me yesterday that you were
going to do that?

NEW MESSAGE FROM ZACHARY WILLIAMS III
We only planned it this morning. I left your apartment
and got the bus to the museum. I was bored.

NEW MESSAGE FROM WILL EVANS
Ok. Are you back at the apartment now?

NEW MESSAGE FROM ZACHARY WILLIAMS III
Yes. Just about to walk through the door.

NEW MESSAGE FROM WILL EVANS
Ok, Captain. I'll see you later x

NEW MESSAGE FROM ZACHARY WILLIAMS III
Ok. Please refrain from sending kisses on the end of
your text messages.

NEW MESSAGE FROM WILL EVANS
Yes, Captain. See you later haha.

MARCH 15TH

Sundiscussion Topic:
Who is the best superhero?

"**G**ood choice of topic, Zac," Ted said with Autumn in his arms. Zac and I were sat at opposite ends of my sofa. "I've always wanted to run very fast so I would pick The Flash. Or maybe Iron Man," Ted answered.

"I would be the Hulk or She-Hulk. Whichever Hulk suits me best. I'd love to turn into an angry unstoppable monster when I get frustrated. I could scare Ted then when he doesn't make the bed after I've told him countless times," Autumn said. Ted laughed and then they kissed. They were due to kiss anyway. I think it had been six minutes since their last kiss. So that kiss reset the kiss meter.

"I'd be Batman," I answered. "Because he's just the coolest."

"I would be the Silver Surfer," Zac then said.

We all watched her silently for a second before Ted said, "And Zac wins another one. Nobody beats him." Ted then suggested afterwards that we should watch *Fantastic Four: Rise of the Silver Surfer*. He had a copy in his room. So we all watched it together, and then afterwards I drove Zac home because

Ted, Autumn, and I had to go to sleep early because I had to drive them to the airport the next day. Zac and I picked up some more fruit and vegetables for her smoothies and soup. And I picked up some to take back to the apartment as well. We're slowly increasing the intake as each week goes. Only ever so marginally, but it is increasing.

"Is everything going ok with the smoothies and soup?" I asked her as we drove to her apartment.

"Yeah. I'm following the journal guidelines exactly as they say. We spoke about this Thursday."

"I know. But are you feeling ok? Are you happy following it?"

"Yes. Thank you, Will. The only thing that annoys me is the loudness of the blender. Natalie wakes up earlier than me and wakes me up using it."

I smirked. "Ok... So I was wondering, since Ted and Autumn are away, if you want to stay with me this week, you can. I don't mind driving you to work each morning."

"Will," she said. "No more than four days, remember?"

I tried not to show any level of frustration. I clenched my jaw and kept my attention on the road. "Ok."

MARCH 16TH

"**G**uys, what do you think I should do about Zac?" I asked Ted and Autumn. Ted was lying across Autumn's lap with his eyes shut as we drove to the airport.

"What do you mean?" Autumn asked.

"I was hoping if we kept seeing each other that she would want to be more than what we're now. But I think I've finally come to the realisation that that isn't going to happen anymore."

"You owe me money if you end it," Ted said.

"Thank you for taking this matter seriously, Ted."

"Why don't you see how things go while we're away? It might be different between you two not having anyone else there. It's only another week, Will. And when we get back I'll have a discreet conversation with her and see how she feels about you. But I like Zac. She's so great."

"Yeah. That's a good idea, Autumn. And I like Zac, and I think she's great, too. But it's like my sister told me. The only person who is going to get hurt if Zac and I continue like this is me. I care about her a lot, and she's doing so well with her smoothies and her soups. She's eating. I mean a couple of months ago she wasn't eating anything. I know eating disorders are difficult to talk about and sometimes people can be offended by the way people speak about them. But I'm becoming scared to talk to her about it because I don't know what to say or do in case it upsets her. She always sends me a photo of her having her smoothie or soup when I'm not with her, and I asked her how it was going last night, and she said it was fine. But I don't know if she's being honest with me or not. And what happens if I end things with her and the progress she is making stops because of me? I'm so worried—"

Autumn placed her hand on my shoulder. "Will. Take a deep breath and calm down." I did as she said and kept my attention on the road. "First things first, wait until Ted and I are back and I can talk to Zac in person about the two of you. Something might happen between you two while we're away. And second, Zac and I message all day, every day, and she tells me about her smoothies and soup. And she really is doing well and she is feeling so much better about herself. And I'm not saying this to make you feel better because that is very insensitive. I am telling you the truth." I took another deep breath and thanked her. She squeezed my shoulder. "You need to stop overthinking everything. It will consume you."

"I just care about her so much. And I panic when I think about the future of our relationship or whatever the hell it is."

"She does care about you a lot, Will. And she does like you a lot. But you know her previous relationship was awful, and it completely put her off them. I know you're nothing like her ex-boyfriend, but you have to understand she let her guard down last time and got seriously hurt."

"I know," I said softly.

"My girlfriend is so wise," Ted mumbled. Autumn smiled down at him and stroked his head.

I helped Ted and Autumn get their suitcases out of the car and then gave them both a hug. "Behave yourself," I said to Ted.

"I will," he said.

"Look after him for me," I said to Autumn.

"I will," she said.

"Make sure he brushes his teeth."

"Oh, I will, don't worry," she joked. And then they waved as they rolled their bags into the airport.

I waved back and watched them for a moment with a smile on my face before I was alerted out of my moment by an impatient driver wanting to unload his bags and passengers, too.

MARCH 19TH

Zac decided to head straight to the apartment after she finished work. It saved me driving to pick her up after work, but I never mind doing that. When I got home from work, Zac was lying on my bed with her back to the door.

"Hey," I said, taking off my suit jacket and hanging it up.

She sat up and sniffled. "Hey."

I could see by her eyes and cheeks that he had been crying. "What's wrong?" I asked, sitting beside her and putting my arm around her.

"My dad called me," she said, fiddling with her hands.

"What did he say?"

"He just shouted at me, and told me to stop being stupid and come home."

"Don't listen to him," I said. "He doesn't know what he's talking about. Just because he's shouting and he's your dad doesn't mean he's right."

She didn't say anything. She continued to stare down at her hands and fiddle with them.

"Why don't you take a bath? I'll bring you a cup of tea. And then I'll quickly pop out and pick up some more fruit and soup and we can have our soup whilst watching a film later. How does that sound?"

She rested her head on my shoulder. "Ok." I sat with her for a few minutes and rubbed her arm before I got up to run her a bath. I added some bubbles, and then went into the kitchen to put on the kettle. I sat beside Zac for five minutes whilst she bathed, and then I left to go fruit, veg, and soup shopping. But before I left I checked her ID to find her home address. I thought about paying her dad a visit and talking to him about Zac. I even took a new tub of ice cream out of our freezer for her mum because she said she liked that flavour of Ron's Ice Cream.

I didn't think I would go. It was one of those ideas that you say you're going to do, but never end up doing. That's what I thought it was anyway. Until I found myself parking up outside their house. My heart started to race as I got out of the car and grabbed the ice cream. I considered turning around as I began to walk up the steps to their front door, but my legs were striving forward. Their house didn't have a garden on the front. But I could see down the side of the house that there was one at the back. Zac's parents lived on a normal street, filled with normal houses. There were two flowerpots either side of the step outside of the front door. I smiled at them because it reminded me of my mum.

I took a big, big deep breath and slowly exhaled before ringing the door. I saw a light flick on in the hallway and then Zac's mum opened the door. She was a very beautiful woman, and she had a kind face. Zac definitely has some of her features, apart from her eyes. Mrs. Williams had hazel eyes and long light brown hair.

She poked her head around the door and smiled at me and said, "Are you going to try to sell me something?"

I laughed. "No, I'm a friend of Zac's. My name's Will."

"Oh. Zac isn't here at the moment. She hasn't been here for a while."

"I know. She is staying with me at the moment. Well, Thursday to Sunday each week... I was just wondering if I could speak to you and Mr. Williams?"

She opened the door and stood aside, allowing me entry. "Please, come in."

"Thank you. Zac told me that you like Ron's Ice Cream strawberry flavour, so I brought you a tub. I work for them."

I passed her the tub and she grinned. "That's very kind of you, thank you."

The staircase to the bedrooms was straight in front of you as you entered. But I followed Mrs. Williams into their living room through a door on the right. Their living room was quite nice actually. It was very modern and they had a huge TV. I was too busy looking around that I didn't see Mr. Williams sitting in an armchair, watching the TV.

Mrs. Williams muted the television and then introduced us. "Harry, this is Will, he's a friend of Zac's. He said he wanted to speak to us."

His eyes met mine and then he scanned me from head to toe. He got to his feet and shook my hand. He was a lot smaller than me. By at least half a foot. It was hard to see that he was a policeman. He just didn't look like one. Maybe he worked in the offices or something. He had dark brown hair, but he was slowly balding. And he had rough skin and was very tan. But the main thing I noticed was the displeased look he had on his face. I don't know if it was because of Zac being mentioned or if he greeted everyone like that.

I sat beside Mrs. Williams on the sofa. "So why did you want to speak to us?" she asked.

"When I got home from work today, Zac had been crying. And she told me that she had spoken to her dad. And it really upset her."

Before I could continue Mrs. Williams turned to Mr. Williams. "You called her?"

He nodded. "Yes, I called her."

"Why? And why didn't you tell me you had spoken to her?"

"I told her to stop being a fool and come home," he said. It didn't seem that he felt bad about his actions or thought that he had made a mistake. Mrs. Williams shook her head and then turned to me.

I faced Mr. Williams and said, "The approach you have taken is a bit vigorous. Shouting at Zac and telling her to stop it hasn't helped and isn't going to help. Eating disorders are very serious. I think if you apologised and tried to support her—"

"Excuse me?"

"I think if you apologise—"

"No, I heard what you said. I'm finding it hard to believe that you said it."

"I'm trying to help—"

"Who the hell are you anyway? Some random guy that she's probably fucking and thinks he knows everything about her and her family."

"Harry!" Mrs. Williams yelled.

"No! I won't allow it! How dare you come into my house and tell me how to deal with my daughter? You little tramp. You have no idea what it's like to go through this. You've never experienced anything like this before. You probably searched it online before you came. So don't come to my house and tell me how to deal with my daughter."

Mrs. Williams didn't say anything. Mr. Williams then told me to leave. I stood and buttoned up my suit. The anger rushing through me was indescribable. I could dismiss any insults or remarks he made towards me. But what I couldn't dismiss was his assumption that I had no idea what it's like to go through this. That I've never experienced anything like this before. And that I searched it online. I clenched my jaw as an attempt to retain my anger. I thought how easy it would be to snap my arm and drive my fist into his face. But that would get me arrested and not make things any better. And it definitely wouldn't help Zac.

"Ten years ago my sister had a serious eating disorder. I was in school one day and my lesson was interrupted because my grandfather had come to take me to the hospital to see my sister because they didn't think she was going to make it. I sat beside my sister in a hospital bed, ready to say good-bye because they thought she was going to die. But somehow, by some miracle, she recovered. And I was going to tell you that I took Zac to meet my sister and mum. And they have helped Zac. And I think she is making progress. We have smoothies in the morning and soup for lunch for dinner and tea. When we're not together, we send each other a photo of our smoothie or soup. I care about your daughter more than anything in the world. I came here to try to help you sort out your relationship with your daughter, so you could support her in the right way instead of calling her stupid. If I were you, I would do everything I physically could to support her and make sure that she is happy." I turned to Mrs. Williams and said, "I'm so sorry to have spoilt your evening, Mrs. Williams. Enjoy your ice cream."

And then I turned to Mr. Williams and said, "And you can go fuck yourself."

Forty minutes after I left to pick up some food, and a bunch of flowers, I walked through the apartment door. I placed the shopping into the fridge and freezer and then I returned to the bedroom. The bedroom was empty, so I checked the bathroom. Zac was still in the bath, surrounded by bubbles.

"Hey," I said.

"Hey," she replied. "I had a call from my mum two minutes ago."

I sighed and dropped my head. "Zac, I cannot begin to explain how sorry—"

"Will, you don't need to apologise. I mean, I'm a little mad, but I'm madder at my dad. I think I should be thanking you. My mum told me to tell you that she apologises for his behaviour."

"Really?" I said. I let out a huge sigh of relief and my heart rate slowly began to return to its normal pace.

"Yeah. Mum said you put Dad in his place. He hasn't said a word since you left their house."

"I just wanted to try to make him understand that he wasn't helping. And I tried to talk to him, but then he interrupted me and started saying things that made me incredibly angry. But I'm so sorry I went without talking to you and asking for your permission."

Zac lifted her hand out of the bath and wiped some bubbles onto my nose. "It's fine, Will, relax." I reclaimed my seat on the chair beside her. "Did you really tell my dad to go fuck himself though?"

I grimaced. "*Yes*."

She grinned and giggled. "Brilliant."

"Brilliant?" I questioned.

"Yeah. I wish I could have told my dad to go fuck himself at least once in my life."

"That wasn't the reaction I was expecting, although it is understandable." I lifted the flowers up so she could see them. "I bought you flowers."

She took them from me and held them above the water.

"You bought me flowers." She smiled and returned them to my possession.

"I bought a vase, too. I'll go and put these in it now."

"Ok," Zac said. "Are you going to join me afterwards?"

"Yeah. I'll come and sit on the chair once I've sorted out your flowers."

"No, I mean, in the bath."

"Oh," I said. "We've never done that before."

She raised an eyebrow at me. "It's not like we haven't seen each other naked, Will."

I smirked. "Ok. I'll be back in two minutes."

MARCH 20TH

Zac woke me up at 2:00 a.m. She was sat cross-legged beside me, the bedside lamp on.

"What's up?" I asked.

"Do you know when you're in the shower?" she said.

I opened my eyes and woke up more due to the irrelevance that I could sense to come from this conversation. "Yes, I do," I said, sitting up slightly.

"Do you ever stand under the water and hold out your arm so the water runs along it and off the edge of your fingers so it feels like you have superpowers?" Her beautiful blue eyes blinked, and she had a blank expression on her face that indicated she didn't feel like waking me up at 2:00 a.m. to ask me such a random question was a bad idea.

"I can't say that I have," I said.

"I'll show you some time," she replied. She pouted her lips and her eyes began to wander around.

"Is that all you woke me up for?" I asked.

"I couldn't sleep." She shuffled around and sat back on the pillow so she was right next to me. I faced her and she faced me. And she had the "kiss me" look on her face. And she was slowly moving in closer to me.

"I have work in the morning," I said.

Her lips parted and they were now inches away from mine. "Ok," she said. She placed her hand on the side of my face and then kissed me. "Good night," she said afterwards, turning off the bedside lamp and rolling over to her side of the bed. I budged over a little and began to play with her hair and scratch her head with my left hand.

"What are you doing?" she muttered.

"I thought this would help you sleep," I replied. "Technically this isn't cuddling."

She shuffled around in her position so I thought that meant to stop, so I took my hand away.

"What are you doing?" she muttered again.

"I thought you wanted me to stop." She remained silent. I grinned in the darkness, and then reached my left hand over again and continued to play with her hair and scratch her head.

I could hear music playing from my bedroom as I entered the apartment from work. I opened my bedroom door to find Zac sat on my bed, nodding her head, her beanie pulled down over her eyes.

"Hey. How was your day?" I asked, slumping onto the bed beside her.

She lifted the beanie from over her eyes. "It was ok. How was yours?"

"Mine was ok. Gets a little boring in the office without having anyone to talk to." Zac smiled and then she rolled on top of me and kissed me. "What was that for?" I asked.

"Well, we have the apartment to ourselves so I thought…"

"Ah," I said. "Can we change the music first?"

"What's wrong with Alex Farrell?"

"Oh, is that who this is? I knew I'd heard it before."

"Are you a fan of his?"

"No. I'm more of a Palmer Hobbs fan."

"Oh. I hate her. She's so stuck up."

"She isn't!"

"Yes, she is."

"Erm, no, she isn't."

"She is, but ok."

"Seriously, though. Can we turn off this music?" She groaned and started to kiss my neck. "Alex Farrell isn't the right kind of music for sex," I said.

Zac sat up and frowned. "But Wham! is?"

I grinned. "Yeah it is!"

"Whatever feeds your panda." She sighed and then grabbed the remote to turn off the stereo. "I have an idea," she then said.

"Do you now? What is this idea?" I asked.

"Can you remember the conversation we had last night?"

"About me scratching your head?"

"No, about being in the shower."

"Oh, yes. The one you so kindly woke me up to talk about."

She went a little shy. "Yes."

"What about it?"

"I could show you now." I pulled a funny face and watched her. "What?" she said, punching me.

"So how do you plan we do this?" I asked.

"We go and get in the shower?" she said with a question-able frown on her face.

"Ok," I said, pushing her off me and hopping off the bed. I got undressed and got into the shower. It's conven-ient that the shower is one of those rainfall showers otherwise it would be an awful idea. Zac joined me a couple of minutes later and caught me completely off guard even though we'd planned to do this. I didn't know where to look. I know we've seen each other naked many times, but I didn't know whether to look or not to look. So I just stared upwards and told myself not to look at her boobs. To distract myself I thought it would be a good idea to count the tiles on the ceiling. It turns out they are thirty-seven, maybe thirty-six and a half; there is one tile that isn't a full tile because of the corner it is on so it completely messed everything up.

"Will," Zac said.

"Yes," I said, trying to figure out exactly what percentage of a tile it was. She put her hands on the back of my neck and then pulled me in and kissed me. She then pushed me back and told me to watch her. She positioned herself underneath the shower water so her shoulder was in the middle of it. She then held out her arm and extended her hand out towards the glass. Then the tiniest, and I mean tiniest, trickle of water began to flow off the edge of her fingers. I was going to laugh and tell her how ridiculous this was, but then she looked over her shoulder to see me, and she seemed so pleased with herself. So I smiled and told her how brilliant this was. We then spent the next fifteen minutes flicking shampoo on the glass or wall of the shower and then washing it off with our superhero shower powers.

MARCH 21ˢᵀ

I woke up this morning to find Zac lying on me. Her head was resting on my chest, and then the rest of her body almost matched the shape of mine.

"What are you doing?" I whispered. I couldn't see if she was awake or not. Her head lifted a moment later and she rested her chin on my chest. Her beautiful blue eyes made a wonderful start to my morning.

"Hey," she said.

"Why are you lying on me? No cuddling, remember?"

"You're too comfy. I wish I'd discovered this sooner."

"So is cuddling allowed now?"

"We'll see. It's too early to think about that now."

Instead of making a sly remark or joke or moving her off me, I just put my arms around her and gave her a little squeeze. And then I shut my eyes. I didn't go back to sleep, but it was nice to simply lie there and hold her in my arms. I've waited to do that for a long time. The main thing I started to think about was how she got there without waking me. Surely I would have noticed a person lying on top of me during the night.

We got up a couple of hours later and she made our breakfast smoothies. I watched her for a moment as she stood on her tiptoes in her Star Wars pyjamas and turned on the blender. Her hair was very wild and full of volume, but she looked incredibly hot.

"So what do you want to do today?" I asked.

"I don't know. Did you have any ideas?" she replied.

"I thought we could go for a walk."

"A walk?"

"Yes."

"Where?"

"There is a lake about thirty minutes away from here. You can walk around it. I thought it would be nice to go outside and do something for once instead of sitting and watching TV all day."

She passed me my smoothie as she sipped on hers. "Ok," she said with a nod.

"I was thinking we could make our soups before we go and heat them up and put them in some flasks, so we can drink them when we're there."

She smiled her tight-lipped smile and said, "That's a very nice plan, Will."

"Thank you, Zac."

We got dressed, and Zac blended our soups and heated them, then I carefully poured them into some flasks. I placed the flasks into a backpack. I also put in a scarf and a big thick blanket for two reasons. The first was that they would wedge the flasks together so they won't rattle around and bump into each other and spill in the backpack. And the second was that Zac would no doubt get cold during this walk because it is very windy there, and even though I told her several times, I still didn't think she put on enough layers of clothing. She had a jumper and a coat and her beanie. I offered her some gloves of mine, but she said she would leave her hands in her pockets. The gloves were too big, but at least they would keep her hands warm. I placed them into the backpack anyway in case she needed them.

As I said, the lake was very windy when we got there. There are lots of trees along the edge to provide cover as you walk so we would be ok. The lake was calm even though the wind was strong. The odd ripple would brush across the surface every now and then. The lake water was a very deep dark blue. Which made sense because the sky was clear, only a couple of clouds were floating by. The sun was out too, and it was fairly warm, but you couldn't appreciate it as seconds later a gust of wind would interrupt.

We walked through the forest, I guess you could call it, along a footpath. The birds would often chirp as we strolled. Since Zac takes the smallest strides we were walking at a slow pace. I almost had to dawdle on the spot to keep at the slow pace because I'm used to walking faster and taking bigger strides. But we were in no rush anyway.

It was nice to actually do something together for once. Couples would pass us and they'd say good afternoon and I would say it in return because Zac was too shy to do it herself. I encouraged her to reply at least once so she said ok. And she ended up saying "Good hello" and then we both started laughing uncontrollably. I almost fell to the ground it was so funny.

She went so shy afterwards. And started to jog away. She stopped after a few seconds. I can't imagine jogging in Timberland boots is the most comfortable thing. She turned to me and hunched up, pulling her coat up so only her eyes were visible. I calmed my laughter as I walked up to her, and then I gave her a hug.

"No hugging," she said, but I ignored her.

Five minutes later we reached the halfway point, so we found a bench to sit on and watch the lake. Zac was already shivering as we sat down. I got out our flasks and placed them between us. Then I reached into the bag and pulled out the scarf and put it around her neck. Then I got the gloves and placed them onto her lap. Then I tugged out the blanket and placed it over her shoulders and tucked it underneath her so it wouldn't fly away. I zipped up the bag and placed it underneath my feet so that wouldn't fly away, too.

When I went to face Zac, she was already watching me. She had this look on her face, just a small smile. She didn't take her eyes off me. And I looked into her eyes, and for a second, I knew she thought I was the best thing in the world. And for that brief moment, I felt whole. I felt like she loved me.

MARCH 22ND

I woke up again this morning to find Zac lying on me the same way she had the day before: her head on my chest, and then the rest of her body almost matching the shape of mine. Once again, I have no idea how she didn't wake me when she climbed onto me. I put my arms around her again and held her. But this time I fell back to sleep.

I woke up to find Zac wafting a plate of toast in my face. Two slices, each with a bite taken out of them. I smirked and sat up, taking the plate from her.

"Good morning," she said.

"Good morning," I replied. "Thank you for my toast."

"You're welcome," she said. I could hear "It's Now or Never" by Elvis Presley playing from the radio in the kitchen. "Your smoothie is here, too." She reached over to the bedside table and grabbed a bottle and spread my legs and put it between them and then closed them so it wouldn't fall over. It was very cold and sensitive against the skin.

"Thanks," I said.

"You're welcome," she replied with a sarcastic smirk. She then leant in and kissed me. "We're having sex once you've finished that," she said.

I coughed on a piece of toast as her directness was unexpected and then I said, "Oh, ok then."

Sundiscussion Topic:
Male and Female Celebrity Crushes

"That's not a discussion," I said to Zac, the topic chooser.

"I know, but I want to know who yours is," she replied.

"So I have to choose a male and female?"

"Yes."

"Ok," I said, removing my phone from my pocket.

"What are you doing?" she asked, bringing her face next to mine and inspecting what I was doing.

"I'm texting Ted. So we can find out what his and Autumn's are. So I'll text him ours first, and he can reply with theirs."

"Ok," she said. "You first."

I peeked down at her nestling her chin on my shoulder. Her big blue eyes intrigued at my answer. She smiled her tight-lipped smile and said, "Come on!"

I rested my head on the back of the sofa. "My female celebrity choice would be Jennifer Aniston. I don't need to think that over. I don't think beautiful will suffice to describe her. They should create a new word just to describe how beautiful she is."

"Ok," Zac said. "And your guy celebrity?"

I hummed. "It would have to be Ryan Gosling. He is an incredibly handsome man."

Zac sulked and nodded. "Interesting choices."

"So what are yours?" I asked.

"Mine are Matthew McConaughey and Natalie Portman."

I nodded. "Natalie Portman would have been in my top five."

"Yep," Zac said.

"So you love Natalie Portman, but yet you've never seen *Star Wars*?"

Zac shook her head. "I didn't think she was in *Star Wars.*"

I shot up. "Of course she is! She's in the prequels!"

"Oh really?"

"We should watch them," I said.

Zac bit her lip. She didn't want to watch *Star Wars*, but I could tell the idea of watching a Natalie Portman movie she'd never seen before enticed her. "Only if you watch *How To Lose A Guy In 10 Days* with me after."

"What's that about?" I asked. Zac raised an eyebrow and gave me an unamused look. "Ok, no need to be all mean," I said. "Who is in that film?"

"Matthew McConaughey and Kate Hudson."

I pouted and considered the offer. "If you watch *Star Wars* with me first, I will watch your film after."

"Deal," she said. I returned to my phone and began to text Ted.

NEW MESSAGE FROM WILL EVANS
Sundiscussion Topic:
Male and Female Celebrity Crushes.

Will: Ryan Gosling and Jennifer Aniston.
Zac: Matthew McConaughey and Natalie Portman.

Please send yours back at your earliest possible convenience – Will.

"Ok. Best friend test," Zac said, shuffling over and sitting on my lap.

"What do you mean?" I asked.

"Well, if you're Ted's best friend, you will know what his answers will be," she replied.

I raised my eyebrows. "Interesting proposition. Shall we place some stakes?"

"Ok," Zac said. "If you get it wrong, we watch *How To Lose A Guy In 10 Days* first, *Star Wars* later."

My phone then buzzed. Zac snatched my phone away and gripped it in her hands. "Tell me your answers," she commanded, pointing her finger at me.

"Hm. I know he loves Jennifer Love-Hewitt. But I think he will say Carrie Fisher or Emmy Rossum. No, he will definitely say both. Carrie and Emmy."

"Ok. And what about his guy crush?"

"He will say George Clooney."

"You seem pretty confident."

"That's because he loves George Clooney." She hummed and then scratched her nose. "Well, check the text and put me out of my misery," I said.

Zac smirked and opened my phone to read the text. A moment later she dropped the phone and started laughing. "I'm leaving!" she said, falling and resting her head on my shoulder. I leant over and grabbed my phone.

NEW MESSAGE FROM TED MAGUIRE
Ted: George Clooney and Carrie Fisher/Emmy Rossum (I couldn't decide.)
Autumn: Jude Law and Rachel Bilson.

I started laughing after I had read it. "Did I get it right?" I jokingly asked Zac.

"How did you know he would say all three?" she said, finding it hard to stop laughing.

"I just did." Our laughing calmed down after a minute or so, then we sat there calmly before Zac started kissing my neck. "What are you doing?" I asked.

"Well, you won, *so…*"

"The reward was to watch *Star Wars* first…"

Zac leant back and said, "So you'd rather watch *Star Wars*

than have sex?" I puffed out my cheeks and thought it over. "I'm definitely leaving this time," she said, about to get off my lap.

"No, wait!" I said, putting my hands on her side.

"Ok, I'm waiting," she said, folding her arms.

"We could do both," I suggested.

"I am not fulfilling some fantasy of yours from being a thirteen-year-old."

"I was fourteen actually." I picked her up and kissed her, then tried to navigate my way to the bedroom without bumping into anything.

We watched *Star Wars* for about thirty minutes before Zac got up and turned it off and put on her film. I'd sent Ted a photo of Zac and me watching *Star Wars*, and he was utterly amazed; he'd been trying to get Autumn to watch *Star Wars* since the day they met. So Zac and I snuggled up together. Yep, we did. She laid her head on my chest as we sat and watched the film. I don't know what has gotten into her recently. I feel like we're actually kind of a couple now. It's weird. Now I'm the one thinking I must have landed in an alternate universe.

I feel like I don't need to explain the plot of *How To Lose A Guy In 10 Days*. Halfway through the film Zac budged over to the other end of the sofa and stuck her feet in my face. She just kept tapping me with the bottom of her feet. "Rub them, please," she whined. So I sat up and began to massage her smelly feet. My bet had really paid off.

"It's a bit unrealistic. Saying that, it's no different from the start of Ted and Autumn's relationship," I said after the film had finished.

"Exactly. And how can you call it unrealistic when you just made me watch *Star Wars*?!" she yelled.

"You watched thirty minutes of it. I'm not having another argument with you because I'm tired of always being right," I said, folding my arms and looking away.

We were silent for a minute or two before she climbed onto me. She tried to lie across my shoulder, but then slumped behind my back and fell onto the sofa behind me. "What are you doing?" I asked, turning to see her head squished between my ass and the back of the sofa.

"What were you thinking when you first saw me?" she asked.

"You're so random," I said, shuffling forward so she could sit up. She rested her head on my lap and put my hand on her head, implying she wanted me to massage her head.

I slowly started to run my hands through her hair, and then she asked again, "What were you thinking when you first saw me?"

I looked down into her beautiful blue eyes, and returned to when I was stood at the top of the stairs in the cinema, seeing her for the first time. "I thought you were the most beautiful girl I had ever seen."

"Na, I don't believe you," she said with a cheesy grin.

"Call Ted, he will back me up. Ask him what my first words were when I saw you."

"How do I know you and Ted haven't planned for something like this and you've already told him what to say to me?"

"*Really?*" I asked, raising my eyebrows.

A smug smile appeared on Zac's face. "Fine." She reached for her phone and called Ted, putting the phone on speaker.

"Hello."

"Hey, Ted, how's the holiday so far?"

"Autumn is walking around in a bikini, Zac. This holiday is even better than the one where I met Santa Claus."

"Tell her I said hello."

"I will. She is swimming at the moment. How are you guys?"

"We're good. I just wanted to ask you a quick question?"

"Ok. What is it?"

"What were Will's first words when he saw me?"

"Erm… He said something like wow or… Oh wait, he said oh my wow. I can't believe I remember that. Why?"

"Oh my wow?"

"Yep. It didn't make much sense at the time, but then he went straight over to you and it provided a little clarity."

"Ok thanks, Ted. Speak to you soon. Enjoy your holiday."

"Ok…thanks, bye."

"Bye."

Zac hung up her phone and placed it onto the table.

"I told you," I said.

"You did," she said. She checked her phone and then said, "Would it be ok if you took me home?"

"Of course," I said. "Is everything ok?"

"Yeah. I just forgot to wash my uniform for tomorrow so I want to get it ready in time."

"Can't you stay a little longer?"

"I'm sorry, I have to go."

"Ok. Let me know when you're ready to leave."

Zac wasn't very talkative during the drive to her apartment. We chatted a little bit about *Star Wars*, and how she liked Natalie Portman in the short amount of time she saw her. We went shopping and picked up some more fruit and vegetables and soup for us both. And she was quiet as we did that, too.

When we pulled up outside her apartment, I asked if she wanted me to walk her to her apartment, but she said no. "Are you sure everything is ok?" I asked.

"Yes," she replied, taking off her beanie and fiddling with her hair before putting on her beanie again.

"Is this about earlier with the oh my wow thing when I first saw you?" She didn't reply. "Ok, so it is," I said. "What are your orders, Captain Panda?"

She smirked and took a deep breath. "I'll see you next Thursday, Horatio."

"Ok. Text me if you need me, Zac."

"I will. Bye." She leant over and kissed my cheek, and got out of the car.

"Bye," I said as the car door closed. I watched her walk up to her apartment block and go inside before driving back home.

MARCH 26TH

Ted and Autumn's flight landed at 4:23am so I went to bed early and got a couple of hours sleep before I had to wake up at 3:00am to drive to the airport.

Ted was wearing an extremely colourful flowered shirt as they emerged from their gate. He looked very pleased with his choice of shirt, and was also very pleased to see me. He was so tan. His light hair appeared even lighter because of it. Autumn's tan didn't appear much different. She was already quite tan.

Ted dropped his bag just before he approached me, and then he gave me a firm hug. "How are you?" he asked.

"I'm good, man. How was the holiday?" I replied.

"It was the best holiday, Will. Honestly I had such a good time."

"Good," I said. "You can tell me about it on the way home."

Autumn then placed down her bags and hugged me. "Hello, Will," she said.

"Did he behave himself?" I asked.

"Oh yes. He was a good boy." I glanced over at Ted and he had a childish smile on his face. We walked out of the airport and found the car. I put their bags into the back of the car, and then got into the driver's seat.

"Are you tired, babe?" Ted asked Autumn.

"No, I'm fine, darling. You put your head on me and get some sleep." Ted did as she said and rested his head on her lap as he did when we went to drop them off at the airport.

"How were things with Zac whilst we were away?" Autumn asked.

"Really good. Really good. It actually felt like we were in a relationship. We're cuddling now!" I glanced up at the rearview mirror and saw a smile on Autumn's face.

"I'm so glad to hear it."

"So tell me about Spain. How was it?" I asked.

"It was lovely, Will. So lovely. Monday we arrived at our hotel and had some dinner and we went straight to bed because we were exhausted from travelling. And then Tuesday I was picked up from the hotel and taken to the museum. Tuesday to Friday I was at the museum from ten until one. An exhibit from our museum was there and I spent a lot of time learning about it when I first started at the museum so I was the best person for the job anyway really. The Spanish museum was having a gala on Saturday, so each day I went in and helped set up our part of the museum display. And each day I'd return to our hotel and find Ted around the pool. It was so lovely and warm. It didn't rain once. The hotel was so quiet. There was hardly anyone staying there. We just had such a good time."

I smiled and flicked my eyes up at the rearview mirror again. She was smiling down at a sleeping Ted and stroking his head. "He told me he loved me," she whispered.

My smile extended. "Did he? Was it a casual wake up in the morning and he said it or did he make a big deal out of it? I'm guessing it didn't freak you out and you love him, too?"

"Of course I do," she said. "It was Saturday, before the gala, and I was super nervous because I had never done something like this. And Ted organised for us to have dinner before we left in this nice restaurant in the hotel that you had to pay extra for. We went down, dressed in our outfits ready to go to the gala. He looked so handsome in his bow tie, and put some product in his hair for once. And we sat down, and they brought us over a bottle of champagne. I thought it was part of the meal, but then he told me he bought it because he had something to tell me. And he took my hand and he kissed it, and it was so sweet, and he told me he loved me, and he wanted to tell me before we came. And then I said I hated him because he was going to spoil my makeup and ruin my mascara."

I sniggered and said, "This is the happiest he's ever been, Autumn. Apart from the time he won one hundred pounds on a scratch card. He didn't shut up about it for the next six months. I don't think it was the money he was happiest about. It was just because he won. He'd not won anything before that."

She laughed and then placed a hand over her mouth so she didn't wake Ted. "Anyway the gala went perfectly, and then the rest of the holiday we spent beside the pool in the sun, drinking cocktails. I'm so pleased he came with me. It was perfect."

"Thank you for taking him, and giving me a break from him for the first time in god knows how long. And I'm glad everything at the museum went ok. Do you think it will help with museum life back here? Like, will you get some kind or promotion or something?"

Autumn hummed. "I haven't thought about that. I guess that would all depend on if the Spanish museum provides any feedback about me or our museum's display. I guess we will have to wait and see."

We all went to our bedrooms when we got back to the apartment. I only got a couple hours more sleep before I had to be up for work. Ted was returning to work Monday as he arranged to have Friday off, too. Autumn had the same arrangement. They went over to Autumn's parents after the woke up. So I had a long day at work half asleep, and then afterwards drove over to Zac's apartment to pick her up. We came back to the apartment. And I laid on the sofa and took a nap.

When I opened my eyes, Zac and her beanie were laid in front of me, her nose almost touching mine, her beautiful blue eyes looking into mine. She stuck out her tongue and licked the tip of my nose. It's strange, I know. And then her tongue vanished and she grinned and then shut her eyes and snuggled up to me.

It was right then that I realised I loved her.

My pulse started to rise and I could feel my heart beating out of my chest. I took a deep breath as I watched her lie in front of me peacefully. I'd never been in love, and now I suddenly felt paralysed. I knew I had strong feelings for Zac, but I didn't know I loved her. And now I knew I had to be with her. Because I couldn't imagine life without her. All it took for me to realise was to have her look into my eyes, lick the tip of my nose, and smile. Sometimes it is the simplest things that make you realise you're in love.

Now what I had to consider was how to tell her. If I did tell her, that is. I don't want to scare her and lose her. But in that moment, I did the only thing I thought I could. I brought my head forward, her nose resting next to mine now. I could feel her breath blowing against my cheek. And then I kissed her. And she kissed me back. She opened her eyes afterwards, and we smiled at one another.

MARCH 27TH

Ted decided to come into work with me today. He thought he would catch up with things at work ahead of Monday, and let Autumn and Zac have some time together. He didn't have anything to catch up on, but I didn't say otherwise because it would be nice to have someone to talk to at work.

Thirty minutes after lunch, so about 1:30pm, Ted and I were at our desks, throwing a tennis ball back and forth between us. We had nothing to do. Nothing at all. His catching up was going super well. But in all seriousness every possible website and social media post was updated. All our emails had been replied to. We didn't have any meetings. So the only productive thing left to do was to throw a tennis ball back and forth between us whilst we brainstormed some future ideas to put onto the website and social media pages.

After we'd been throwing the ball backwards and forwards for fifteen minutes, Autumn appeared at our office door.

"Hey!" Ted said.

"Hello, darling," Autumn said with a grin, holding the door open. She was looking back along the corridor. "Come on," she said, almost like she was calling a dog to come in from outside.

And then Zac slowly walked in with her arms crossed and her head down so all I could see was the bobble on the top of her beanie. She looked like a child who'd been brought by her mother to come and apologise to one of the teachers at school.

Autumn shut the door behind them. I leant over my desk and tried to look at Zac.

"Hello," I said.

She glanced up and said, "Hi."

I looked back at Autumn. "Why is she being weird?" I whispered.

"She's feeling shy because she thought you would be mad about her coming into your office uninvited," she replied.

"Aw," I said. "I'm not mad. Why would I be mad? I'm happy you're here."

"Because this is your work and you're busy and stuff," Zac answered.

"The first part is true, but the second part isn't. We've been throwing a tennis ball around for a while now to pass the time."

Autumn walked over and sat on Ted's lap and kissed him. Zac and I watched them, and then we looked at each other. I held up my hand for a high five, which she returned.

"How come you decided to visit?" Ted asked.

"We thought we'd be good girlfriends and come and visit our boyfriends at work and see how they were," Autumn replied.

My face suddenly dropped and I was about to correct Autumn. But Ted beat me to it. "Woah! You can't say the G word in front of Zac."

Autumn apologised to Zac. "Zac, I'm so sorry. I forget, please forgive me."

"It's ok," Zac said with a smile.

"So what have you two been doing today?" I asked.

"That's one of the reasons we came to visit you. Zac made an interesting discovery." Autumn looked over at Zac, hinting for her to take over.

"I put your smoothie in the freezer this morning for you," she began to say.

"Oh shit, I'm so sorry, Zac. I completely forgot to have my smoothie this morning. I had my soup for lunch though. I swear I did."

"He did," Ted supported.

"That's ok. It's my fault. I forgot to tell you that I put it in the freezer for you so it would be nice and cold," Zac said, now moving over and sitting on the edge of my desk. "When I remembered I had left the smoothie in the fridge, I went to take it out, and it had frozen. And then I had an idea. I grabbed a spoon from the draw and took off the lid and scooped out some of the frozen smoothie. And although it looked kinda weird, it actually tasted kinda nice. I told Autumn to try some and she liked it, too. So we dug around the kitchen to find a takeaway tub because they're better to contain ice cream in, instead of a bottle. And we created some more smoothie and poured it into the takeaway tub and froze that, too. Once it had frozen we took it out and came here to show you, so you could try some. We thought it might help with a future ice cream idea." She placed the takeaway tub in front of me and gave me a spoon.

It didn't look too presentable, but after all it was a frozen smoothie in a plastic takeaway tub. I scooped a small amount up and placed it into my mouth. And surprisingly, it tasted fantastic. "This is great," I said, scooping up some more. The frozen smoothie wasn't as easy to scoop as ice cream; it was more like a block of ice. "Try some, Ted," I said, passing it back to Zac so she could take it over to him.

He took the spoon and tried some. He liked it, too. "It looks horrible, but tastes great," he said. I sort of faded away when they started chatting about it, because although Zac's frozen smoothie had just given me an idea, another one was approaching me, too.

I stared at the frame on our office wall. Inside the frame are two photos. The first is of me and Ted when we were kids, and we're sitting in a sandbox in Ted's back garden, and we're playing with our toy dinosaurs. Ted is holding a T-Rex and I am holding a Brachiosaurus (one of the really big ones with the long neck). And the second photo is of Ted and I holding the same dinosaurs two or three years ago on our sofas, trying to replicate the image. I'm sure you're wondering why this is relevant to Zac and Autumn bringing in some frozen smoothie, but when Zac said, "So we dug around the kitchen," an idea popped into my head.

"Ted, when is the next meeting to propose the new ice cream ideas?" I asked. I think I interrupted their conversation, but I can't be sure as I'd just reemerged from my daydream.

He rubbed Autumn's knee as he stared up at the ceiling, trying to find the answer to my question. "I think my dad is going to New York in the next month or two to meet the recipe creating people, and then once they've selected some flavours, we have all the surveys and taste tests with our ice cream fans and then some ordinary people so the results aren't biased."

"I know how it works, I just wanted to know when the meeting was."

"Why?" he asked.

"Because I have two ideas."

"How long have you had these ideas for? Why didn't you tell me?"

"I only thought them up thirty seconds ago."

"Did my ice cream help?" Zac asked, all excited. I rose from my chair and took three or four paces before I was in front of Zac. Her arms were still crossed and she looked up at me, waiting for me to answer her question, but then her eyes started to wander as her shyness increased.

I put my hands on either side of her face and then kissed her. She blushed and hunched her shoulders. She smiled her tight-lipped smile over at Autumn and Ted. "Aw," Autumn said.

"I'm sorry," I said. "It was like an eureka moment for me, and you and your frozen smoothie provided me with a lot of inspiration."

"That's ok. Glad I could help," Zac replied.

"I told you he would like it," Autumn said.

"Can we keep your frozen smoothie, please? And can we have the recipe, too, please?" I asked Zac.

"I want some credit for handing my recipe over to you," she joked.

I then pointed to Ted and said, "No."

"What?" he said with his mouth ajar, pretending he wasn't going to say anything.

"You were going to say something like 'he'll make it up to you later.' I could sense it."

"I wasn't!" I raised my eyebrow slightly and tilted my head. "Ok, fine. You win."

Autumn and I laughed while Zac wrote down her recipe on a pad for us. She ripped off the sheet and handed it to me.

"Thank you," I said to her. "You know what this means," I said to Ted.

He changed his view from Autumn to me, and took his hand off her knee, his eyes widening. "What does this mean, Will?"

"It means we're going to need some big whiteboards and lots of coloured pens so we can draw up these ice cream ideas of mine. We can do some ice cream tub designs, too."

"I love doing ice cream tub designs," Ted said with a childish look on his face. He looked back at Autumn. "Will and I have work to do, gorgeous, you're going to need to vacate this area."

"Of course, my darling. I'm glad Zac and I could help." She got off his lap and stood, then leant over and kissed him.

As I watched them, Zac wrapped her arms around my waist and rested her head against my chest, the top of her beanie tickling my chin. I put my arms around her and hugged her back. It was a nice hug. This was a big moment for us. This was the first time we had ever hugged outside of our apartment.

"I'll see you later," she murmured.

"Ok, Captain," I replied. She let go of me and then looked up at me and fiddled with her beanie. She smiled her tight-lipped smile and then left our office. Autumn followed behind her.

Ted and I got straight to work. Ted went into his dad's office and asked him if we could present two ideas of ours to him Monday. Ted didn't even know what the ideas were yet and he was already asking to present them to his dad. It just shows how much we trust each other really. But also the other thing was if we did spend hours working on them we could take them to his dad and he might say he isn't interested, so it could be a waste of time. Ted's dad agreed and said we could have fifteen minutes with him Monday.

Ted and I were suddenly fueled by excitement. We grabbed two big whiteboards, the kind that has tripod legs like what some schoolteachers would use. And then we got some whiteboard pens and some notepads. We moved back our desks a little and brought our chairs out from behind them so we could sit in front of the whiteboards. We'd also written on a piece of paper "Do not enter. Geniuses at work" and taped it onto our office door. We'd also shut the blinds so no one could see Ted and I working on our super-secret project.

I stood in front of the two boards as Ted sat in his chair and waited for me to present my two ice cream ideas to him. I wrote at the top of the first board on my left "Captain Panda's Paradise" and then I wrote at the top of the second board on my right "Dinosaur Disaster." Then I drew an outline of a large ice cream tub on each board.

"Ok," I said with my back to him. "I know you're excited, but please let me explain my ideas first and then you can add your comments afterwards."

I turned back to Ted who was nodding. "Ok, man. Let's hear what you've got."

The first thing I did was write down the list of ingredients from Zac's list onto the Captain Panda's Paradise board. And Zac's piece of paper looked like this:

-Bananas
-Milk
-Yoghurt
-Blueberries

That is the order I put them into the bottle to be blended. You can sometimes add frozen fruits and oats. It just depends if you want to mix it up. Zac x

"This is the list that Zac gave me. So obviously Ron's Ice Cream wouldn't make it the same way as she did because although it tasted nice and interesting, it didn't look very appetising."

"Of course," Ted said with a nod, trying to not get over excited.

"I'll start with Captain Panda's Paradise. I'm thinking we could have a light banana ice cream, almost like banana and vanilla blended together. If it was too strong I think no one would really like it." Ted nodded and allowed me to continue. "So we have the banana ice cream base. And then what I thought would be brilliant would be to have a blueberry ripple. You know so like numerous blueberry lines running through the banana ice cream?" Ted nodded again. I drew a dome on top of the lid and then drew some lines through it, not breaching the outline. The dome represented the banana ice cream and then the lines represented the blueberry ripple. I drew a line off each and labelled them as such.

"I'm sure you're still wondering why I have called it Captain Panda's Paradise. It is because I thought we could add small white chocolate pandas into the ice cream. I thought about adding milk chocolate pandas, too, to sort of symbolise the black and white of a panda's fur. But milk chocolate is brown so that wouldn't really work; that's why I thought it would be best to only have white chocolate pandas." I drew a few small squiggly circles inside the dome, but I made sure they didn't interfere with the ripple lines. I then labelled them as pandas. "As for the design on the tub, obviously we have the Ron's Ice Cream template. But the design idea I had for this was that we could have a panda as a pirate. He is holding a sword and wearing a pirate hat, and the treasure is blueberries and bananas. He's a friendly pirate, not an angry, bloodthirsty pirate. I'm not going to draw that because it would look nothing like I just described."

"I can visualise what you're saying," Ted assured.

"Ok, great. I think because Ron's Ice Cream has started selling very well in China, too, the panda ice cream could be a hit over there because pandas live in China, right?"

"Right," Ted replied.

I stepped next to the whiteboard with "Dinosaur Disaster" written on it. "The explanation behind this one is a bit simpler. I thought we could blend chocolate and vanilla ice cream together, so when you open the tub it looks like the ice cream is swirling like a vortex. And then I thought we could add milk chocolate T-Rex skulls, and maybe other dinosaur bones. And the idea is you dig through the ice cream to the find the remains of the dinosaurs."

I could see the excitement in Ted's eyes. He stood and started clapping. "You thought all that up in thirty seconds?" he asked.

"Pretty much," I replied. His applause continued. "So what do you think?" I asked.

"I love it," he answered. "So what is your plan now? Where do you want to start?"

"I think we should start right away on making a visual representation of what the ice cream will look like. That's the most important part. If we waste all our time on tub designs, it could all be for nothing because they'll have some proper artists design one if they decide to go with the flavours."

"Ok. The ice cream visuals will take me an hour, maybe not even that long. I can just generate them from previous ice cream images and then fiddle with the colours and things. The most time-consuming part is going to be making chocolate T-Rex skulls and pandas, but I can make that happen," Ted said, already dragging his desk out to begin the visuals on his computer. Ted is pretty good at graphic design. He studied it at college. "Why don't you prepare what we will say to my dad? I know it's kinda self-explanatory, but it'll help to have some printouts or details or whatever so he can keep them."

"Yeah, that's what I was going to do. I thought we could print it all out later onto the A2 paper-sized boards and take them home with us so we could show them to Zac and Autumn. We could have a practice presentation with them. I'd like Zac to see the flavours before we show your dad, too, since she was the main source of inspiration behind it."

"That's a great idea, Will. I'm so pumped up right now! This is going to look fantastic!" Ted said, jumping up and down on his seat.

Meanwhile I typed up some details about each ice cream and what audiences they would appeal to.

"Did you have an idea for the design on the tub of the dinosaur flavour? We got so excited we forgot to mention that," Ted asked, clicking his mouse and focusing on his computer screen.

"I actually had a funny idea for that one. I thought we could have a paleontologist in a museum display with a chocolate T-Rex skull, and then there's a human bite mark taken out of it."

Ted sniggered. "Yeah that does sounds funny."

"Or we could have an ice cream meteorite heading straight for earth. So it's implying that the dinosaurs were wiped out by an ice cream meteorite instead of a real one."

Ted sniggered again. "That's funny, too. If I have time, I will draw both of them up."

"You just take your time and make sure the visuals look as realistic as possible."

"Don't worry, Will," Ted said, taking his vision away from his computer screen for a moment to look at me. He squinted at me dramatically and said, "I got this."

Ted finished the visuals in forty-seven minutes, and they looked fantastic. I thought he would struggle creating the chocolate pandas and T-Rex skulls and bones, but he nailed it. And then two hours later, he'd finished the tub designs, too. I didn't have anything to do during that time, so I ate the rest of the smoothie ice cream that Zac had left us, and then I sat beside Ted and watched him create the designs. We printed everything onto A2-sized boards. They came out so well. We laid them out in our office and admired them for a couple of minutes, and then Ted placed a hand on my shoulder and said, "I'm proud of us. These look great."

"I agree," I replied.

"*So*, how were things with Zac while we were away?" Ted asked as I drove us home.

"Good. Did you not hear the discussion I had with Autumn when we drove home from the airport?"

"Nope. I was asleep."

"I said it felt like we were actually in a relationship."

"That's good! Did you speak about it to Zac at all or was it just the feeling?"

"No, we didn't talk. We kissed and cuddled a lot while you were away. And when she first created the rules cuddling wasn't allowed. And kissing was only allowed in the bedroom."

"*Wow*."

"Joke all you like. But it was nice, you know, to wake up and see her lying on me or be holding her."

"I know what you mean. I love waking up to see Autumn's head on my chest."

"Yeah. I think Zac might be some kind of ninja."

Ted laughed. "What makes you say that?"

"Because I'll go to sleep in bed and I wake up and her entire body is lying on me, and I think how on earth did she get there without me noticing? It's scarier on the sofa. I'll close my eyes for two seconds and then when I open them she's lying in front of me. Scared the hell out of me the first time."

Ted laughed again. "So what do you think is going to happen now?"

"I don't know what we're anymore. I feel like we're slowly merging into something serious if that makes sense."

"Maybe in ten years you might start holding hands."

"That's not funny."

Ted sniggered and then said, "Speaking of something serious..." I glanced over to him quickly and then turned my attention back to the road. "I wanted to ask you what you think about Autumn?"

"You know I think she's great. She's funny, smart, and she likes you, which is a bonus. It's just like having another sister."

"Ok...because I wanted to know what you thought about me asking Autumn to, erm, marry me."

I didn't say anything. I flicked my head from Ted to the road and then back to Ted and then back to the road.

"Your wide mouth and silence isn't a positive sign."

"It's just you've only been together for a week."

"It's been a month actually. But Will, I love her. And her face is the only face I want to wake up to for the rest of my life. And I don't think I've ever been so...happy. I feel like I've matured a lot since I've been with her, too."

"Yeah, it's weird how grown-up you are now. I'm starting to think she murdered the real Ted and replaced him with you."

"I'm serious!"

"I know you are! I think it's the fifteen-year-old Will in me thinking about you getting married, picturing me being the best man at your wedding. It's a little hard to believe. The maturity of this conversation is starting to make me uncomfortable."

We laughed as we came up to the set of lights at the bottom of our road. I stopped the car and asked, "You're not going to ask her, like, now though are you?"

"I wasn't going to do it right away, but I was definitely thinking about asking her later this year. But I thought about asking you first. I would ask my dad, but I know he will be no help. I've seen you for ninety-nine percent of my life for the past sixteen years, and I'd want you to be my best man. So your approval and thoughts would mean a lot to me. I don't know if I'm being silly and I ask her and then it scares her and she leaves me."

"Ted. You told her you loved her after a couple of weeks, and she told you the same. I think if you ask her later this year your relationship will be a lot stronger, and you will be even more in love with one another. I'm happy for you, man. I think you and Autumn are perfect together."

Ted patted my shoulder and then we were quiet as we drove up to the apartment. "I was thinking," he then said.

"Yes?"

"I think Autumn and Zac are going shopping with Autumn's mum next Saturday. I think Autumn might be shopping for a birthday present for me. But she is taking Zac with her so I don't know if she is going to buy you one, too. Since yours is only a couple of weeks after."

"Ok?"

"So because I know she is definitely away, I thought we could go down to the jewellery shop and maybe take a look at some engagement rings."

I wanted to laugh because I never thought Ted and I would be having this conversation at this stage of our lives. "Absolutely, Ted."

"Thank you," he said.

I pulled into our parking spot and turned off the ignition and we sat there for a moment.

"Can we go inside now, please? I'm trying to not get emotional," Ted then said.

I smirked. "Let's grab the boards and show the girls the flavours."

Ted told me that it would be best if I presented the flavours to the girls since they were my ideas and he didn't really know the full story behind them.

Autumn put on her glasses and sat on Ted's sofa with a notepad and pen. And Zac just put on her beanie and sat on my sofa with a cup of tea. Ted was my board holder, so I could easily take away one board to reveal the next.

"I'll start with Dinosaur Disaster first," I said, taking away the first blank whiteboard, revealing a plain tub with the ice cream poking out of the top. "This idea was inspired by my love for dinosaurs with my best friend, Ted." I flicked my vision between Autumn and Zac. Autumn was nodding along, paying attention. And Zac was sipping away at her tea, staring at the dinosaur board. "As you can see I have made a mix of vanilla and chocolate ice cream into a vortex, tornado-type swirl as the base. And then added some milk chocolate T-Rex skulls. I was thinking we could maybe add other dinosaur bones to generate some more variety, but the fun idea I had was that eating the ice cream is like digging for dinosaur remains, and I believe that it will be a huge hit with children." I removed the board to reveal the first tub design with the ice cream meteorite heading towards earth. I picked that board up and held it myself, so the other design was visible. "As I previously mentioned, eating the ice cream is like digging up dinosaur remains. That is why we added the caption: 'Dig 'em up!' The design I am holding is implying that the dinosaurs were wiped out by a giant ice cream meteorite sixty-five million years ago, and the ice cream in the tub is from the meteorite." Zac smiled her tight-lipped smile, but other than that, no other interest was shown. "And the second design is a paleontologist in a museum, looking at a large milk chocolate T-Rex skull with a giant bite mark taken out of it... And that concludes Dinosaur Disaster."

Autumn blankly stared at me and then wrote something down on her pad, and Zac put down her tea and gave us a small applause. I leant the two tub designs against the sofa with the other boards. Another blank whiteboard was now protecting the next idea I was most looking forward to showing to Zac. "My next idea is called Captain Panda's Paradise," I said, moving the blank whiteboard, revealing a plain tub with the ice cream poking out of the top. I decided to avoid looking at Zac because I didn't want to know what her reaction would be. I wanted to wait until the end. "Captain Panda's Paradise has a light-tasting banana ice cream, almost like banana and vanilla blended together. Then it has a blueberry ripple running through it. The captain of my ship, Zac, and her saying 'whatever feeds your panda' inspired this idea." I couldn't help but look over at her. She was sat with her legs tucked up against her chest and her tight-lipped smile had reached its maximum width.

I paused and watched her for a moment as she examined the board. She looked so intrigued. "Then inside the ice cream is white chocolate pandas. I thought about adding milk chocolate pandas, too, to sort of symbolise the black and white of a panda's fur. But milk chocolate is brown, not black. I believe Captain Panda's Paradise will be the dark horse of our ice creams, and any other ice cream. I think some people may find it silly, but since Ron's Ice Cream has started selling very well in China, the panda ice cream could sell millions over there because pandas live in China. I also think the blueberry ripple will taste so good, that people will buy it just for that."

I removed the board to reveal the tub design for Captain Panda's Paradise. "This was the only idea I had for the tub design. We have a panda as a pirate, and he's the captain of course. He's holding a sword and has a pirate hat. And instead of the treasure being gold and jewels, the treasure is blueberries and bananas. He's a friendly pirate, not an angry, bloodthirsty pirate...and, well, that's it. We'll be much more well-spoken and professional on Monday, but I wanted to show Zac, and you, Autumn, our ideas since you both helped with the creation of these flavours. I would also like to thank my friend, Ted. Without his design work, none of this would have been possible. Thank you."

Ted leant the final board up against the sofa with the rest of the boards and then we high-fived. "So what did you think?" Ted asked, going over to his sofa and sitting beside Autumn.

"I loved it," Autumn said. "It's very creative and unique, and it appeals to good audiences." He kissed her and then he asked Zac what she thought. I sat beside her and awaited her reply.

"They're nice," she said. "I can't believe you made an ice cream flavour for me."

"Do you like it?" I asked.

She put her arms around me and gave me a hug. "This is the sweetest thing that anyone has ever done for me. I love it. Thanks, Will."

"You're welcome." I glanced over at Ted and Autumn. He had his arm around her, but they were both smiling at me, and giving me the thumbs-up.

MARCH 30TH

So this morning we went into Ted's dad's office and presented the two new flavours to him. We did a practice run-through in our office before we went in and that seemed to sound pretty good. And then when we presented it to Ted's dad, I thought we nailed it. But Ted's dad didn't show any sign of interest or pride towards it.

After we had finished our presentation Ted asked, "So what do you think, Dad? I mean boss, I mean Dad. What do I call him?" He turned to me as if I should know the answer.

"Dad, boss, Robert, or Rob will do, Theodore," he said. Ted's eyes and mine bulged as we slowly made eye contact with one another. Ted's dad only ever called Ted, Theodore if he was in a lot of trouble. "Whose ideas were these?" Ted's dad asked.

Ted, being the caring best friend he is, quickly threw me under the bus. "It was Will's idea. It was all Will's idea. I just helped him do the designs! Don't get mad at me, please!"

I nodded at Ted and mouthed, "Thanks, man." Ted's dad continued to stare at the spread of boards we had presented. Instead of hiding them all behind each other we leant them against the wall so he had a view of each one after we had presented them.

"I love them," he then said.

"What?!" Ted blurted.

"Will you shut up for a moment?"

"Sorry, doss, I mean bad. I'll shut up now. Sorry, Dad."

Ted's dad watched his son for a moment in disbelief. "Will," he then said.

"Yes?"

"You came up with these ideas all by yourself? Nobody else helped you?"

"Yes, I came up with them myself."

"You didn't steal them from a company that creates ice cream ideas or you didn't collaborate together to present me this?"

"*No*...I came up with them in our office Friday afternoon when Zac and Autumn came to visit us."

"So you're the only person in the world that deserves credit for these ideas?"

"Well, I would like to give some credit to Zac for Captain Panda's Paradise. She inspired the idea massively. Without her it wouldn't exist."

"I see. Is that the girl you slept with a couple of months ago and we got him the card and stuff?" he asked Ted.

"That is correct, Father," Ted replied.

"So she's your girlfriend now?" he asked me.

"They have a complicated relationship. They basically spend the weekend together and sleep together, but Will wants something more although she's too scared for commitment or any kind of relationship," Ted answered.

I shut my eyes and pinched the top of my nose; I don't know why, it's just what people do when they're embarrassed or annoyed.

"Will."

"Yes, boss?"

"I love these ideas. They're fun and enjoyable. They look tasty. It's something I would like to see associated with

Ron's Ice Cream. And the audience, like you said, the panda one would sell fantastically in China, and the dinosaur one will do great with kids. Everyone else around the world will buy them anyway, but those are the target audiences that it will appeal to."

"Thank you," I said. I felt like the only thing missing from this meeting now was an ashtray and a cigar hanging out of the edge of Ted's dad's mouth.

"You've just saved me a hell of a lot of money, Will. And earned yourself a hell of a lot in return," he said.

"I don't understand," I replied.

"When Ron's Ice Cream wants to make a new flavour, the first people we have to go to is a company in America to create a few ideas for us. And they have to do all these surveys and tests and see which one will sell the best. Every statistic possible. But I can honestly sit here and say that we don't need to do that because these ideas you have presented are exactly what I would have been hoping to see from them. They're fun and quirky. They're... they're different. Unique. I think that's what I like about them most. So, now, I can save God knows how much money, millions for sure, and skip all the flavour idea creating people and move straight onto flavour-testing people."

"Dammit, I wish I had said I helped now," Ted said.

His dad got up and sat on the front of his desk as he observed the boards again. "The tub designs are great, too. I love them. Obviously we'll get some proper graphic designers to make official tub covers, as these are rough designs. But the idea behind them I love, too. I think we will use them. Who came up with the ideas for the tub designs?"

"That was Will, too," Ted answered. "I can't believe it took you thirty seconds to come up with this," he grumbled.

"So the dinosaur tub designs are options? They're not the front and back of the Dinosaur Disaster tub?"

"Yes, they're options. We didn't think about having one on the front and the other on the back," I answered.

Ted's dad nodded and continued to analyse them. "I'm thinking we put both the dinosaur designs on the same tub then. The paleontologist on the front and the meteorite on the back or the other way around. That could work, right?" Ted and I glanced over at each other and nodded back to his dad. "We'll have plenty of time to go over that anyway," he added. He turned and pressed a button on his desk phone. It immediately started to ring on loudspeaker. Jeremy then picked up.

"Yes, boss."

"Jeremy, will you come into my office for a moment, please?"

"Yes, boss."

I don't think Ted's dad managed to end the call before Jeremy was knocking on his office door. "Come on in, Jeremy."

The door opened and Jeremy stepped inside. "What can I do for you, boss?" he said with a notepad in his hand.

"We're going to need some new employees to take over our social media and website department. So do we have somebody already working in the office who would be very capable of taking over Ted and Will's roles in a few weeks or do we need to get some new employees? Either way we're going to need new employees to take over someone's job."

Ted's eyes widened. "Is he firing us?" he whispered.

His dad noticed the indiscreet whispering and said, "No. You're getting a promotion of sorts."

Ted grinned. "Really? Are you finally quitting?"

I sighed and so did his dad. "Return to being quiet, please." Ted turned back to me and shrugged.

"Exactly how soon will you need them to be ready to take over? Because sometimes a few weeks translates to this week," Jeremy replied.

Ted's dad pouted his lips. "Let's say a month."

"Ok, boss. I am more than capable to do their roles if needed. We will just need to install a couple of files onto my computer as I won't be able to work from their office."

"Ok, great. For now, let's find somebody new because if you're ever off ill then we don't have anyone to run them."

"Yes, boss," Jeremy said.

"That will be all for now, Jeremy." Jeremy exited the office and shut the door behind him without another word. "I'm making you two project managers," Ted's dad said as he returned to his chair behind his desk and placed the tips of his fingers to together like an evil mastermind.

"Project managers?" I asked.

"Project managers," he replied.

"Care to shed some more light on the whole idea behind that? Do you not think you should reconsider? This is a rushed decision and is a bit reckless."

Ted's dad was reading something on his computer. Ted shuffled over and nudged me with his foot. "Shut up," he whispered. "This is going to be the best thing ever."

"But what if it goes wrong and it turns out my flavours are a huge failure and become the worst ice cream in history? That's not going to be the best thing ever."

Ted opened his mouth and then shut it again. Then it reopened and he said, "Let's make sure we work hard to prevent that from happening and make it as perfect as possible."

"When you two are done talking," Ted's dad began, "I'd like to talk to you both."

"Sorry," we both said in unison.

"Ted, Will. After seeing the new flavours you presented to me, and the work you two put into it, in the time you did it, it shows me that the skills you have developed since you started working here are being wasted behind your desks. Even though your maturity is questionable at times. Mainly you, Ted." He paused to allow Ted to react.

Ted looked at his dad and then at me, and then said, "That's fair, I suppose."

"You two are ready to take on a bigger responsibility now, and you can begin to learn about another area of Ron's Ice Cream. So let's meet again at the same time next week, and the three of us will sit down and plan how we're going to create Captain Panda's Paradise and Dinosaur Disaster."

"Yes, boss," Ted and I both said in unison.

"I'm proud of you both. Good work." Ted and I nodded as his dad returned his attention to his computer. "You can leave now," he said, flicking his eyes from his computer to us and then to the door.

"Do you want the flavour boards and tub design boards with you, or shall I email them to you?" I asked.

"Leave me the boards, please. And if you could email them to me as well in case I need to email them to anyone or print them off."

"I will do."

"Thank you."

Ted and I left the office, and then we high-fived.

APRIL 3RD

Zac had taken on an extra shift today so I didn't see her yesterday. She is going to a party tonight with Natalie, but not until late in the evening, so I picked her up and told her we could chill for a few hours, and then she could get ready and I'll drive her and Natalie to the party. So we had sex, and then had our bowls of soup. And now Zac was in the shower, getting ready. I was lying on the bed as she did so, watching some television. And then her phone started to ring. It was Natalie. I thought I would be ok to answer it and let her know that Zac was in the shower.

"Hey, Natalie. It's Will. Zac is in the shower at the moment."

"Oh, hey, Will. I was checking that she was getting ready. Are you still ok to pick me up later?"

"Yeah she's getting ready. And yes, once Zac is dressed we will drive over and pick you up."

"Ok. Thank you. See you later."

"See you later."

I hung up, and I was about to place her phone back on the bedside draw before her phone returned to its home screen. And the photo she had set as her wallpaper was a photo of me on my sofa. I was just sat there, smiling, I can only assume at the television. I didn't even know she had taken this photo, but to have it as her wallpaper is kind of a big deal, isn't it? To me it is anyway. I smiled and then placed the phone back on the bedside draw.

Zac emerged from the bathroom ten minutes later with a towel around her body and one on her head. I still don't know how girls tie that towel around their heads. It will always be a mystery to me.

"Am I your phone screensaver?"

"No," she quickly replied. "Matthew McConaughey is."

"That's strange, because I just saw it, and it's a photo of me on my sofa."

Her eyes bulged and she rushed over to her phone and snatched it up. "It's Matthew McConaughey," she said again. "Why were you on my phone?"

"Natalie called, so I answered it and told her you were in the shower. And then when I went to put the phone down I saw the photo of me."

"It's not you," she said. "It's Matthew McConaughey."

"Why didn't you tell me he changed his appearance to look like me and then came to sit on my sofa for you to take a photo of him?"

She looked away. "Am I the screensaver on your phone?" she then asked.

"Of course you are," I replied.

"What?" she said, seeming surprised. I rolled over and grabbed my phone. I opened it and checked the photo. It was a picture of Zac and me. We were lying on my sofa and she had fallen asleep. She was wearing her beanie. She looked so beautiful and calm in the photo. I put my phone into her hand.

She looked at the photo and then asked, "When did you take this?"

"I'm not sure, last week or the week before?"

"Change it, I look horrible."

"No! I knew you were going to say that. I like it."

"Whatever feeds your panda," she said grumpily and threw the phone back to me.

"I want to know why I'm your screensaver, please."

"I don't know," she said. I could see that she felt uncomfortable, so instead of teasing her about it I decided "I don't know" was good enough.

"Ok," I said. "You need to get ready, otherwise we're going to be late to pick up Natalie."

Zac looked beautiful when she was dressed. She was wearing her typical outfit. But she still looked beautiful. She always does. I didn't want her to leave. I drove her over to her apartment, and we picked up Natalie and then I drove them to their friend's house where the party was being held. Zac and Natalie were going to get a taxi back to their apartment and then Autumn and her mum were going to pick Zac up from there ahead of their shopping trip tomorrow. I returned to the apartment and watched some TV with Ted and Autumn. And then I went to bed early because they were kissing, so I thought I would give them some space.

APRIL 4TH

My phone binged and woke me during the early hours of the morning. My phone read 1:32am. I squinted and read the screen to see I had a text from Zac. I assumed she was just letting me know she was home safe.

NEW MESSAGE FROM ZACHARY WILLIAMS III
Are you awake?

NEW MESSAGE FROM WILL EVANS
Yes, why?

NEW MESSAGE FROM ZACHARY WILLIAMS III
Could you come pick me up?

NEW MESSAGE FROM WILL EVANS
Of course, is everything ok?

NEW MESSAGE FROM ZACHARY WILLIAMS III
Yes. I just don't like it here and would like to come home.

NEW MESSAGE FROM WILL EVANS
Ok, I'll come and get you now. I'll be 20 minutes x

NEW MESSAGE FROM ZACHARY WILLIAMS III
Ok. Thank you.

Zac was sat outside on the step of her friend's house. It was freezing and she was only wearing her Timberland boots, ripped jeans, small T-shirt and her beanie.

"What are you doing outside?" I said, rushing up to her and putting my coat around her. I started shivering almost the second after I took off my coat. "You're going to make yourself ill," I said, rubbing her arms. I couldn't believe how cold it was, and I couldn't believe even more that she was outside in it. She was shivering like crazy. "How drunk are you? How long have you been out here?" I asked.

"Ten minutes and I'm sober. I only had one drink," she said. "I'm just tired."

"Right, let's get you to the car." I helped her stand up and then put my coat on her properly and zipped it up.

Once we were in the car I turned the heating up to its highest possible setting. "Why were you outside?" I asked. I put my hand on her thigh and it was so cold.

"I didn't want to stay inside."

"Where is Natalie?"

"She was kissing some guy, I'm not sure."

"Is everything ok? You seem a little upset." She crossed her arms and stuck her hands under her armpits and shook her head. "Are you sure?"

She nodded and then said, "Can we go home, please?"

"Of course. Are you feeling a bit warmer now?" I asked as I began to drive back to the apartment.

"Yes. Thank you," she replied.

Zac was quiet for the first five minutes of the drive home. I kept looking over to check if she was ok, but she was staring out of the window.

"It's nice that you think of my apartment as home," I said, making conversation.

"I guess so," she replied.

"Are you sure everything's ok?" I asked.

"Yes!" she snapped.

"Ok," I said, deciding that I should just drive home. I know she didn't mean to snap at me. She just needed some sleep.

She then shuffled around to face me, and she looked like she was going to say something. She'd opened her mouth as if she was going to say something, but she remained silent and stared down at the gear stick. I kept looking out of the corner of my eye as we drove along, and then she eventually said, "I-I-I...kissed someone."

We came up to a set of lights, which provided a moment for me to talk to her. "What do you mean you kissed someone?" I asked.

"There was a guy at the party...and I kissed him."

To be honest my stomach felt that bad, I thought I was going to throw up. I could feel a huge lump in my throat, and my hands wanting to tremble. The car was so hot I had started sweating so I couldn't pass it for shivering. My heart had now started beating two or three times its normal rate. But I knew I couldn't say anything. I couldn't be mad at her. Because I was stupid enough to agree to her rules.

I said the only thing I thought I could say. "I'm not your boyfriend. So I don't know why you felt like you needed to tell me."

"Will..."

"What?"

"Don't be like that."

"Don't be like what? I'm stating a fact: I am not your boyfriend."

"I know, but we've spent a lot of time together and I wanted you to know—"

"That it was nothing serious...like you and me," I finished for her.

"It didn't mean *anything*, it was a stupid mistake and I wish it never happened."

"Ok." I was so angry and frustrated and upset. I didn't know how react to this situation. I knew I was being a dick. But I just wanted to get home and go to sleep. If there was anything to talk about, we could talk about it in the morning.

When we got home and got into bed, Zac wouldn't leave it until tomorrow. She nudged me a few times, but I dismissed it and ignored her. Then I could sense her sitting there cross-legged, watching me. Then she started kissing my neck and nibbling my ear. "Will, will you please talk to me?"

"We'll talk tomorrow. Go to sleep, Zac." We said this backward and forward four or five times. And then she said those two little words that made me bite my lip to prevent myself from jumping on her.

She put her hand on my shoulder, leant over me, and whispered into my ear, "Make me." So we had sex, and then she left me alone, and fell asleep.

When I woke up, Zac was already dressed and about to leave with Autumn to go shopping with Autumn's mum. She didn't say hello, good morning, I'm leaving now, or good-bye. She just left. I guess she was probably avoiding the confrontation about her kissing some other guy last night.

I got up and made my smoothie, and Ted had one, too. And then we got dressed and drove to the jewellery shop in town. I didn't bother telling Ted about Zac kissing another guy because I didn't want to dampen his day. Searching for an engagement ring for the girl of his dreams didn't need to be spoilt by me whining about Zac kissing some other guy.

A gentleman asked us if we needed any assistance as we entered, and Ted said no thank you. And then the gentleman told him if he needed any assistance that he need only ask.

"So do you have any idea what you're looking for?" I asked. The store wasn't huge. But there was plenty on display. Watches, necklaces, earrings. Everything.

"When I spoke to my mum about searching for one, she told me when she and Dad went to buy one for her. She said there was such a large collection, but suddenly, one caught her attention, and she just knew it was the one. So I'm hoping that is going to happen to me."

"Ok. So are you going to actually buy one today or are we scouting?"

"I guess if we find the right one, I'll get it today."

"That is a bold move, sir. But I am here to support you, so you do whatever you need to do."

"Thank you."

We found a huge glass cabinet displaying at least one hundred engagement rings, starting from ridiculous prices to utterly ridiculous prices.

"You're going to need to sell a kidney to afford this, Ted."

"You're obviously forgetting who my great-grandfather was then. I got left quite a lot by him."

"I didn't know."

"Yeah. I've always kept it to myself. I've never touched it. I was waiting until I really needed it. Buy a house or whatever."

"You're not going to spend it all, are you?"

"No. Of course not. Autumn would kill me if I did that. She'd rather have the house." We both laughed.

"That's true," I said.

We continued to scan through all the rings. Nothing caught my attention. There was just such a huge selection. Nothing stood out to me with some variety.

"What are you thinking, man?" I asked.

"I have my eye on two," he replied.

"Which ones?" I asked.

He put his hand on the side of my neck and pulled my head next to his. He pointed. "That one there to the left about three back. And then that one over there near the back right. About five in."

"I see them," I said. "Why don't you take a look at them?"

"Do you think I should?" he asked.

"Of course. They will look differently in your hand. We have most of the day to look, and you don't have to get one today or from here. This is a very big deal so you should select carefully."

"I really like those two," he said.

"Right, well, let's get that guy to take them out for us." I walked over to the counter and asked him if we could take a look at them. He told us to sit down at this table that had a small mirror on it. I wondered what it was for, but then I realised it was so you could see a larger reflection of the jewellery on your hand.

Ted was on his phone as the rings were placed in front of us. "Put your phone down!" I said.

"I'm just checking to see if Autumn has texted me," he replied. "Ok," he said, returning his phone to inside jacket pocket. He picked up both rings and held them. "If you were Autumn, and I was proposing to you, which ring would you want to see appear as I opened the box?"

I leant forward and examined the rings. Ring descriptions are not my best subject so I will have to describe them as I see them. The first one had a silver ring, and then on top of the ring was a diamond in a bracket holding it in place. It was a lot more beautiful than I just described. It was breathtaking. Ring descriptions aren't my specialty.

And then the next ring was *huge*. This one had a silver ring, too, and then on top of that was a huge wide diamond. It didn't have height like the last ring, but it was very wide. And then surrounding that diamond was probably eight smaller ones, almost creating like a diamond flower.

"Which one do you like most?" I asked.

"I like the big one," he said.

"See, I don't think that reflects Autumn. She doesn't want big and bold. That's not who she is. Obviously she wants you to make her feel like the only girl in the world. But buying her the biggest ring isn't what she'd want. She'd want you to buy her a ring that made you think of her when you saw it. She'd rather it be smaller and cheaper or whatever, and it be meaningful, than it be bigger and more expensive and not meaningful. Plus Autumn wouldn't be able to work with that on the end of her finger. She'd have to drag it around with her and it would get in the way."

Ted placed the bigger ring down and now examined the smaller one. "I understand what you're saying," Ted said. "She just wants a ring that shows that I love her."

"Exactly. That's why people get married."

He smirked and twiddled the ring in his hands. "I'm going to get this one," he said.

"Really?" I asked.

"Yep. This is the one."

Ted already knew Autumn's ring size somehow. And he asked the gentleman what the price would be, and how long it would take to come in. The gentleman nodded his head and took away the rings, and then went to complete Ted's requests. When he came back, he informed Ted that the ring could be here in ten days' time. And then he told him the price. And I won't tell you the exact figure, but you could have gotten yourself a fairly nice car for that price.

Ted didn't seem bothered by its price. "How much was the other one? Just out of curiosity," Ted asked. And then the gentleman told him that it was three times the one of his choice. Which could have gotten you a very nice car.

Ted was on his phone as he was paying for the ring. I was stood there thinking *what is more important than buying an engagement ring.* Ted ordered and paid for the ring and then he walked over to me afterwards.

"Why were you on the phone?" I asked.

"I missed a call from Autumn and she left me a voicemail."

"Is everything ok?" I asked.

"Yeah. She just said that she hopes we're having a good time, and that she loves me." He gave me a hug after he placed his phone into his pocket. "I'm gonna get married," he said. "Me. Ted Maguire. I'm getting married."

"She hasn't said yes yet."

He laughed and then he said, "I have something to show you. Let's go back to the car."

Ted drove us out of town and out into the countryside. I had no idea where he was taking me. I thought he might murder me and bury my body out here.

"Where are we going?" I asked.

"You'll see soon," he said. Two minutes later he switched on the indicator, even though there wasn't another car in sight. And then he pulled into the drive of this huge stone house. A gate prevented us from access, but there was a numeric keypad outside the window. Ted rolled down the window and entered a code, and then the gate opened.

I frowned because I had no idea where we were and why we were there. And then as I focused on the gate, I saw a small golden plaque on it that read *Ron & Annie's.* I turned to Ted. "Is this your great-grandfather's house?"

"It certainly is," he replied.

We drove into a courtyard and parked the car. I got out and rotated three hundred and sixty degrees and admired the house in amazement. There were actually three stone houses. They were all joined together. And if you looked at them from the road and higher up, they should form a giant straight C. The biggest one was at the front where we came in through the gate. And the smallest one was in between that one and the medium one at the back.

I didn't even know this place existed. In all my years of knowing Ted, I'd never been here. I'm not sure how often he has been here. He's never mentioned it.

"Why are we here?" I asked.

"Because, Will, when I ask Autumn to marry me, if she says yes, I would want us to live together, and I was thinking we could live here."

"That's a great idea," I replied.

"They're not actually separate, these houses. There is a door from each house into the next. They just added three front entrances onto them because it's so big.

"Oh, I thought they were."

"Nope. So Autumn and I would have the big one at the front." He turned and pointed to it, and then he pointed to the one at the back. "And you would have that one."

For a second I thought he was joking and I smirked and turned to look at it.

"What do you think?" he asked.

I turned back to him. "Are you being serious? I can't tell if you're joking."

He laughed. "I'm serious!"

"Ted, I don't know what to say."

"Say yes," he said, putting his hands on my shoulders, and then jokingly dropping to his knee.

"All right, get up," I said, helping him up.

"Shall we take a look around?" he asked.

"Yeah!" I said. He pulled a set of keys out of his pocket and then we walked to the biggest section at the front and opened the door. Ted showed me around for at least an hour and told me about all the history of it. I can't describe everything I saw. All I can say is that it's great. It's so wonderful and fantastic and amazing. The old-fashioned stone on the outside misleads you, because you expect to enter the house and for it to be old-fashioned, too. But everything was so modern. The kitchens and bathrooms were immaculate. Ted told me that his dad had refurbished it a couple of years ago and had been renting it out. But now that the renters had moved out, he wanted Ted to have it if the proposal to Autumn went to plan. And I couldn't believe he would want me to stay with him. I know we've been friends for a long time, but at some point I thought we would have to go our separate ways and live alone. Almost like when you move out of your parents' house.

My phone started to buzz as we exited and made our way back to the car. Natalie was calling me, which I thought was strange. Maybe she was trying to call Zac, but her phone was on silent. Zac's phone is always on silent.

"Hi, Natalie."

"Will. I've been trying to call you! Where have you been?"

"Sorry. Ted and I are out in the countryside so the signal isn't great. What's up?"

"You need to come to hospital. Zac and Autumn were in a car crash."

"What? Are they ok?"

"I don't know. I'm in the waiting room waiting to find out now. But you need to come to the hospital, now."

"We'll be right there."

Ted and I broke every speed limit possible as we drove to the hospital, and we arrived there twenty minutes later. We burst into the waiting room and found Natalie sitting there.

"How are they?" I asked, rushing over to her.

"Zac is fine. I just saw her, but I came back to here to wait for you," she said. "And Autumn is being operated on. I don't know why, but I think she is going to be ok."

I rubbed my face with my hands and dropped onto a chair across from her. "Can we see them?" I asked. My heart rate was beyond a normal level. I think it was beyond any possible level. I could feel every part of my pulse thumping and echoing around me.

Before Natalie could answer, Zac's mum appeared. "How is she?" I asked, rising to my feet. "Can I see her?"

She put her hand on my forearm. "She is fine. Don't worry. You can come and see her with me now."

"Do you know how Autumn is?" I asked. "Have you heard anything about her?"

"No. I haven't. I have been with Zac."

I took a deep breath and tried to compose myself. I turned back to Ted, who was blankly staring forward. "Ted," I said.

"Go," he said. "Go and see her. I'll text you if I hear anything about Autumn."

I nodded. "Ok." Natalie, Mrs. Williams, and I walked through the ward for a few minutes and got into an elevator to the third floor. We turned left as we exited it. Then we turned left again into a smaller room.

There were maybe ten hospital beds and I saw Zac on the third one, sitting with her legs crossed. She looked unharmed. She looked like her normal self. Her dad was sitting on a chair at the end of the bed. He was about to stand and most likely cause a scene and not let me see Zac, but Mrs. Williams told him to sit down and remain quiet. Which he did.

When Zac saw me, she looked horrified. "What are you doing here?" she asked loudly.

"What do you mean what am I doing here? You were in a car crash, Zac. I had to see that you're ok." I knelt down beside her and went to take hold of her hand, but she flinched and moved it away.

"I'm fine. You don't need to be here."

I opened my mouth, but I didn't know what to say. I didn't think she would react like this. I only wanted to see that she was ok. She looked so angry and frustrated with me. "I was worried about—"

"I'm fine. Now go."

"Have I done something wrong?"

"I don't know why you're here. I don't want you to be here. So please leave now, Will." She looked over at her dad and he stood from his chair, indicating that if I didn't leave he would assist me.

I got to my feet and looked down at Zac. "I just wanted to see that you were ok." Zac didn't even make eye contact with me. She was looking in the opposite direction. Natalie and Mrs. Williams were standing behind me. They looked slightly shocked and upset, too. But I presumed that was because of Zac being in hospital, not because of the way she had reacted to me being here. I forced a faint smile at them both, which they returned, and then walked back the way I came. I didn't bother to say good-bye or try to stay. All I know is I felt broken as I left. I had no idea what had happened to her, or why she didn't want to see me, and then she just told me to leave.

When I returned to the waiting area, Ted was still sat there. I sat beside him and blankly stared forward. "Have you heard anything about Autumn?" I asked.

He shook his head. "How's Zac doing?"

"She looked fine. She was sat on a hospital bed like nothing was wrong. Her mum said that they were waiting to run some final tests and scans on her. To make sure that all her vitals and everything were ok. And when I saw her she got so angry with me for being there, and she told me to leave…"

"I'm sorry."

I could feel my bottom lip beginning to tremble. I wiped my eyes and sniffled my nose. He squeezed my shoulder and then sat back in his chair. "You should go home," he said.

"No, it's fine."

"Go home," he said again. "I'll text you when I hear how Autumn is doing. I don't want you sitting here all upset."

"Are you sure?" I asked.

"They probably won't let you see Autumn even if you do stay." He said.

"I know, but I still want to stay and find out if she is ok." Ted took my hand and placed the car keys into them. "I'll see you later."

"Ok. Please let me know how she is doing when you find out, please."

"I will."

I drove home and sat down on the sofa. A few tears rolled down my cheek as I did, and then five minutes later I fell asleep. And when I woke up, Zac was sat on the edge of the sofa, rubbing my shin.

For a second I thought I was dreaming.

"Hey," she said.

"Hi. How are you feeling?" I asked.

"I'm ok. How are you?"

"I'm ok. Have you seen Autumn?"

She shook her head. "They wouldn't let me in. Have you?"

"No. Ted told me to go home and he would let me know if he heard anything. Did you see him?"

"No." She took off her beanie. "I wanted to come and talk to you about today, at the hospital, and about last night."

I sat up and made eye contact with her. Zac's mood had completely changed compared to earlier. I scratched my head before saying, "We've basically merged into a relationship, Zac. I know it's an unusual one, but I thought that's what we had become. I've wanted to talk to you about it, but I could never find the right words. The way we have been recently is more than just sleeping together. I certainly know that. I want to be with you, and I thought you wanted to be with me. I don't think there is anything scary about that. I know you've been hurt in the past, but if you're worried about me hurting you or cheating on you, then you clearly know nothing about me... A relationship is just like coming home. That person is home. That's all it is, Zac. And if that isn't what you want, I don't think I can see you anymore. As much as it hurt hearing that you kissed somebody else, I could get over that. That wouldn't be a problem unless it became a reoccurring thing. But today, at the hospital, when I didn't know what had happened to you... It could have been so much more serious. You could have... You could have... Something a lot worse could have happened. But you just dismissed me like I was nothing. And it felt like you'd forgotten about all the time we had spent together, and you didn't care about me, the parts of my life and the people I have opened up to you about. And it felt like you didn't care, and it felt like you had ripped out a part of me, and simply thrown it away. And I can't begin to explain how much that upset me. So if being me with isn't what you want, then I won't be able to see you anymore. I can't see you if you're wanting or spending time with other people. My feelings for you are too strong. And if you don't see other people, but want to continue doing whatever we're doing, then I can't do that either. Not if you can just dismiss me like you did at the hospital. I'd rather deal with the pain of not having you in my life than deal with the pain I'm going through now."

I wiped my eyes and remained still and facing forward. I didn't know if I loved Zac or hated her. I didn't know if I wanted to her to leave or to stay. "It's been a long day. Let's get some sleep and we can talk about this tomorrow. I can't think straight until I hear about Autumn," I said.

Zac got to her feet and said, "Ok."

She held out her hand for me to take it, but I declined. "I'm going to stay on the sofa tonight. I want to wait up for Ted."

Zac walked over to me. As I stared at the floor her socks came into view. She rested my head against her, and ran her hands through my hair. And then she placed me onto the back of the sofa, and she sat on my lap. She started to kiss my neck, and I looked up at her and our eyes met. I quickly picked her up and went into my bedroom. We got into bed and then I let her go and got out.

"Good night, Zac," I said, standing by my bedroom door before closing it behind me. I returned to my seating position on the sofa. The time on my phone read 10:38 p.m. It seemed so much later than it was. And the later it got, the more concerned I became. I stayed awake for another hour before I fell asleep again. I woke during the middle of the night at around 1:00 a.m. I quickly glanced at my phone and only saw the one on my phone's clock.

I could hear lots of smashing and breaking and yelling. The source of the commotion appeared to be coming from Ted's bedroom. My heart started to race because I thought someone might have broken in or was trying to break in. I raced into my bedroom to check that Zac was ok. She was fast asleep. Undisturbed.

I closed my bedroom door and then walked over to Ted's bedroom. He should have been home by now. I had to push open the door, as there was something stacked behind it. And when I opened the door and stepped inside, I could see Ted standing there, yelling and crying and throwing things against his wall. His room was turned completely upside down. It looked as if a tornado had torn through only moments ago.

After a few seconds he noticed me standing there and stopped. He started crying even harder. "She didn't make it..." He wiped the tears off his cheeks, but they were replaced by more immediately after. "When Autumn's mum finally appeared and told me how she was doing, she told me that they were just about to turn off the life support machine. That I had two minutes to say good-bye. She just looked like she was asleep. My beautiful girlfriend just sleeping. She had some bandaging on her head. That was it. She looked as beautiful as when I first saw her. They said... said that she hit her head too hard during the impact. Her side took the full force of the crash, and there was too much swelling on her brain. There was nothing they could do. Two fucking minutes to say good-bye. I thought they were joking. I thought it was a joke. And then I saw all the doctors gathered around her and all the machines she was hooked up to. I didn't know what to say to her. I couldn't stop crying. I just told her I loved her and told her to wake up. I thought she was going to wake up any second and tell me that she was ok and that she loved me, too. And that everything was going to be ok. And then just like that she was gone. I'd lost her. My beautiful angel taken away from me. I don't know what to do, Will. Why isn't she here?"

Ted screamed and then he continued to smash anything he could get his hands on. I stood there crying, watching him, before I walked over and wrapped my arms around him.

He struggled to break free, but my grip didn't budge. And then he stopped struggling. He cried and yelled into my shoulder as I cried and kept my arms around him. "Tell me this isn't real, Will. Please tell me this isn't real," he repeated.

I don't know how long we were stood there. It could have been minutes. It could have been hours. Ted was so exhausted that he just collapsed in my arms. I cleared up the mess on his bed the best I could and then put him in it. As I exited his bedroom, I saw Zac stood like a statue in the living room. She saw me crying and she instantly knew then what had happened. She placed her hands over her face and then she started to cry. I paced over and put my arms around her and I started crying even more. She sobbed into my chest and let out a loud cry. I took her to my sofa and rested her on me. I couldn't think of a word to say to make any of this better. Every inch of me was in pain. I was numb. I couldn't imagine what Ted was going through, how he must be feeling. And I couldn't stop thinking about Zac and how she was feeling.

I tightened my grip around her and held her close to me. Zac exhausted herself like Ted and she fell asleep on me, too, leaving me sat there with her in my arms, staring forward. I glanced over at the clock and it read 4:26am, and the next time I glanced over to it, it read 8:08am. I rubbed my face with my hand, then picked up Zac, carried her into my bedroom and placed her into bed. I woke up three hours with Zac lying on me, her head resting on my chest. She lifted her head and stared up at me. Her beautiful blue eyes were red from crying.

NEW MESSAGE FROM TEDS DAD
I'm so sorry to hear about Autumn. We adored her so much. Do not worry about work. Jeremy will take over. Take as much time off as you need. The new flavour project is on hold until your return. Please take care of yourself and my son. Everyone sends you their love.

I got up and made Zac and I a smoothie. I just tried to find something to do for a second to take my mind off Autumn. But it didn't work. I brought them to my bedroom, and Zac and I sat on the edge of the bed.

She stared down at her smoothie and had a sip. "About us," Zac said.

"We don't have to talk about that now," I replied.

"I need to."

"Ok."

"I need some time. Time to think about Autumn, and time to think about you. Just give me a few weeks and I can talk to you. But please wait until I contact you first."

"Whatever you need, it's yours."

"I just need some time," she whispered, her eyes tearing up again. "I can't believe she's gone. I'm never going to see her again." She put down her smoothie and then she started to cry. She put her arms around me and cried into my neck.

I held her for a few minutes and cried myself before I asked her if she wanted to go home. And she said she did.

So we got up and packed her things, and then I drove her home.

I walked her inside and we stopped outside her apartment door. "Do you want me to come in?" I asked.

She was looking down at my feet, and she shook her head. I stepped forward and kissed her forehead, covered by her beanie, and then held her in my arms for a few minutes. I stepped back and was about to say good-bye before she placed a hand on the back of my neck, pulled me in, and kissed me. It seemed before the kiss had even started, it was ending, and she was closing her apartment door behind her.

I watched it for a moment, in hope she would open it again, but she didn't. So I began to walk back to the car. Then I could hear her crying. I stopped and returned my sight to her apartment door. My whole body started to tremble because I knew I couldn't go back there and put my arms around her and hold her and let her know that I loved her. But I had to walk away. I felt so helpless, and I started to cry as I forced myself to walk away.

APRIL 14TH

"Let's go," I said to Ted. He put on his black suit jacket and nodded. I opened the apartment door and allowed him to walk through it first. I closed the door behind us and we began to walk downstairs.

I watched him as he walked downstairs, his head staring down at his feet. He hadn't said a word since that day. Not one. Losing Autumn has been so hard on everyone. But I know this has destroyed Ted. And I don't know if he will ever recover from this.

Ted stared at the car door as I unlocked the car. He didn't open it. He just looked at it. I walked around to his side, opened the door, and helped him into his seat. I got into the driver's seat and placed the key into the ignition. I waited to see if Ted was going to put on his seatbelt. He didn't. I told him to do it three times before I leant over and did it for him.

I drove us to the church, unclipped Ted's seatbelt, and helped him out of the car. The church was already full when we walked in. Everyone was there, Autumn's family, friends, Ted's parents, Natalie, and Zac. Ted and I walked to the second row and took our seats. And then I switched off. I could say it was a lovely ceremony, and that everyone said such caring and loving words about her, but I honestly don't know what anyone said. I couldn't believe that this was Autumn's funeral. I keep thinking that it was a dream, and any second I was going to snap out of it, and I was really sat on my sofa with Zac as we sat and talked about today's Sundiscussion with Ted and Autumn. This isn't real. She isn't really gone.

Autumn became such a big part our lives, and we all loved her, and now we were losing a member of our family. It's too hard to understand.

Ted and I were one of the last few people seated in the church. The sound of everyone leaving the church switched me on again. Everyone was leaving to bury Autumn's coffin. Ted and I got to our feet and followed them. Ted and I stood together as they lowered Autumn into her grave. He looked so empty and lost. I saw Zac and Natalie amongst everyone. Zac was crying. And I had to fight everything inside of me to not go over to her. They didn't come over to us or say hello afterwards. They left like everyone else.

Ted and I were the last ones stood around Autumn's grave. Her parents stayed for a long time, too. But they left us alone after a while.

"I'm going to stay," Ted then said.

"Are you sure?" I asked.

"You go home. I'm going to stay. I don't want to leave her alone right now. I'll see you later."

I knew me trying to stay wasn't what he needed. He needed time alone, and time with her. So I placed my hand on his shoulder and gave it squeeze and told him to call me if he wanted me to come and pick him back up. I knew the cemetery shut at 7:00pm. So I knew Ted should return home within an hour after that. But it turned 8:30pm, and he still wasn't home, so I got in the car and drove around to try to find him. I drove the route I would walk home from the cemetery to our apartment. And I couldn't find him on any of the streets. And then I returned to the cemetery to find him sitting on the wall outside the closed gates.

I parked the car upon the curb next to him and got out. "They had to close the gates," he said.

"Why didn't you come home?" I asked him as I sat next to him.

"I was going to wait until they opened again."

"You can't sit here all night. You'll freeze. Let's go home. I'll drive you here tomorrow."

Ted then opened his hands. He was holding a red engagement ring box. He held it in the palm of his hand and offered it to me. I took and opened it. The ring sparkled as I did so. I smiled down at it and took it out of the box to examine it further. Then I noticed there was something engraved on the inside of the ring. I tilted my head and the ring so the last little bit of daylight could help me see it better. The engraving read: Thanks For Slapping Me. I could feel my eyes tearing up again so I returned the ring to the box and back into Ted's hands. His hands were so cold. If he stayed out here any longer he was going to make himself ill.

I helped him to his feet and said, "Let's go home."

APRIL 17TH

I opened the apartment door to find Autumn's mum sitting on my sofa, and Ted sitting on his.

"Hello, Will," she said.

"Hello, Mrs. Baker," I said, closing the door behind me. I didn't ask her how she was. I didn't think it would be appropriate. The kettle flicked off in the kitchen. Ted got to his feet and moved to the kitchen to make Mrs. Baker a cup of tea. I placed the bags of food onto the kitchen side, and began to take the items from the bags, placing them into the fridge.

"Have you been here long?" I asked her.

"Only been here two minutes, darling. I've heard that Ted has been at the cemetery the past few days, so I thought I would visit after he came home. I stopped by to talk to him, and to give you two something." When Mrs. Baker said darling, it made me picture Autumn, and how she used to call everyone darling, mainly Ted.

Ted carried Mrs. Baker's tea over and placed it onto the table in front of her.

"Will you sit down with us, please, Will?" Mrs. Baker asked.

"Of course," I replied. I took the final item from the bag and placed it into the fridge, then sat beside Ted on his sofa. I saw the tears in Mrs. Baker's eyes before she even began to speak.

"When we were on our way, driving to the shopping centre…" She stopped and sniffled her nose. "You must have accidentally called Autumn somehow, and you left her a voicemail while your phone was in your pocket."

Ted's head lifted. I then remembered where Ted and I were when he said he was checking his phone. We were in the jewellery store, looking at engagement rings.

"She overheard that you two were at the jewellery store, searching for an engagement ring." Ted placed his hand on his pocket, hinting that the ring was in there. He retrieved it from his pocket and placed it on the table. Mrs. Baker smiled. "She was so shocked when she listened to your voicemail. And then she became so happy and excited."

"What did she say?" Ted asked his voice croaky.

Mrs. Baker was already crying. And I was about to start as well. "Well, after she stopped screaming, she told Zac and I what she heard. She acted out the conversation between you two. She was talking so fast. You know how fast she talks when she gets excited." Ted smiled and wiped his eyes. "I spoke to Zac at the funeral. I didn't know if she may have told you already, but she said she hasn't seen you since the day after. I told her that I was going to come and see you, to tell you. I thought you would want to know that she heard what you were doing. But the main reason I wanted to speak to you, was to tell you what she would have said if you would have asked her to marry you." She paused and wiped her eyes. I wiped mine. Ted didn't wipe his, even though tears were dripping onto his lap. He didn't flinch, budge, or move. Time must have stood still for him in that moment. Waiting to find out if Autumn would have agreed to marry him if he had asked.

Mrs. Baker smiled. "She would have said yes, Ted. She would have said yes. I thought she was crazy to agree to marry a boy after a month, but she didn't care. She knew how she felt about you, and there was no changing her mind."

Ted covered his face with his hands and he started to cry even harder. Mrs. Baker wiped her eyes and then grabbed her bag from beside her. She placed it onto her lap and pulled out two yellow parcel-type envelopes. "Autumn wanted to be prepared for your birthday since it is very soon. She spoke to her grandmother, my mum, and Autumn told her that she didn't have a lot of money to spend on presents for you. So her grandmother recommended doing a portrait. You know, like a school photo where you sit on a stool and smile. She said 'back in the day' that's what she and her girls used to do for their boyfriends." She passed Ted his, and then she passed one to me. "Don't open them until I've left, please. Autumn thought it was a great idea and that is what we were doing that day. She got the voicemail when we were driving to get the photos done. So they were taken, and then on our way back that's when..." Mrs. Baker retrieved a handkerchief from her bag and dabbed her eyes. I changed my sight to Ted for a moment. The tears from his eyes were dripping onto the envelope. "Autumn insisted that Zac had one taken for you, too, Will. Because your birthday isn't long after Ted's. Believe me, I know how strange things are between you and Zac, that's all Autumn and Zac were talking about before she heard your voicemail, Ted." She paused and wiped her eyes with her handkerchief. "I had completely forgotten about them until I got a call a couple of days ago, telling me that they were ready for collection. And today I went to collect them and I brought them straight to you."

Ted nodded. "Thank you."

Mrs. Baker bit her lip. "You know, Autumn and I had a conversation a couple of days after the two of you met. And she was telling me how great you were. And how she thought you might be the one. But she told me about how you met."

Ted smirked. "You should take a look at the inside of the ring."

Mrs. Baker opened the box and she placed a hand over her mouth. "Oh, it's so beautiful, Ted." She lifted the ring and then read engraving on the inside of it. "Thanks for slapping me. That's funny," she said as she laughed. "She told me... She told me the truth about how you really met. And she said if she ever...died, then she would want me to tell you, and well, if I died, I suppose she'd want your kids to tell you." She paused and apologised. "She saw you enter the museum, and she thought you were so handsome, and she just wanted to talk to you, but she was too shy to do so. She thought it would be weird to walk all the way over to you to say hello. So she pretended that she was rehearsing for the tour, and she was going to casually bump into you and say hello and then the two of you could chat. But she completely misjudged it. She only meant to brush your arm, but somehow hit you in the face. And well, that gave her a fairly good excuse to give you her phone number. It seems that love at first sight took its cause with you two."

Ted took the ring from her and returned it to his pocket. "I'll always be glad she hit me," he said.

Mrs. Baker smiled at us both and then she got to her feet. "I'm always here if you ever need to talk," she said, hugging Ted.

"Thank you," he replied.

She smiled and placed a hand on the side of his face and then made her way towards the door. She stopped as she opened it, and looked over her shoulder. "She was always so happy with you, Ted. She always used to tell me. Told me how much fun she was having and how she enjoyed spending so much time with you. You made her so happy, and you made her feel so special. I hope you know that. You made her the happiest girl in the world. And I cannot thank you enough for the love and happiness you gave my daughter." Her face winced as she tried to compose herself and then she left seconds later.

I wiped my eyes and left my photo on my sofa while I went into my bathroom to splash some water on my face. When I returned to the living room, Ted was staring at the envelope, still crying. I sat down and held mine in my hands. It was roughly the same size as an A4 piece of paper, maybe shorter and wider. I ripped the top of it and removed the frame. It was a photo of Zac. You could see by her expression that she clearly didn't want to have her photo taken. Autumn must have been behind the camera lens with the photographer because Zac's eyes were focused only just above the camera. I can picture Autumn saying, "C'mon, Zac, smile!" Zac was smiling her usual tight-lipped smile. She looked so beautiful.

I smiled at the photo and went into my bedroom, placing it on my bedside draw. I wasn't sure how long it would stay there for. I guess it would depend on if I heard from Zac or not in the coming weeks.

Ted was still staring at the envelope thirty minutes later when I came out of my bedroom. I sat on my sofa and watched him.

"I don't know if I can open it," he said. He made eye contact with me and then his attention returned to the envelope. "Can you open it for me?" he asked, holding it out to me.

I took it from him and opened it. I stared at the photo for a few seconds. Autumn was sat, moving a piece of her hair whilst smiling into the camera. It was a sort of caught off guard, but not fully caught off guard capture.

"She looks as happy as her mum described. She looks as happy as a girl who knows she is going to marry you," I said, placing the photo into Ted's hands. He smiled and then his tears restarted. It was the happiest I had seen him for a long time.

APRIL 18TH

The next day I woke up earlier than usual. So I got up and made myself a cup of tea. As I was doing so, Ted emerged from his bedroom, dressed and ready to go see Autumn. He was holding a copy of the novel, *The Hobbit*. Before I could ask him about it he said, "Autumn told me she always wanted to read it. I thought I would read it for her."

I smiled. "Do you want a drink?"

"No, I'm going to make my way over there now."

"Ok," I said. "I'll see you later."

During the mid-afternoon, an hour or so before Ted would be home. My phone started to ring. I hoped it was Zac since I had been waiting for her to call since the day I dropped her off at her apartment. Then I thought it would probably be my mum or Rosie, checking in to see how we were. I answered it without even checking who it was.

"Hello."

"Hi. Is that Will Evans?"

"Yes it is. May I ask who this is?"

"It's August...Bishop. You gave us the tour around Ron's Ice Cream?"

"Oh, hello. How are you?"

"I'm great, thank you. Yourself?"

"I'm doing ok, thanks. What can I do for you, August?"

"Well, Madeline has been pestering me every day since our afternoon around Ron's Ice Cream to call you about becoming a 'matador' as she calls it."

"Aw, that's adorable."

"I know it's been a while since then. I've been so busy filming. But I thought I would call you anyway and see if there was anything we could maybe do together. Do you still work there? Not that I thought you would be fired, it's just sometimes it happens. Sorry, I'm rambling."

"I still work there, don't worry. I've actually been away for a few weeks. I was about to start working on two new flavours. But it is on pause until my return. I could give you a call when I do, and we could see if there is something we could involve you in with that?"

"Ok, great! Does my number show up on your screen?"

"It does. Is it ok if I save it?"

"Of course, as long as you keep it to yourself."

"Promise it will stay with me and only me."

"Thank you... So how did things go with you and, Zac, was it? Did it work out?"

"Erm... Well, your gift was great, she loved that and she was so happy. But we've had gone through a lot recently, and we're taking a few weeks apart."

"Ah, I'm sorry to hear that. I hope everything works out between you two."

"Thank you. Me too. But I'll call you soon about working together. I'll speak to you soon, August."

"Ok, Will. Thanks. Bye."

"Good-bye."

After I put down the phone, I realised I had to go back to work. If I left it any longer, the new flavours project would be taken over by somebody else. I needed to return to work as well. I couldn't sit around in the apartment all day staring into blankness.

Later on that day, Ted and I were sat on our sofas watching *Star Wars: Episode IV — A New Hope*. I thought if there were anything that could bring him the smallest amount of happiness or distract him for at least a minute, it would be this film. Halfway through the film he asked, "What day is it?"

I didn't even know the answer. I had completely lost all track of time. "I think it's Thursday."

"What's the date?"

"I don't know. Let me check my phone. It's Saturday the...."

He laughed. "Only two days off."

"Yeah...It's the eighteenth," I said. "How are you feeling man?"

He sighed. "I feel like it's been a second since I was meeting her. I just miss her so much."

"I know you do. Me too."

"I know she wouldn't want me to be this much of a miserable zombie, but I can't help it."

"I know, man. Is there anything you need? Are you hungry?"

"Can we order some pizza?" he asked.

"Yes, of course. I'll phone up and order some now." I stood and went to grab the menu from the kitchen draw.

"Will," he said.

"Yes?"

"Can I have a hug?"

"Of course you can have a hug." I walked over to him as he stood and we gave each other a firm hug.

"Thank you for being here for me," he said from over my shoulder.

"I always will," I replied. "You smell," I added.

He laughed. "I'll take a shower now."

"Ok, man. You need anything else other than pizza?"

"Just a shitload of ice cream afterwards."

"I think I can make that happen." After our embrace separated, Ted went into his bedroom to shower. And I paused *Star Wars* with the remote, and called the pizza delivery place to order some pizza.

APRIL 19TH

I fell asleep during *Star Wars: Episode VI — Return Of The Jedi*. We'd decided to watch the next two movies. When I woke up the TV had been turned off. Ted wasn't on his sofa, and I had a blanket placed over me. I reached for my phone to check the time. It said 5:11am. I got to my feet and then waddled to my bedroom. I climbed into my bed and fell asleep. The startling and deafening sound of my phone ringing woke me a few hours later. I had fallen asleep with it right in front of my face.

"Hello."

"Hi, Will. It's Natalie."

"Oh, hi. How are you?"

"I'm good, thanks. Yourself?"

"I must admit, I have been better."

"Yeah. I wanted to talk to you about Zac."

"Is she ok?"

"Not really. It's like I've been living with—"

"A zombie."

"Yes… I think you should come and see her."

"She said I had to wait until I heard from her. That she needed some time, and then she would call me."

"She was never going to call you, Will. She was just hoping that she could leave it for so long that you would both forget about each other."

"Oh."

"I know losing Autumn has been awful for you both. But I think the last thing you need is to lose each other as well."

"I know, Natalie, but if she doesn't want to be with me, then there's nothing I can do about that. I can't keep seeing her if that isn't what she wants."

"Come here and see her. Then you can talk to her about it."

"I don't know if that would be a good idea, Natalie."

"She's been sat in her room listening to 'She Will Be Loved' by Maroon 5 for about an hour straight now. I don't know if she's eating or sleeping either. And I've heard her throwing up nearly every other day. She's even been sent home early by work some days."

"Ok. I will let you know if I am coming over."

"Please come, Will. I don't know what else to do."

"Like I said, I will let you know."

"Ok...good-bye."

"Bye."

I hung up and dropped my phone back onto my bed. My clock read 10:47 a.m. I rubbed my face with my hands and massaged my cheeks. Then I got to my feet and walked to the kitchen. I needed to wake up first before I could decide what I was going to do. Ted then emerged from his bedroom.

"Hey. How are you?" I said.

"I'm ok. I overslept. I'm going to go to the cemetery soon. How are you?"

"Ok, man. I'm ok. I just spoke to Natalie. Do you want a cup of tea?"

"Please. What did Natalie say? Who called who?"

"Let me make the tea and then I'll tell you."

"Ok," he said, walking over to his sofa and sitting on it. I made two cups of tea and then sat on my sofa, placing our mugs on the table. "So what did Natalie say?" Ted asked.

"She called me five minutes ago. She said Zac isn't doing so well. And she thinks I should come over and see her... But I said I hadn't heard from Zac. She said she would contact me when she was ready. Natalie then told me that Zac was never going to call me. That she was just hoping that she could leave it for so long that we would both forget about each other. But Natalie thinks she might not be eating or sleeping either. And she's heard her throwing up some days. And she said that Zac has been sent home early by work some days. But..." I paused and took a deep breath as I thought over what Natalie had said to me. Ted's face was blank, but he was listening. "But..." I didn't know how to word the next part without it upsetting Ted. I looked down at my hands, trying to word what I wanted to say.

"I know," Ted then said. "Losing Autumn has been hard for you both, I'm not the only one who loved her. You need each other to help get through it."

"Yeah," I said. "I don't know what to do. I can't stop thinking about her."

Ted leant forward. "Do you love her?"

"More than I can put into words." I answered.

"Then stop sitting here like a miserable arse. I do enough of that for the both of us. Drive to her, and tell her."

"I don't think that is what she would want though."

"For God's sake, Will, you're an idiot sometimes."

"Why am I?"

"When a girl says one thing, she doesn't mean that at all, she means the complete opposite to what she said. If she says she's fine, she isn't. If she says she doesn't want something, it means you better get that thing as soon as possible. If she says she's tired, then there's something on her mind. It's always the opposite. Now go over there, grab her, and kiss her, and tell her that you love her. If she really doesn't want to be with you, then at least you can both begin to move on. But don't stay here wondering what you two could have been; go and find out. I would give my left arm to have one more day, one more hour, one more minute, one more second with Autumn. Don't let her go, Will. You'll only regret it if you do." He exhaled and then took a sip of his tea.

I smiled and said, "Ok. I'll call Natalie now and tell her I'm on my way."

"Hello."

"Hey, Natalie. I was going to come over now, is that ok?"

"Yes. She doesn't know you're coming though. So I'm going to have to get her into the living room somehow."

"I'll text you when I'm outside."

"Ok. See you soon."

Ted asked me to drop him off at the cemetery before I went to Zac's. Ted exited the car and grabbed his foldable chair and his novel off the backseat of the car. Then he said, "I hope it all goes ok, man. I'll see you later."

I thanked him and then began my drive to Zac and Natalie's apartment. I texted Natalie once I was outside, and she buzzed me into their apartment block. I walked up the stairs to the seventh floor, my heart rate raising as each floor passed. I kept reciting what I would say to her, but I knew rehearsing or preparing wasn't going to help me. I had to speak from my heart if the opportunity arrived.

Once I reached the seventh floor I walked along to their apartment, number two. Natalie was waiting for me in the doorway.

"Hi," she whispered.

"Hi."

"Zac is sat on the sofa."

"Ok."

Natalie held open the door and escorted me inside. After I took a few paces into their apartment, I saw Zac on her sofa. She had tucked her legs up to her chest and wrapped her arms around them and her head rested against her knees. She was wearing the beanie I bought her when we first met, which instantly put a smile on my face.

"Zac," Natalie said. "You have a visitor."

She raised her head and looked in our direction. Her beautiful blue eyes captured me as always. She had such big bags under her eyes. She looked so tired and exhausted. Her cheeks had lost their rosy color. Glum would be the best word to describe her. But she still looked as beautiful as I had ever seen her.

Only now had I realised I had missed her ten times more than I had originally thought. I don't think she shared the same feelings. Her face had a large amount of shock and horror on it. She turned to Natalie and shouted, "Why is he here?" And she turned to me and shouted, "Why are you here?"

"I told him to come."

"Why?" Zac yelled.

"Because you can't just ignore him. You two need to talk and sort things out...Will, take a seat, please," Natalie said, pointing to her sofa.

I walked over and sat down across from Zac. Natalie sat down next to me. "Ok, Will, do you want to be with Zac?" Natalie asked.

"Yes," I said.

Natalie nodded and then she turned to Zac. "Zac, do you want to be with Will?"

As I looked over at her, I already knew what Zac's answer was going to be. She was staring at the floor, not even making eye contact with me or even looking in my direction. She bit her lip and shook her head. "No," she said softly.

The whole idea of me coming over to pour my heart out and win her over was now obliterated. Natalie and I looked at each other. I could feel my eyes beginning to water. So I got to my feet and decided it would be best to leave before either of them saw me crying. I just wanted to get as far away from Zac as possible and hoped that the farther away I was, the less the pain would be.

"Zac," Natalie said. "Walk Will to his car so you can say good-bye." I looked over my shoulder at Zac and expected her to ignore her and remained seated. But instead she sighed and got to her feet. She walked past us and put on her Timberland boots, and then walked to the door.

"Good-bye, Natalie," I said.

"Good-bye, Will. I'm sorry."

"Don't be. It's ok."

Zac walked silently behind me as she walked me to the car. I didn't have anything to say to her. I think we'd said enough inside the apartment. I felt like telling her to go back inside because it was pointless her coming to the car.

I walked down the couple of steps to the road and then unlocked the car.

I sighed and turned around to Zac. I thought I would make our good-bye a short one. But then I saw she was crying. "Why are you crying?" I asked.

"Because it's sad," she replied, her voice cracking.

I decided to say one final thing to see if there was any chance we could be together. If that didn't work, then I could accept that she didn't want to be with me, and I could go. I walked back up to the steps towards her and stopped in front of her. Our shoes almost touched. Her arms were folded and she was looking away to her right.

"If you can look me in the eye now, and tell me you don't want to be with me, then I will get in my car now and leave and you'll never have to see me again."

She didn't say anything. She shook her head and continued to cry.

"Why?!" I asked. "Why can't you just look me in the eye and tell me that—"

"Because I love you, ok?" she snapped. Her head sharply turning to face me. She shut her eyes, forcing more tears to run down her cheeks. She placed her face into her hands and dropped her head.

I put my arms around her and brought her close to me. "I love you, too." I rested my head on the top of her beanie and tightened my arms around her. That feeling I had by the lake of being whole was returning.

"Is this the part where you say something romantic?" she mumbled.

"Something romantic," I replied. She laughed and nudged me. I brought her from out of my grasp, put her hands down, and wiped her face with my thumbs. "I can offer you two options," I said.

She sniffled and then said, "Ok."

"The first is that I play this all casual and say, 'You wanna get something to eat?'"

She nodded. "Ok. And the second?"

"The second is that I can take a step forward and kiss you, and say something romantic. Not the actual words 'something romantic.' I'll tell you what I wanted to tell you inside your apartment."

She wiped her nose with her arm. "Ok."

"Or three, I could combine them both," I said.

She nodded. "Number three sounds good."

So I took a step forward, kissed her, and then told her, "You're the best thing that has ever happened to me. And I have missed you so much. I've missed waking up to your beautiful weird self lying on me or in front of me. And I've missed questioning whether you're actually a ninja or not."

I paused whilst she finished sniggering. "But most of all I've missed looking into your beautiful blue eyes, that have enticed me since the first time I saw you, and realising just how desperately in love I am with you... And I'm never going to let you go." And then I asked her if she wanted to return inside to have something to eat.

She held my hand as we returned to her apartment. It was nice, and new; we'd never held hands before. Natalie was sat with her back to us and her head to the floor when we reentered their apartment.

"Hey," Zac said.

"Hey," Natalie grumbled.

Zac and I walked around her and sat on Zac's sofa. "Is it all right if Will stays for soup?" Zac asked. "He might be staying for soup more often from now on."

Natalie raised her head and saw me sitting there.

"She told me she loved me," I said, all excited. "The feeling's mutual," I added.

The surprise on her face was almost comical. Her eyes moved over to Zac, who was clinging to my arm. "You told him you loved him?" Natalie asked loudly.

I peered down at Zac. She went all shy as she nodded her head against my arm.

"I can't believe it! I'm so happy for you two! It was so saddening, watching you leave."

We smiled and then I said, "So what do you want to do? We don't have that long before you need to get ready for work tomorrow."

"I have the week off work," Zac then told me.

"How come?"

"They were worried about me so they told me to take the week off and let them know if I was feeling better."

"You could spend the week with me if you like."

"Yeah, please do," Natalie interrupted. "You need some

love, and so do I. I haven't been able to have any guys around since I've been keeping my eye on you every second."

"Thanks, Natalie," Zac replied.

"Anytime," she replied.

"So what do you think?" I asked Zac, and flicked the bobble on the top of her beanie.

"Will you make me breakfast in bed?" she asked.

"Yes, I will bring your smoothie to you each morning."

"I have one or two slices of toast as well now."

"Ok, I'll make you toast, too. Am I allowed to take a bite out of each corner piece like you?"

"No. Only I can do that," she commanded.

"Ok, Captain Panda," I replied.

"How is the ice cream going?" she asked, suddenly sitting up, her grip not loosening on me, though. She rested her chin on my shoulder, her breath tickling my neck.

"We haven't been at work since the accident. The new flavours project is on hold until we return."

"Ok," Zac said, kissing me.

"Just to clarify," I said. "Are we in a relationship?"

Zac smirked. "Yes. Is that ok?"

I shrugged. "I guess so. That is why I came over."

So Zac, Natalie, and I had a bowl of carrot soup each. And I thanked Zac for the portrait she had taken for me for my birthday. She got really embarrassed about that, and she said she was going to throw it away when she got to the apartment. But I told her she would do no such thing. And I just didn't take my eyes off Zac, and I don't think I ever want to.

We returned to my apartment and chilled out there for a bit, and then Ted arrived home later that evening. He congratulated Zac and me, and then he made us fajitas to celebrate since that was the only thing Autumn had taught him to cook. And I'll give him credit, he did a great job, and they tasted fantastic. Zac ate at least one or two, which surprised me because that's the first time I've seen her eat anything other than toast, smoothie, or soup since, well, since we met, I think. I didn't mention it to her or ask about it. Clearly she felt comfortable eating them, and I didn't want to make a big deal out of it so I let her be.

Zac woke me up during the middle of the night. I thought something was wrong because she's normally her silent ninja self. "What's wrong?" I asked.

"I was just checking that you still love me, or like me."

"Of course I do," I replied, lifting my arm and allowing her to tuck into me and rest her head on my chest.

"It's ok if you don't," she mumbled.

"Shut up and go to sleep," I said as I shut my eyes again. And I predicted what she was going to say next so I placed my hand over her mouth. She hummed and then I moved it away.

"What was that for?" she whispered.

"You know what it was for. Those two little words you've used on me before." She giggled and then kissed me before resting her head back onto my chest.

APRIL 20TH

I've spent today taking care of Zac. She is ill. I'm not sure what is wrong with her. I don't know if she had a bug or the flu. Or there was something wrong with the food she ate last night. But if there were something wrong with the food last night, surely it would have disagreed with me, too. I thought it might have been because her stomach isn't used to eating fajitas. I don't know.

I woke up this morning at six or seven a.m., and she was sat up. She looked so pale. I was about to ask her if she was ok, and then she threw up. And she threw up everywhere. Normally when I see sick seconds later I'm sick, too. But I managed to bypass that and quickly get to my feet and help her to the bathroom and over the toilet to throw up in. She was so weak. She could barely hold herself up. I had to stack a pile of cushions that she hadn't thrown up on beside her. It held her up, so if she did need to throw up she only had to lean forward slightly.

Meanwhile I ran a slow bath with a small amount of bubbles in whilst I cleaned the bedroom. I wiped and mopped the floor first, and then scrubbed the rug and put that into the washing machine. Every two minutes I poked my head around the bathroom door to check if she was ok. But I didn't know what the definition of ok was at this moment. Her eyes were shut and she was breathing. I didn't know if she was sleeping or was just so exhausted that she couldn't keep her eyes open. One time when I came to check on her, her head had drooped forward. By then the bath had filled with water. I checked that the water was mild enough; I didn't want it to be too cold, and I didn't want it to be too hot, even though she likes hot baths.

Her clothes were covered in sick as well and it smelt horrible. I got some on myself and I kept gagging, but still didn't throw up.

Once I'd taken off her Star Wars pyjamas, I picked her up and placed her into the bath. I left a jug from the kitchen beside the bath so I could pour some water over her hair as she had somehow managed to throw up into that, too. There weren't many things she hadn't thrown up on.

I held up her head with my right hand as I rinsed her hair with the jug in my left. Then I shampooed and conditioned her hair. The washing machine started to bing as I was conditioning her hair. I could now put the bedding into the washing machine and then I could put the spare bedding onto my bed ready for when Zac got out of the bath. I couldn't let Zac go though because she would sink under the water and drown. But I had thought this through, too. I placed one of those cushions that you wear on planes or trains for comfort. You know, the one you wrap around your neck and it's a cushion, but also a neck support. It kind of looks like a jigsaw puzzle piece. Anyway, I placed that around her neck and watched it for thirty seconds just to make sure that it would actually float, and it did.

The bedding was still covered in sick, but I just crammed everything into a small ball and stuck it into the washing machine. I shivered afterwards, and then rushed back to the bedroom to put the spare bedding onto my bed.

Afterwards I knelt beside the bath and searched online how to wrap a towel around your head so her wet hair wouldn't drip everywhere. I sat her up and attempted to do so, but it looked nothing like it should have so I decided not to do that. I picked her up and stood her on the bath mat, then tied the towel around her, which wasn't easy. I then sat with the hair dryer on the lowest setting so it wouldn't be too vigorous or burn her. It seemed like I was drying her hair for at least an hour. She still hadn't said anything or opened her eyes or flinched. Nothing. She was like a flimsy doll. Once her hair was dry, three days later, and a lot more fluffy and full of volume than normal, I put her into a fresh pair of Star Wars pyjamas and then placed her into bed.

I walked into the kitchen and grabbed a few bottles of water and a special bottle because it could be tipped upside down and it wouldn't allow the water to leak. I then got into bed and spread my legs either side of her, and placed her head onto my lap. I thought it would be the best position for me to keep an eye on her in. I placed the television remote and the water and special bottle within reaching distance, as I wouldn't be moving anywhere for a very long time. I pulled the covers up to Zac's chin, so about my hip, so she was nice and warm. She did look rather snug.

She started to become the tiniest bit responsive when I tried to give her some water. The bottle had a special nozzle on it and her lips would slightly pout as she drank water. She would occasionally let out a little moan, too, but she didn't speak or move.

I sat and watched TV for the next few hours and may have fallen asleep for ten or fifteen minutes. But Zac was slowly regaining her colour. At around 5:30pm the front door opening waked me. Ted had come back from the cemetery. I glanced down at Zac, and she was awake, watching me, still all snug.

"How are you feeling?" I asked.

Her beautiful blue eyes met mine. "Better, thank you."

Ted poked his head around the bedroom door. "You ok?" he asked.

"Yeah. Zac wasn't very well. She was throwing up this morning, so I've been looking after her and making sure she drinks water."

"Your balls must be a bit squished."

I laughed. "Yeah, they are. I've needed a pee for about two hours as well now. I've been trying to drink water carefully so my bladder doesn't feel like it will explode."

"Are you feeling better?" Ted asked Zac.

Her eyes moved over to the door and she said, "Yes, thanks. I'm very comfy."

"You look it," Ted replied. "Do you guys need anything? Are you hungry?"

"Would you bring us two bowls of tomato soup please, man? I prepared them earlier so they're already in the fridge."

"Two soups coming up," he said before fading out of view. He reappeared five minutes later with a bowl of tomato soup and then returned to the kitchen to grab the other. He placed them both on my bedside draw so I could reach them. I thanked him and then he left and went into his bedroom.

"Right, let's sit you up so you can eat your soup."

"I'm too weak to move." I knew this already and was already lifting her up, moving her head from my lap to my chest, so it would be easier to feed her soup. I moved my head slightly so it would be easier to see her. I let the soup cool for a few minutes before I picked up the bowl and rested it on her lap, but still holding it. I scooped up some soup and then brought it towards her.

"What are you doing?" she groaned.

And then I suddenly had this big moment of realisation, and I knew there was only one way I could respond to her question.

"I'm feeding my panda."

She slowly moved her head to look at me, and she looked into my eyes as if I had said the most romantic thing of all time. She forced a smile and then for the next ten minutes I slowly fed her soup. And then once her bowl was finished, I had my cold bowl of soup. It didn't bother me that it was cold. I was more bothered about Zac feeling better.

After I finished my soup Zac needed to pee, but she was too tired to move, so I had to carry her and put her on the toilet, then leave to let her pee and return a minute later to carry her back to bed. I placed her in bed and tucked her in, and then I went for a pee myself since I'd needed one for hours. And then I wandered into the kitchen to stretch my legs and wash our soup bowls.

I got into bed afterwards. Zac rested her head on my chest and fell asleep while I watched a Matthew McConaughey film she had told me to watch called *Sahara*. It was really good. I enjoyed it a lot more than I expected. I remember she mentioned it when Ted was talking to Autumn about that pirate gun in the museum. In *Sahara* they go searching for treasure, too.

APRIL 21ST

Zac pretty much returned to her normal self the next day. I think being asleep for nearly twenty-four hours must have helped.

She wasn't in bed when I woke up, and I shot to my feet and poked my head around the bathroom door to see if she was being sick, but she wasn't there. Then she appeared at the bedroom door with two smoothies in her hand.

We sat in bed and drank them, and I kissed her every few minutes because now I could. With her permission, of course.

We got up an hour later and went for a walk. Zac wanted some fresh air. I made sure Zac was all wrapped up in scarves and her beanie so she was as warm as possible. If she did have any bugs or flus, then going outside and being cold wasn't going to help her get any better any soon.

She said she wasn't feeling great when we returned to the apartment, and she asked if she could be taken to the doctor to find out if she did have some kind of illness. But she wouldn't let me take her. She wanted Ted to take her. Why, I do not know. But all I cared about was her being well, so we waited for Ted to come home, and then he took her to see a doctor.

They were gone for a couple of hours, and I started to become worried. I didn't know if she was ok or what the doctor had said or were saying. I tried calling them both, but it went to their voicemail. So I waited and waited until it was 8:30pm-ish, and they casually strolled through the front door.

"Where have you been?" I asked. "I've been so worried."

"Relax, Will," Zac said. "Everything is fine."

"What did the doctor say?" I asked.

"He said I had a small bug, and he gave me some medicine, and he said I will be fine in a couple of days. That it will pass soon."

"Is she telling the truth?" I asked Ted.

"Yes. The doctor said she'll be fine in a couple of days."

"Ok," I said, kissing her and then hugging her afterwards.

"I'm going to make myself some soup. Do you want some?" she asked.

"Yes, please," I said. I slumped back onto the sofa and took a deep breath and let myself relax. Zac walked over, wearing oven mittens, and placed my bowl of soup on the wooden table a few minutes later. We were having vegetable soup. I think vegetable soup is my favourite. I always add some pepper into the soup to make it a little more interesting. Zac adds some weird leaf stuff into hers. I think it might be rosemary or basil, I'm not quite sure.

I turned on the TV and watched it as I allowed my soup to cool. I also wanted to wait for Zac and Ted to join me so we could eat together. "What are you having to eat, Ted?" I asked.

"I'm having spaghetti letters on toast," he replied.

"Nice food for grown-ups," I joked.

"I know its *baby* food," he said. "But I like it."

Zac and Ted continued to fiddle around in the kitchen, and I was wondering what was taking them so long. "Are you two coming to sit down?" I asked.

"We'll be two seconds. You go ahead and eat," Zac replied. I sulked and shrugged my shoulders. I brought my feet around and leant forward to stir my soup. But as I stirred it, I felt something heavier than a vegetable chunk at the bottom. I thought it must have been a piece of carrot or something and during the process of the soup being made, this large chunk of carrot somehow managed to slip through.

I scooped it onto my spoon and brought it to the surface. And it wasn't a carrot. It wasn't even a vegetable. It appeared to be a baby's dummy. I frowned down upon it and thought how on earth a baby's dummy could have gotten into my soup. I was about to look over at Zac and tell her that I had discovered a dummy in my soup before Ted walked over and placed his plate of spaghetti letters on toast beside my soup. And on the toast the spaghetti had been spelt like this:

YOURE GOIN
TO B
A
DADDY

My frown increased at how coincidental this all was. And then I stopped being an idiot and realised what was going on. I changed my attention to Zac, who was leaning against Ted's sofa with her arms crossed, looking at me from a side angle. I then looked at Ted. He was smiling at me all casual.

"I'm going to be a dad?" I asked.

"Yes," Ted replied. "You two morons are going to be parents."

I grinned and looked back down at the soupy dummy on the end of my spoon. The thing I was trying to think of was how, because Zac and I always used protection. And then I figured it out. Two little words. Just those two little words of Zac's. "Make me." They had now turned us into parents.

I returned my sight back to Zac. She was now biting the end of her thumbnail.

"We're going to be parents," I said to Zac.

"I know," she replied with tears falling down her face. I looked back at the dummy on the end of my spoon, and then I started to cry.

I got to my feet, stepped over to Zac, and put my arms around her.

"I love you," I said.

"I love you," she said.

"Are you ok?" I asked. "How are you doing?"

"I'm a little scared," she began. "I've got a human growing inside of me and I'm going have to give birth and I'm gonna be huge and I don't know what to do about work and what are we gonna do when the baby gets here and I'll need to pee all the time—"

"Hey, hey, hey," I said. "Whatever you want or need to make you as comfortable and relaxed as possible, I will make sure that happens. I will do everything I can to make you and the baby as happy as possible." She smiled and kissed me. "So is this why you have been throwing up? It's been morning sickness?"

She nodded. "Yep."

"Can we come in yet?" was then said from outside the apartment door.

I frowned and turned to it. "Who's outside?" I whispered to Zac.

"Your mum and Rosie," she answered.

"Why are they outside? Is this what took you so long to come home?"

"Maybe," she replied mischievously.

"Or maybe it's because she had to pee on six pregnancy

tests, and do a million breathing exercises to calm down when she found out she was pregnant," Ted said, walking over to the apartment door and opening it.

Rosie yelled, "I'm going to be an auntie!" as she entered. I opened my arms to embrace her, and she moved straight past me and hugged Zac.

"Hello, baby boy," Mum said, putting her arms around me.

"Hello, Grandmother," I replied.

"Oh my lord, I'm going to be a grandmother. I really am getting old."

"No, you're not," I replied.

"Are you ok?" she asked.

"I'm going to panic a lot later when everyone is gone. But I'm so happy," I said. "I can't believe I'm going to be a dad."

EIGHTEEN MONTHS LATER

OCTOBER 27TH

Today my beautiful daughter, Evie, took her first unaccompanied steps. She only managed two before she stopped and slumped onto her bottom. Zac and I were so thrilled. Normally when we let go of her to see if she'll walk, she just wobbles and then slumps onto her bum. Evie seemed pleased with herself though and let out a little giggle. She started walking towards me after Zac let go of her. I think she was more interested in the biscuit I was eating. She continued to crawl towards me, but by then the biscuit was gone, and then she didn't seem so interested in me after that.

I never thought someone so small could make me so happy. She owns my heart, she really does. Well, she and Zac have equal shares. She's exactly like Zac. She's like Zac 2.0. We even bought her a little blue beanie so she and her mum could be matching.

Not long after she was born we used to joke about how she looked nothing like me, but Zac would say that she had my teeth, but then I'd say she doesn't have any teeth. It sounds silly, but we thought we were hilarious at the time. Comedy geniuses. Maybe our poor parent jokes are already taking over.

I'm so proud of Zac. Just when I thought I couldn't love her anymore. It was seeing her hold Evie for the first time, and I knew as long as I had those two in my life, I would never be unhappy again. Zac's pregnancy was an interesting nine months, to say the least. It was basically a gradual development of Zac's emotions amplifying as each day passed. The first twelve weeks were fairly normal. Zac was nervous and worried, but they were normal emotions for her to feel. We went to the doctor and found out that Zac had to start eating a lot more otherwise it would harm the baby, so we created a whole new food plan with the doctor. It meant she would have to have bigger and more frequent bowls of soup, and fish, that would be our dinner. Zac found it difficult to start with. She obviously didn't want any harm to come to the baby in any way, but she wasn't used to eating so much. But after a few weeks she was eating enough. And I remember that tight-lipped smile Zac gave me when she had her the target set for her. An indescribable rush of happiness and proudness and love ran through me. And I couldn't believe how lucky I was to have a future with her.

Eight weeks in we woke up one day and Zac's pregnancy boobs had kicked in. I thought she must have sneaked out in the middle of the night and had a boob job done. It was fantastic.

And then about week fifteen we woke up and she had a small bump on her stomach. At first we were so happy and excited, and I was thinking that this is going to be such a happy and loving time for us both. And I thought this doesn't seem so bad. It seemed to be going pretty well so far. We saw the ultrasound a month after that so about twenty weeks in, halfway through the pregnancy. And we found out we were having a baby girl. And I just looked at the monitor and saw her, sleeping I assume, I doubt she was watching television, in Zac's tummy, and I couldn't wait to meet her. Ted was going to have some serious competition when she arrived because we were going to be such good friends. Zac and I smiled at each other and we kissed. And I didn't think anything could spoil these nine months for us.

But once we passed the twenty-week stage, that's when it all went downhill. When I say downhill, I mean Zac turned into The Hulk. I don't think I've ever been insulted as much in my entire life. It was a roller coaster of emotions. I would pick her up from work and we'd drive home. During the car drive home she would be fine and happy. And then once we got home she would become this evil, hungry, demanding monster. She just wanted chocolate and fish all the time. I know it's an odd combination, but that was what she demanded. I read in one of my many, many, many pregnancy books that being pregnant can change your appetite. One minute I was cooking fish and running to the shops to stock up with chocolate. And then the next I was being bullied senselessly. And then having to cuddle my bully senselessly. And then go away because I was being annoying even though I hadn't said a word. And then be called back as she wanted a foot massage. I gave her thousands of foot massages during her pregnancy.

But I can't describe how proud I am of Zac. There are no words. Growing and carrying a baby inside of you for nine months. Nine months. I don't think I could have done it for a day. I know I joke about her being angry and mean, but I loved every second of it. I was going to have a daughter with the amazingly angry girl I loved. And that's the greatest gift I could receive. I didn't plan on it happening so soon, but I'm glad it did.

One thing that annoyed Zac was that she could no longer lie on her front, and she could no longer climb onto me during the night and lie on her front on me. During the first few weeks she could, but once the bump appeared, we had to change our sleeping positions. My mum bought her one of those pregnancy pillows, the ones that are shaped like a question mark or a snake, I guess. To help her sleep at least one part of me had to be touching Zac. So I would play with her hair until she fell asleep, and then leave my hand on her shoulder. And if I rolled over or if it slipped off, she would instantly know and wake up. And she wouldn't take hold of my hand and just place it back up there. She had to make me aware of it.

Shopping for baby things was the best part. Clothes mainly. Just seeing how small she was going to be. I found myself saying "aw" more than anything during those nine months.

We made picking a baby name a Sundiscussion Topic. Ted suggested that we call our first daughter Sofa Cushion Lightning Bolt. And although it was a very great and cool name, Zac and I immediately told him that we wouldn't be calling our daughter that. I actually suggested what I thought was a sensible choice, and I said we should call her Zachary Williams the fourth. And Zac then told me to cough. Not actually cough, but something that is much ruder and more offensive, but also sounds very similar to cough. And then Zac said she'd had a conversation with Autumn once, that if she ever had kids she would call them Andrew if it were a boy, and Evie if it were girl. Because she liked those names. So we decided to call her Evie.

There was no way any of us were going to beat Zac to naming the baby anyway.

One thing I do miss so dearly is sleep. I haven't had a full night's sleep since probably that twenty-week stage. I think Evie could sense that I was enjoying being asleep so she would then start kicking Zac. And this woke her up and then she woke me up. It's the same now. She cries almost every night. I never let Zac get up even though we agreed that we would alternate who got up to check up on her. I let

Zac stay in bed, and then I'll walk into Evie's room and pick up my angelic daughter screaming like there is no tomorrow. Then we'd go for a walk to the kitchen; by then she has calmed down, and I would see if she wants some of some Zac's breast milk from the fridge. Then I'd rock her in my arms for a few minutes before she went to sleep and I'd place her back into her crib.

Zac spends every possible second she can with Evie. She obviously went on maternity leave from the cinema. She left about thirty weeks into her pregnancy, and then she had twelve weeks off. But when she went back to work, she just couldn't leave her. She'd spend all day with her and then when it came to putting her to bed she couldn't leave her. She had a chair beside her crib and she would read her bedtime stories, and she just wanted to sit there all night and watch her sleep. But then I would pick her up and carry to bed. Even though she had her own she still loved to be babied over.

So, I told Zac to do a week at work and see how she felt. And if she didn't want to do it then I could understand and didn't have a problem with her quitting. Evie would stay with either my mum or Rosie or Zac's parents during the day.

Yes, Rosie decided to stay in England. She set up this Internet marketing business thing. She's tried explaining it to me so many times, but it still doesn't make much sense to me. But she works at her computer from her home. Yes, she has her own place now, too. Evie spent the first three days with her. And then she stayed with my mum for a day. And then Friday she stayed with Zac's parents. Her dad and I smoothened things out, but then Zac told him that she was pregnant, and then he wanted to kick my ass again. But we're ok now. I think ok sums it up perfectly. Mrs. Williams loves me, and she was incredibly happy at Zac's pregnancy so one out of two isn't so bad.

So the first week of work had passed and I thought she would be ok and she would come home and realise she could work again. But Ted and I pulled up outside and she got into the car and told us she had quit. I glanced over to Ted, who had started laughing because he bet she would, and I bet him she wouldn't.

So Zac quit and became a full-time mum, which is what she wanted anyway so that didn't bother me. I fully supported it, and my new job role meant we could afford to do that anyway. Ted and I were just about finishing the new flavours project at the time, too. And I hadn't found out what royalties we were getting from the ice cream yet.

Ted and I returned to work two weeks after Zac announced her pregnancy. And because we were made head of the new flavours project, it meant we could no longer just work from our little office. It meant we had to travel backwards and forwards to America to have lots of different meetings. Ted's dad came with us most of the time to overlook everything. But we flew to America and back at least once a month, which was kind of difficult during Zac's pregnancy. But we made it work.

I spoke to Ted and his dad once we returned to work and told them that I had spoken to August Bishop, the actress who I'd given the tour to a few months ago. And she said she was interested in becoming an ambassador or having some other involvement with us. They thought it was a great idea so I called her and told her that the new project was under way, and that they would be released within a year. And that we wanted her on board from the start. And we wanted her to be in the television advert for them.

She agreed to do so, but only if she could have her sister in the adverts as well. And we agreed to that. So that was pretty much the first bit of business I did towards the creation of the new flavours. We'd not even tried any ice cream samples yet and we already had one of the biggest actresses in the world to be the face of them.

Testing the ice cream samples was the best part, I must admit. I ate so much ice cream during that time. But I remember the first thing Ted said to me when we walked into the office. Our office had been taken over by our replacements upon our return. But Ted's dad had turned one of the two conference rooms into a new office for us both. They never get used anyway. But we couldn't believe how much space we had. The first thing Ted said to me when we walked into our new office was, "We're going to have such great paper basketball contests in here." And then the second thing he said to me was, "So are we still moving into Ron's house?"

And over the next nine months we secretly started setting up the house, ready for when the baby arrived. We bought nearly every baby accessory possible. Ted bought this Thomas The Tank Engine train set, and I think we played with that more than Evie did. Everybody would see us lying on the floor with Evie, playing with her and her toys, and they would say "Aw, look at them playing with her." But really, it was Evie who was playing with us. We spent hours playing with that train set. And then when Zac picked Evie up and fed her, we would still be playing with the train set.

I still remember the day Evie was born like it was yesterday. It was a horrifying and wonderful day. I saw things that I never want to see again. It put me off having another child ever again. It was like watching a horror movie. But at the end the murderer and the victim fell in love. Evie was placed straight into my arms after she was born. Her precious little life trusted to be given to me first. And I looked down at this beautiful tiny crying baby, and I knew two things at that moment. The first was that I was going to do everything I could to make my precious daughter feel as happy and loved for as long as I lived. And the second was that I was never going to have a healthy bank account ever again.

When we left the hospital for the first time with Evie, Ted and I decided to go straight to Ron's house. Zac wasn't paying much attention because she was too busy watching over Evie, making sure she was ok. I don't think Zac even let herself blink, she became so instantly protective. We kept telling her that there had been an accident so we had to take a huge detour. And then when we drove into the countryside she became very suspicious. She didn't believe the detour anymore. And then we pulled into the drive of Ron's big stone house. Ted opened the gate and then we parked inside the courtyard. Natalie was already leant against her car when we parked and got out of the car because Ted had invited her to live with us in the small middle stone house. Mum had visited a lot over the past few months as well to maintain the garden. She was the only one besides Ted, Natalie, and I who knew about our moving in.

Zac didn't believe us when we told her this was where we would be living from now on. She kept telling us to take her back to the apartment so she could sit down with Evie. We walked through Natalie's part of the house first, and then we wandered into Zac and my part of the house. It was only when we walked out of our bedroom and into Evie's room that Zac finally started to believe us. The room was filled with toys and swings and play mats and stuff. And obviously a nice crib for Evie to sleep in. She looked so happy, and that was the look I wanted to keep on her face for the rest of her life.

When we went into Ted's part of the house to complete the tour, there was a dog in the living room. Well, a very small Labrador puppy. And that was when Ted revealed a surprise of his own. He had bought himself a dog, and he had called it Sofa Cushion Lightning Bolt. A very sensible name for a dog. We all refused to call her by that name, so we called her Sofia instead. Since it is sofa with an I in it. We moved into the beautiful stone house that day. We returned to our apartment and packed all of the things we hadn't already taken over discreetly. If Zac asked where something went, we either told her that it broke or we got rid of it. But she didn't notice too much.

Once we moved in, a couple of months after that Captain Panda's Paradise and Dinosaur Disaster were released. We had one launch party at each factory. The first was in America, and the next one was in China, and then the final one we had back home in our factory. I wanted Zac to come with us because without her Captain Panda's Paradise, which turned out to be a record-breaking selling ice cream, would not have been possible. But she refused to leave Evie's side. We talked about bringing Evie to America and China with us. But we decided that it was too soon to take her on a plane, and the flights were too long as well. Zac and Evie came to our factory's launch party, though. August was in the country as well so she came along with her fiancée, Ethan. We asked her to come along to one, and she said she would be in England for the premiere of her next film, so she would be in the country for a couple of weeks. We'd already filmed a couple of adverts with her and her sister. We were supposed to go and overlook the filming, but we couldn't because Zac was about to give birth. But Madeline, August's little sister, got her wish and starred in the ice cream commercial with her older sister. The advert came out really well actually.

The whole project went well surprisingly. I was expecting something to go wrong throughout the entire thing. I didn't tell Zac that August would be attending, and she was so star-struck when she saw August. I was holding Evie at the time so Zac just gave her a big old hug. There is a photo in our bedroom of August holding Evie with Zac. August and Evie got along very well. Ethan and I were having a chat while the three of them were socialising. He was telling me about this new film August had a role in. I definitely remember him saying there was tap dancing in the film, but I can't remember if he said she was a tap dancer or not. But he said she had a small role in it, and it was going to be a huge film so Zac and I had to see it. Some teenager who was seventeen, eighteen, or nineteen wrote the story. That's why everyone is talking about it, because he's the "next big thing." Oliver Green or Pink or was it blue, I know his surname was definitely a colour. And then he told me about this astronaut film August was the lead role in was coming out in the coming months, too. I couldn't really absorb what he was saying because I was too busy watching Zac, August, and Evie.

And then August started to turn to Ethan. And Ethan and I both knew what she was going to say next. Those famous words.

"I want one," she said. I think it frightened Ethan a little. And then he held Evie and it didn't seem so frightening then.

Zac and I had to leave early to put Evie to bed so we did the announcement and popped some champagne and had a photo and then returned home.

So, yeah, you're all caught up. My beautiful daughter has just taken her first two steps. I still can't change her diapers, though. I'll do anything Zac asks towards our daughter, but even when I've stuck wet wipes up my nose and put on gloves, I still nearly throw up. So Zac is the diaper changer. But the past nine months have been the best of my life. My family is perfect. And I have a great job to support my family. The new flavours are selling really well. I get commission from both ice creams, and I was given an upfront bonus as well, which nearly caused me to pass out. The commission alone could mean I could quit myself and live off it. But instead of working five days a week now I only work two or three. Which is great because now I get to spend more time with Zac and Evie.

Zac receives commission from Captain's Panda's Paradise, too. The commission is split between us. It's her idea really. I just put it into action.

Ted still visits Autumn once a week on a Sunday. We took Evie to see her a couple of weeks after she was born. I'm sure Autumn is really proud of us all. I wish she was here to see how grown up we're all being. We all miss her so much.

Ted hasn't dated anybody since. Although Zac and I suspect that there might be something developing between him and Natalie, but we're not sure yet. We're keeping an eye on them. I just want Ted to be happy. He deserves to be happy. And I think Evie has really helped bring a small amount into his life. They always put a smile on each other's faces.

I'm sure you're wondering if I popped the question and asked Zac to marry me, and the answer is no. And there is a very good reason behind that, I promise. I want to wait until Evie is old enough. I'm not sure how old yet. But I had a nice idea of how I would like to propose. It's not glamorous as most would like. But it would be meaningful for Zac and me. I was thinking we could take Evie to the cinema where we first met. And I was thinking that Evie could help me propose. I could pretend to tie my shoelaces and then she would walk around and pass me the ring afterwards. It was just an idea. But I would definitely like to wait until Evie is old enough. She will remember her mummy and daddy getting married. It would mean a lot to me for her to see it. It would set an example of what my daughter should expect a gentleman to love her like. But she will have to wait until I am no longer living to have a boyfriend. As long as I am alive I will guard my daughter with a shotgun.

But, in all seriousness, I want her to see how much her parents love one another. To see how much I love her beautiful mother...the girl from the cinema who I fell in love with at first sight.